Nancy Jasin Ensley has worked in the healthcare field for 56 years in multiple roles. Her poems and four books are available on Amazon, Barnes and Nobles' websites and in the national Library of poetry. "The Tire swing" is a memoir chronicling her metamorphosis from a frightened, abused child to a nurse, educator, mother, wife and great grandmother. *"A Rainbow in December"* is a story filled with intrigue, power struggles, murder and romance. Join the protagonist, Melinda Strigow in her stormy ride to find her pot of gold.

To my beloved mother who taught me the magic of the written word. I love you for your courage and talent.

Nancy Jasin Ensley

A Rainbow In December

The Obsession with Power and Money

Austin Macauley Publishers™
London • Cambridge • New York • Sharjah

This is a work of fiction. Names, characters, businesses, places, events, locales, and incidents are either the products of the author's imagination or used in a fictitious manner. Any resemblance to actual persons, living or dead, or actual events is purely coincidental.

A CIP catalogue record for this title is available from the British Library.

ISBN 9781398405943 (Paperback)
ISBN 9781398406568 (ePub e-book)

www.austinmacauley.com

First Published 2022
Austin Macauley Publishers Ltd
1 Canada Square
Canary Wharf
London
E14 5AA

To my amazing parents, family, and friends, my wonderful husband and all of the authors of every book I have read, I am eternally grateful. I could not have taken on the task of writing a harrowing murder mystery without the encouragement and patience of my children, grandchildren, my husband, John, and friends who supported me as I developed a story twisting and turning through my protagonist's life. A special thank you to the editors and project managers at Austin Macauley Publishers. With me always is my God, who shakes his head at my discussions with my characters at three in the morning and for giving me the gift of a passion for writing.

Table Of Contents

Chapter I
The Bus Stop

Early November: It was much colder than the weatherman had predicted when he gave his report at 5 am. The wind chill made the temperature feel like fourteen degrees below zero. Wind gusts stirred the light dusting of snow into miniature funnels dancing haphazardly along the street. The wind seemed determined to unwrap Melinda's blue wool scarf from the loop she had carefully arranged. Millie, a reconstruction of her name she tolerated, marched her feet up and down. She wished she had donned her unfashionable boots instead of the ones with two-inch heels and minimal insulation.

The streetlight rattled in tune with the wind, the glow cast Millie's shadow in a staccato dance on the desolate street. The buses in this part of Moline were few and far between. The cheap, under-maintained apartments and boarded up skeletons of businesses, left vacant when the economy took a plunge, were poor attractions for buses, cabs or any form of public transportation. The bus stop was near the corner of Vanguard and Ashton Streets. Vanguard was also known as route sixty-three. About two-hundred feet adjacent to Vanguard, Ashton St veered to the south and continued under an overpass towards Iowa.

The intermittent glow in the darkness beneath the overpass could only be seen if someone determinedly looked in that direction. There was a moment when the light from the burning cigarette shone on a face. The shadow moved quickly towards a car and disappeared.

Melinda Sherman's stomach grumbled its dissatisfaction with the half cup of coffee and two bites of toast she had ingested for breakfast that morning. She was starting a new job. She had to be there by 6 am to begin orientation. Melinda needed this job. After pounding the pavements, e-mailing renditions of her resume multiple times and making calls, she was sure she had landed the only available job in Rock Island. She was so weary of hearing "We have filled that position" or "You seem to be overqualified", the thought of pole dancing at one of the cheap clubs started to look enticing.

If someone sends a resume that seems to fit a job description, how could that person be overqualified? She thought. She had almost unleashed that question on the last person leaving that message but recanted when she realised she would be addressing a robot.

The headlights bounced along the pitted pavement as they approached the bus stop. Melinda had walked gingerly down Volmer Street from her small apartment. There were two ways to access the street. Glenda Rd. ran north and south on the west end of Volmer; Ashton bordered the east end, a short distance from the Expressway. Melinda anxiously checked her watch. It was 5:28 am. She dug into her small purse for tokens. As she looked up, it seemed odd that the headlights' beam appeared to be lower than those from a bus.

The road met her head so violently that it cracked, driving fragments of bone into the soft tissue of her brain. Her tiny purse flew into the air and the wind dumped it near some bushes in front of an abandoned house. The icy tires ran over her right leg, twisting it in her fashionable boots. Those boots were one of the few possessions she had managed to keep from the divorce. Her pelvis twisted and separated near the head of her femur. The vehicle turned east on Ashton, then slowed under the Expressway overpass. It stopped, the snow veiling its taillights.

Blood oozed from the depression in Melinda's skull down the side of her face. The red river slithered along the frozen pavement until it met with a discarded beer bottle and congealed. Crystals formed on the tiny pool, glistening in the dismal light. Melinda had pulled her hair back off her face in a loose bun, which allowed tiny ringlets to bounce against her cheeks. Her cheeks were pale, one of them scraped as if the claws of a cat had attacked it. Gravel and dirt were imbedded in the wounds. The wind blew her blue scarf towards Vanguard. It wrapped its tails around a splintery telephone pole. The tails of the scarf eerily motioned like outstretched arms. They caressed the tattered garage sale signs and posters of lost people and animals.

The Rock Island downtown bus bumped along Ashton Street at 5:42 am. The header announcing the bus's destination could barely be seen. Only one of the light bulbs behind it was working. The bus driver was crankier than usual because he was six minutes behind schedule. On one of the stops before his turning onto Ashton, he had to assist an elderly man with a walker up the three steps into the bus and down the aisle, depositing the passenger's oversized bottom into one of the seats. The old man's wife shuffled behind him mumbling orders and swearing unashamedly. Jeffrey Collins was standing next to the driver, preparing to exit at the Volmer Street stop. He peered out the front window.

"Stop! Stop the bus, man!" he yelled, attempting to grab the steering wheel himself.

"What the hell!" The bus driver grumbled.

"There is something lying in the street. It looks like a person!" Jeff screamed as he wrestled with the bus driver to turn the wheel away from the form.

The bus driver slammed on the breaks and the bus careened to the left. Its huge tires just missed Melinda's lifeless body. Jeff bounded off the bus while the driver tried to calm the other four passengers. Jeff's plan to visit the apartment on Volmer Street to set things right would have to wait.

Chapter II
The Glass Ceiling

She had finally made partner in the firm—one of a very small, elite group of women who had battled and survived a masculine dominated business world. Staring through the floor to ceiling window in her office, her pulse quickened as the city awakened. Bodies moved like tiny dolls in and out of the buildings. The muffled sounds of taxi's honking, riveters' machines pounding steel, sirens screaming, filled her senses. It was like an orgasmic climax; a symphony to accompany her feeling of power. There were only two more hurdles blocking her way to the pinnacle. The first one would be easy to overturn, but number two was much more of a challenge. She sighed and returned to the pile of papers and folders on her desk.

Jacob, Balingsford & Treacher Financial Consultants, Inc. was one of the largest, most profitable corporations of its kind in the Midwest. The home office was in Chicago with satellite offices in other parts of Illinois, Ohio, Indiana and Kentucky. The consultants catered to celebrities, politicians, medium and small business owners, physicians and restaurateurs. The clients appreciated the hands-on oversight of the staff. The founding partners insisted on ethical practices and a personal review of projects. Thus, the firm's spotless reputation, stewardship and fairness were maintained.

Douglas Jacob and Martin Balingsford were graduates of Northwestern University. Young, full of energy, armed with book smart business knowledge, brains and $23,320 in savings, they had set out on their journey to success. The first office of Jacob and Balingsford, LLC was humble, to say the least. The door to the one room flat, located above Marshall's Cleaners, could only be opened by lifting it about an inch so it would clear the buckled wooden floor under the carpet. It seemed that the constant flow of steam from the presses below moistened the wood, allowing it to take the shape of a tortoise shell.

To seat the deadbolt and the tumblers in the lock, one had to gingerly lift and pull the door just a few inches. The dull green, shag carpet was practically worn away by footprints and other traffic. The room smelled like the bottom of an ash tray. Stale food added to the ambiance. There was a dingy tan couch with buttock prints in the cushions. The poor couch leaned to one side, ejecting any person sitting there on to the floor. Across from the couch was an old roll top desk whose roll top no longer was operable. A chair, with hair oil stains on its headrest, and an army cot from the Spanish-American war (or at least it looked that old) were against the wall across from the couch. An apartment refrigerator, a camping stove and a microwave, Doug had pilfered from his parents' house, completed the food processing area in a small alcove next to the bathroom.

Douglas Jacob could have played Ichabod Crane on stage. His spider-like arms and legs dangled from his torso. There was an irregular bend to the bridge of his nose, the result of a battle with a swing when he was five years old. His chin protruded slightly so that his lower lip covered the upper lip, giving the appearance that he was mulling over some radically important decision. Dark brown eyebrows almost met in the middle, covering the furrow between them. The worry lines were imbedded there from hours of sleepless nights while he studied laboriously to maintain a 4.0 GPA.

His deep blue eyes, set behind long dark eyelashes, had the ability to stare directly at a person without blinking for long periods of time. This expression would make the recipient of the stare fidget in their chair. Sometimes they would turn away wondering whether Douglas was having a seizure or harboured some sort of brain tumor. Those eyes made up for his other odd features. After being subjected to his gaze, some people even said he was kind of handsome. Douglas slept on the cot (when he slept, which was very little) on his back with his arms crossed over his chest—unmoving except for his breathing. He probably would have landed on the floor had he dared another position because the cot was so narrow.

Martin (he hated that name) was fondly known as PC, short for pizza-cake, by his friends and family, not only because he loved both delicacies but also his comment "a piece of cake" resounded with every challenge. He was five feet, eight inches tall, with black, curly hair he cut close to his head. Working out at the gym and making quite a mark on the wrestling team at Northwestern, pumped up his muscles enough to make up for his lack of height. Wanting to look more distinguished, he had attempted to grow a moustache. For some odd reason, it grew in a pale reddish blond colour, which made him look like Yosemite Sam. He attributed the red hew to his mother's Irish ancestors.

Martin slept on the lopsided couch when he crashed in the office. He was a very restless sleeper, tossing and turning, punching and groaning. Doug wondered if he was dreaming of having sex with his many lady friends or recalling a wrestling match in his sleep. His antics caused the couch to thump repeatedly, keeping the mice in their caves and Douglas's rationed sleep interrupted.

In the summer a feverish breeze was the only air conditioning available to the tenants of the small apartments surrounding J & B's and the cleaning establishment A cacophony of sounds—people yelling, babies crying, multiple strains of music mixed with the pounding of bass and rap, sirens and an occasional gunshot, filtered into the small window and mixed with the tapping keys of their typewriter. No business was too small or poorly moulded for these two men. No stack of receipts and carton of dishevelled paperwork too arduous, no client too poor to pay up front were turned away. Each of them was so different in physique and attitude but very much alike in their mission and goals. Every check or cash payment was divided into twenty percent living expenses, eighty percent savings. Eventually the eighty percent was divided equally between savings and investments. During those early years from 1962-1967, the two partners rode the post war roller coaster of the manufacturing revolution.

In 1963, they could purchase a small office on the outskirts of downtown Chicago. It was a palace compared to their original digs in Moline, Illinois. They purchased two desks, three file cabinets, a couch, a copier, two comfortable chairs and one of those new electric typewriters. It seemed wise to splurge on professionally made business cards and marketing. To serve the clients that had contributed to their early success, they bought the cleaner's building from the owner who had retired, remodelled what they could afford and hired both Henri Treacher and a secretary to man that satellite.

Henri was an exchange student who had stayed with the Jacob family while Doug was in high school. He was a brilliant student. His ability to predict investment opportunities and foretell investment disasters, even as a youth, was amazing. After graduating from secondary school in Germany, his homeland, he took the risk of moving to the United States, even though there were still those whose sentiment was less than congenial towards any German citizen. He graduated with honours from Princeton University in New York and received his Masters' degree in business. After graduation, he took a position with a small Wall Street investment firm, enhancing their account base within two years. Henri had kept in touch with Doug and his family. He was intrigued by the maturity, honesty and fiduciary caution with which both Doug and Martin performed while developing their business.

Martin was a natural born salesman. In college, he was the one who could talk any girl into a date and occasionally into bed. He was the smooth talker, the wheeler-dealer, the master of ceremonies. Douglas was more serious, the deep thinker, the man who could put together charts, graphs and spreadsheets with tender, loving care. Doug could add several columns of numbers in his head without using any of his appendages. Douglas Jacob could clean up dishevelled accounting ledgers and businesses on the verge of bankruptcy, in short periods of time—almost as if he had a magic wand waved over drowning businesses. Abracadabra! All fixed—back to work.

Henri was doing well in the Moline office. The business was growing at the Chicago location as well. Within five years, the business had reached a point where Henri was invited into the partnership. Henri excelled at purchases and sales in the stock market. He always was candid and fair with clients.

Samantha Reynolds' goal to become the first female partner in a financial consulting firm seemed attainable when she was hired as a receptionist for the building in which JBT's new offices were now located. Far from the one room flat over the cleaners, the ninth-floor offices at One Prudential Plaza, in Chicago, were posh. There were picturesque views of the big city from the offices of the partners and the upper echelon of bean counters who managed the spreadsheets and reams of paperwork flowing through the business. The building design offered floor to ceiling glass windows in the larger offices. Jacob, Ballingsford, and Treacher owned several satellite offices in other States including the original one in Rock Island.

Samantha was housed in a circular station in the front of the lobby of One Prudential Plaza. Every sound, even whispers, echoed through the center of the building to the arched ceiling and back down to the entrance. Glass elevators moved up and down to the various floors. The design was very much like some of the large hotels in the city. A large modern sculpture stood in the center of the lobby. It was carved from marble into curves with hollow places near the bottom and top. It was titled "Wisdom". The curves represented knowledge and the openings at both ends represented limitless power. Water fell gently, in sparkling sheets, from the upper opening down through the three curves to a marble collecting pool surrounding the sculpture. Sounds of ocean waves and birds chirping softly over a speaker system, gave the feeling of being in a park, when one closed their eyes near the fountain.

Samantha greeted visitors and clients as they entered the building. No one could have access to the elevators without a plastic card key, like some hotel room keys. Residents and some special clients and consultants were given a key card that would allow access at any time. Others were given a key card that would only allow access for the date stamped on the card. Computers were becoming a necessary piece of equipment in businesses, hospitals, hotels and even some homes. Samantha would check appointments of those visiting the various businesses in the building and prepare a key card for that visitor. She would call the business if there was no appointment scheduled to obtain authorisation.

Samantha Reynolds was a handful, according to her parents, Joe and Marlene Reynolds. From the day she was a toddler until she left home immediately after her high school graduation, she had them scratching their heads, frustrated with how to handle their independent child. Joe worked as a carpenter for a small company in Bettendorf. Marlene was a grade schoolteacher who gave up her career to stay home with the children. Samantha was the youngest of the three Reynolds kids. Susan and Sherrie were her twin sisters—four years older than Sam. The family went through good times and bad as most families did in the fifties and sixties. The twins and Samantha had their share of squabbles, runny noses, skinned knees and communicable diseases.

Their parents took them to church every Sunday, to Sunday school and Bible study. They ate meals together, took inexpensive vacations, occasionally, when they could afford it, laughed, cried and lived. Samantha was always a puzzle to her family, her sisters and her acquaintances. As a baby, she rarely cried. She could read by age three and preferred playing by herself, building things with blocks or Legos. Often, she would find a hiding place and read until she fell asleep. By age five, she could recite the names of all the presidents in order, the capitals of every State, do math problems at a fifth-grade level and insisted on picking out her own outfits. She avoided human touch as much as possible, pulling away if anyone came too close to her.

Her parents took her to doctors who could not find any deficits. She was not autistic. She was exceptionally smart and probably bored in school at her grade level. Samantha was a beautiful child. Her auburn hair and large green almond-shaped eyes were framed by porcelain skin. When she smiled, which was rare, her eyes would sparkle. The corners of her mouth seemed hesitant to curl into a full smile. She was obedient, never fussed or was defiant. There seemed to be a shield around her that made her feel like she did not belong, not with her family, not at school, not at play. She was content to read and learn as much as she could. Something inside needed verification—to be in control.

When she graduated from high school at the age of sixteen, she asked her parents if she could go to college. She wanted to leave home and live on the college campus. Joe and Marlene wanted her to stay home but gave in to her request. She received a full scholarship to Northwestern University, picked up her two small suitcases and headed to Chicago. Her parents had arranged for her to stay with Marlene's sister, Veronica, who worked for a legal firm, was single and had a condo a few blocks from the University. Both of Sam's parents were uncomfortable with their youngest daughter living in the big city and being around kids older than her at college.

Jeff yelled to the bus driver to wait as he jumped from the bus into the cold air. As he approached the still body lying in the street, his feet slipped in the icy blood that had pooled on the ground.

"My God!" he hollered as he stooped over Millie's twisted body. "It's a woman!" Her face was covered with blood, dirt and snow. He did not move her. Stooping close to her and putting his face near her mouth he thought he heard air slowly exiting her pale lips. The bus driver had run out of the bus and stopped near Jeff.

"Call 911! Go to that house just down the street. I saw a car in the driveway. Hurry!" Jeff yelled to the bus driver. The four other passengers on the bus peered out the windows that faced Volmer St.

The bus driver ran as fast as he could down Ashton towards the car that had backed into a driveway about fifty feet from where he had stopped the bus. He ran to the driver's side and pounded on the window. His panting breath fogged over the cold glass. Mary Skeldon's heart was beating rapidly as she stared at the outline of someone pounding on her window. She was already late for work again. Getting her three kids ready for school, showering and dressing, feeding the dog and gulping down her coffee, always seemed to take longer as the week wore on.

It probably was because she stayed up until two in the morning working on an assignment for her statistics class. The assignment was due that evening after work. She had to manage without any help. Her husband had died in an automobile accident a year prior. She had little time to grieve as she had to shoulder all the responsibilities, work at a job that was physically and mentally exhausting and continue to take classes to obtain her college degree. She was smart and had a great sense of humour, both of which had helped her dig her way out of the ghetto.

She was trying hard to hold things together. It was more of a challenge than she had ever faced. She was living in an environment that gave her few choices. She had to keep it together for children. She earned a minimum wage as a Nurse Aide attempting to pay bills and school tuition. Neither she nor her husband had a Will, though there was very little to pass on. Her husband's tiny death benefit lasted about six weeks.

She finally could see the frightened eyes of the bus driver and took a chance, cracking the window open just enough to hear him.

"Stop! Please, someone has been hit or something back down the street." He pointed towards his parked bus. "It's a lady, he thinks, and there is blood! I need to use your phone to call for help." Saliva sprayed on Mary's car window as he spurted the words through the opening.

"Okay. Stand back! Did you hit someone with the bus? I…I'm late for work. Crap!" Mary pulled her car farther into her driveway. She started to get out of her car but thought twice about that, jumped back in and slammed the door shut. *What if it is a crook or rapist or something!* The bus driver ran back towards her car and screamed.

"No… No! That is my bus…but I didn't hit her. Ma'am, I won't hurt you. I need to call now!" Mary softened a little when he called her ma'am. She wrestled with fear. There had been an increase in rape and robbery in the neighborhood. She could see the guy was wearing a uniform and cap and he looked terrified. She looked at the man pounding on her car window and wrestled with being late again for work.

"Back away from the car," she shouted through the tiny window opening, "Tell me your name and what you want."

"Please, my name is Paul. Someone is lying on the ground near my bus! A guy from the bus is staying by her. She is barely breathing. Please, lady, let me use your phone to call 911 and the cops." Though it was cold, Paul was perspiring. He stepped away from the car as Mary cautiously opened the door.

"Okay, for heaven's sake… Did you hit her?"

"No! No! The guy saw her on the ground when he was ready to get out of the bus. C'mon, ma'am. I need to call right away!"

"You either are a pretty good actor or I'm a dumb shit. I'll let you in to make the call. I have a gun and I know how to use it." Mary tried to look tough…all five feet, one hundred pounds of her. She followed the trembling bus driver on to her porch, made him stand several feet away from her as she unlocked the door. She bowed slightly as Paul passed through the door.

Geesh...a gun! Why me? I should have retired from this job months ago. Paul stepped into a dark hallway just as a large figure moved towards him. A low sinister growl echoed in the darkness. "Wha…what is that?" he stuttered as he backed up against the wall.

Mary laughed, "That's just Bruno, my dog. He won't hurt you as long as I am here." Mary turned on a small lamp and there stood a very large, black dog with slobber coming from a sinister mouth with huge white teeth.

"It's okay, boy," Mary said as she pointed the pistol at Paul's chest.

"Damn it, lady…put that down! I just need the phone and I will get out of here!"

"The phone is over there on the stand. Don't make any funny moves." Mary followed Paul as he backed towards the phone, picked it up and dialed 911.

"A lady is hurt really bad on the corner of Ashton and Volmer. I stopped my bus and there is a guy who is staying with her. He said she was barely breathing. Come quick!" After leaving his name and Mary's phone number, he begged Mary to put the gun down. The emergency service called, and Mary verified the location of the accident.

Mary hung up the phone and put the gun back in a locked drawer. Then she ushered Paul out on to the porch. She called her work and told them what had happened. She said she would get there as soon as she checked to see if she could help in any way. Paul was shivering as he stood on the porch and started to walk back to the bus. Mary locked her house and got into her car, slowly coming alongside the bus driver. "Get in," she called to him.

"Are you sure? Do you still have that gun?" Paul continued to walk.

"No. It wasn't loaded anyway. Get in. You have to be freezing." Paul slumped into the passenger seat warily looking Mary over to make sure she wasn't still packing.

"You should have seen your face when Bruno growled, and I picked up my gun. You would have made a good character in a scary movie." Mary chuckled. "I called my work. Maybe I can help the person you hit."

"I didn't hit her! A guy on the bus saw her lying in the street, I tell you."

Jeff had wiped some of the blood and dirt away from the injured lady's face and realised it was Melinda.

"Millie…God, what happened? Please stay with me. Don't die!" Jeff knew enough from his two years in the Army not to move her. He talked to her softly, encouraging her to hang on. In the distance, he heard sirens and prayed they were for her. His voice cracked as he remembered the good times they had had together. One time she surprised him at work with a picnic lunch. She wore bib overhauls, a bright red and green flannel shirt and a straw hat. She had painted freckles on her nose with an eyebrow pencil and smeared red lipstick on her cheeks. She had braided her long curly hair into pigtails.

Jeff told her she was the "puritest gal" he'd ever seen. He followed her to a park nearby and they sat next to a pond eating bologna sandwiches with hot mustard and cheese. They laid on a blanket, holding hands and stealing kisses. Those "just in love" feelings are hard to describe. The passion pushes into your chest, up into your throat and down to your private parts. It's more than tingles and chills. It makes you dizzy. You look in each other's eyes and you want to dive inside them. When you touch, every fiber of your skin trembles. You want to touch every part of that person. The warm feeling surrounds you, wraps around your beating heart. You never want that feeling to end. That's how Jeff felt about Melinda.

"Warm…got to keep her warm." His coat was little protection against the biting wind and the cold ground where she lay still, so very still. Jeff laid on the ground next to her and blew breaths against her neck. The smell of blood and her perfume mingled. Tears filled his eyes. Footsteps made crunching sounds coming towards them.

"Are there two victims?" Jeff heard a woman's voice say. Then hands touched his shoulder. He looked in Mary's face as she searched for Melinda's wrist. "I'm Mary. I live down the street. The bus driver called 911. It sounds like help is on the way. I am a nurse's aide. Does she have a pulse? Are you hurt also?"

"No. I'm trying to keep her warm. I'm her…um…friend. My name is Jeff. I can feel her breathing but it is very shallow." Jeff took Mary's hand and guided it to Melinda's limp wrist.

"I think I feel a very faint pulse. Thank God, the EMTs are finally here."

An ambulance, fire truck and rescue squad vehicles pulled onto Volmer Street and several people rushed towards Jeff, Melinda and Mary. Paul had returned to his bus to let the other passengers know what was happening.

In the dim morning light, again the glow of a cigarette lit up the face of someone standing under the viaduct across Vanguard street, a few yards from the scene at the corner of Volmer and Ashton. The person turned and walked towards the black car parked under the viaduct.

Chapter III
Opposites Attract

Doug Jacob married Frannie a few months after he graduated from college. Francesca Romonoff had spurned Doug's many attempts at turning her head or getting her attention. Some of his efforts resulted in the wrong kind of attention. She ignored the single long-stemmed rose he left on her desk in advanced calculus class. She barely acknowledged his chivalrous gestures, such as the times he barrelled past groups of fellow students, often knocking them down, so he could open a classroom door for her. His fraternity was to host a luncheon for the ladies in Frannie's sorority.

Doug rented a tuxedo he couldn't afford, wore contact lenses he hadn't worn in years, so she could see his pleading eyes, and doused himself with Brute cologne to the point of asphyxiation. He bribed three of his fraternity brothers with beer he bought with the few dollars he had left from his meager wages at the campus commissary, so he could be assigned to wait Francesca's table. After all his preparation, Frannie barely noticed the poor chap until his lack of depth perception from the outdated contacts caused him to pour hot tea on his heart throb's blouse instead of her teacup. He certainly was noticed as Frannie jumped up from the table pulling her lovely blue silk, tea- soaked blouse away from her skin.

"You idiot!" she screamed. "You stupid idiot!" These were not the terms of endearment he had so hoped she would be saying to him. He almost landed in one of her sorority sisters' lap when Frannie pushed him out of her way as she hastily exited to the powder room. Douglas grabbed a napkin from the table, knocking over the vase of flowers used as a center piece. He caught up with the frustrated Francesca outside the powder room and began to blot the front of her blouse and the same time blubbering apology after apology.

"Leave me alone! I need to get cold water, you freak!" Francesca batted Douglas's hands away from her blouse and ran into the bathroom closing the door in a rather unceremonious manner. Not to be deterred from heroism, Doug grabbed a glass of ice water from a nearby table, ignoring the sign that clearly read *Ladies Room,* darted into the room and threw the water on the chest of his imagined lover.

"Oh, my God…are you crazy?" Francesca glared at the bewildered Douglas Jacob. She attempted to unbutton the wet, tea-stained blouse as she spouted obscenities to Doug who could only look at her beautiful breasts heaving with anything but passion. She managed to put the garment on backwards, stomp past her suitor and march into the lobby of the club. She grabbed her coat without looking back. Francesca charged into the parking lot, jumped into her car and peeled on to the street. Doug didn't make any points on that fiasco. He was a very persistent young man in all his affairs.

Once Douglas made up his mind to pursue something or someone, he revved up his motor, researched the pros and cons, developed a plan and followed it, full steam ahead. Part of that determination came from his genes. His Jewish parents and their ancestors had always found paths to success despite roadblocks, disappointments and failures. Doug's mother and father had exited Germany just before Hitler began his purge of the Jews and any other non-Arian form of humanity. They traveled to France where they established a small clothing business. Doug's mother was an accomplished seamstress and his father had excellent business skills. Reasonable pricing for quality goods brought them earnings enough to cover living expenses. The profits over and above these were placed in savings.

When the Nazis' march drew closer to France, the Jacob parents and Doug, now only nine months old, found a cheap fare on a cargo ship leaving for the United States. After two years of barely getting by on the savings they had accumulated, they moved from New York City, teeming with refugees, to Chicago. They started a clothing business once again which thrived in a city growing rapidly. The city offered the good life. Dresses and suits made to order with fine stitching and quality fabric charmed the well to do. The business grew, and the family lived comfortably, saving enough to send Douglas to a prestigious college. Doug's father died at age fifty-eight from a heart condition. Douglas had inherited business savvy from his father. He and his mother ran the business for five years after his father's death. His mother succumbed to a rare form of Dementia. He visited her every day he could in the Nursing Home where she resided until she died at age seventy.

Francesca Romonoff was not going to be held back by any male, female or discriminatory barrier from her goal to be a broker on Wall Street. She loved playing with figures, placing that green stuff in the most profitable slots. Her parents had come from Russia to America when the Russian-Jews were threatened extinction, along with millions of others led to gas chambers, prison camps and other horrific forms of persecution and death. Francesca and her two brothers watched their parents struggle to make a living and to fit into a country and culture foreign to them, when they escaped to the United States. She vowed she would become wealthy enough to give her parents peace and security, while she worked to be accepted, if not revered, in a masculine dominated business world.

She had seen many of her friends, who were intelligent women, trod the investment track to success only to fall under the dominate rule of a man. They became Stepford wives, mannequins dressed in petticoats and white gloves, genuflecting to their husbands, losing their independence and numbing their brains. Something about that poor Jacob fellow fostered a tiny bit of interest, though she fought it in every way possible. Was it the sincerity in his eyes or simply his persistence, despite her frosty chagrin? Perhaps the fact that he was at the top of his class, with the promise of a lucrative career commiserate with her own goals, that awakened her attention.

The Spring Fling was a special event put on by three fraternities and sororities on the university campus. Doug volunteered to participate by chairing his fraternity planning committee, despite his lack of interest in social activities. Francesca was head of the committee for decorations. The dance was one of the philanthropic activities of these fraternities and sororities to raise money for a nearby Children's Hospital and fund trips by students to less fortunate countries. Silent raffles and ticket purchases usually brought in thousands of dollars. Choosing the perfect theme was of utmost importance. Votes were turned in by the six participating groups. There was a cost for each entry. Those funds were added to contributions from benefactors and from sales. "Unforgettable Moments" was the theme chosen for that gala in 1960.

Francesca, Doug and their committees met often during the months before the dance to advertise, select food and table decorations, solicit donations for the silent raffle and, most importantly, prepare decorations to match the theme. Francesca and her team not only wanted to impress the students and faculty but also the community leaders and business moguls who often attended. During the planning sessions, Francesca and Doug shared similar traits and talents. Both were on a path to success and valued their independence. Unlike most of his classmates and friends, Doug respected a woman's abilities and desire for a career. Because his mother had taken over the clothing business when his father died and fostered its continued success, he was not prejudiced against women having a career and becoming successful. Every detail, including the type of table favors and the sherbet to cleanse the guests' palates between courses, was planned and executed. Francesca's team arranged for students to take black and white photographs of activities, special memories and events that occurred on campus. She submitted them to the committee. Faces with winning smiles and tears of sadness, graduations, parties, class presentations, sports events, couples holding hands or caressing under one of the large trees, faces filled with awe and anxiety during orientation, a star-studded sky as seen through the campus Observatory telescope, and touching good-byes were captured by the contestants.

The moments depicted in the photos that were chosen were enlarged and framed, hung with gold chains from the rafters in the hall where the dance was to be held. Each table was adorned with a vase etched with Birds of Paradise. Lighted ferns, sprays of stephanotis and roses were placed in each vase. Pale yellow and blue voile was draped from one picture to another tying the pictures of the memories together with the school colors. The tables holding the donations for the silent raffle were draped with the same filmy voile material.

Doug and his team worked tirelessly to obtain donations from businessmen and community leaders to ensure the raffle would provide generous revenue. Fran began to view Doug in a more favorable manner. His ability to delegate duties to his fraternity brothers, a charisma that elicited cooperation and support from powerful businessmen and faculty and his maturity was evident in the profits from the event. Douglas admired Francesca's artistic flair and her ability to motivate people and to squelch disagreements. He was already in love with her because of her beauty and stoic character. Now that they had a chance to work together on this project, Doug was mesmerised. Francesca saw an opportunity to climb the business ladder using Doug's talents as a steppingstone.

The Unforgettable Moments gala was a huge success. Eighteen thousand dollars was raised, the largest amount in the history of the event. Douglas and Francesca continued to see each other to finalise post event details. Soon they were going on actual dates. Doug yearned to make love to this beautiful and mysterious woman. They had kissed and held each other close after dinner dates, movies and campus events, but their passion was put on hold as they used their energy to excel in classes and to establish a place in the business world. This required creating connections with wealthy entrepreneurs in the area. Douglas graduated Cum Laude and was accepted in the Masters' degree program. Francesca also applied for a Masters' degree in Business.

Doug and Martin were fraternity brothers and shared similar career goals. Both wanted to enter the world of the financial elite by providing management services and solid, ethical business advice. Though Martin, at times, gave the more conservative Doug pause with his ability to charm the most cautious client, they made a good team and shared similar values. Doug married Francesca two months into their Masters' program. Martin was their best man. Their passion burst as they tumbled into bed at the hotel following the reception. Even Doug's most erotic dreams couldn't match the feelings when Francesca appeared in a pale blue silk nightgown with a slit on the side that exposed her shapely leg. The cleavage of her ample breasts peaked out from the lace bodice. He yearned to feel the warmth of her body beneath him and to please her until they exploded in a climax of excitement together. They experimented by caressing areas that made both tremble.

After several bouts of love making, with short cat naps in between, they stood on the balcony of their honeymoon suite in Casomel, arms wrapped around each other. The ocean breeze lifted the whispers of the surf caressing the sandy beach up to where they stood. The sun spread finger paintings of purple and yellow across the horizon. Everything was good.

Jeff begged the EMTs in the ambulance to let him ride to the hospital with Melinda, but they had been instructed by the police that all were to remain on site. His chest ached as he watched the crew wrap her wounded head with bandages, start IV and oxygen, place a splint on one of her legs and gently lift the stretcher into the ambulance.

I should have tried to see her sooner. I didn't mean to let her down. The thoughts raced through his brain as he walked back towards the bus. The bus driver was talking with one of the policemen.

"I swear, officer, I did not hit that girl! Here… here ask him!" Paul's hand was shaking as he pointed to Jeff. "He was on the bus and saw her lying in the street. Hey, mister, tell these guys, um…cops she was already lying in the street." Paul was sweating, despite the chill of the wind. He took off his cap and wiped his damp forehead with his sleeve.

Jeff approached the policeman and confirmed Paul's story. Jeff began to tremble and tears filled his eyes as he told the police he was coming to see her at her apartment down the street and was standing at the front of the bus when he noticed a form lying in the street. He was shocked to discover it was Melinda. He told them she was barely breathing, and he found a weak pulse. Lying next to her to keep her warm was all he could think to do.

"She was so cold and so still. I need to get to the hospital and see how she is doing. Please, can one of you take me?"

Hal Putnam had been on the police force for twenty-six years. He was considering retirement when the Mayor visited him a week prior to ask him to consider taking the present Chief of Police's place. The present Chief was fighting a battle with cancer and would not be able to continue working. This took Hal by surprise. He had asked if he could have a week to think about it and the Mayor agreed to let him have that time.

"What is your name, son?" Hal asked as his thoughts returned to the present.

"Jeff Collins, Sir."

"What is your relationship to the victim?"

"I am a good friend," Jeff stammered as he stared after the departing ambulance. "Can I answer these questions later? I need to get to the hospital." Hal had learned to read people. He could tell if they were lying or trying to con their way out of a situation. Jeff seemed legitimately upset and worried. Hal surmised Jeff was much more than a friend to Melinda. He felt he could get more answers if he questioned Jeff at the hospital.

"Okay, Mr Collins, tell my partner, Sergeant Jones, the policeman with a moustache, to let you into our squad car and he will take you to the hospital. Is there any reason that Ms Strigow would not want to see you?"

Jeff wasn't sure if she would want to see him if she was conscious—not after what had happened the last time they were together. "I sure hope she will see me. We were close once—very close."

Hal thought Jeff might be helpful in finding out more about the victim. He kept that thought to himself as he directed his team to take pictures and make impressions of fresh tire marks turning left on to Ashton Boulevard, gather and mark Melinda's purse and scarf, and complete their preliminary reports. He told his partner that it would be alright to take Jeff to the hospital and that he would follow in another squad car.

Paul, the bus driver, boarded his bus after apologising again to the four other passengers. The policemen had obtained statements from the passengers and Paul. They were told they may be contacted again as the investigation progressed. The bus could proceed to its original destination.

A car pulled away from the shadows of the overpass, crossed over Vanguard and slowly drove on to Ashton Boulevard, after the police, ambulance and bus had left. It slowed down in front of Mary Sheldon's house and pulled into her driveway. There was no sign that someone was at home. Bruno's fierce growl and bark could be heard as the intruder backed out of the driveway and disappeared down Vanguard.

Chapter IV
Tangled Webs

The red Ford truck looked as though it had been the loser in a demolition derby. It had dents along the body and a rusted bumper barely hanging on to the frame. Frayed duct tape and one screw barely held the bumper in place. The truck rattled to a stop in the driveway of 4126 Morrow Street. A tall man wearing a torn pair of blue jeans, mud covered work boots and a frayed vest covering a sweatshirt, stepped out of the truck, stamped out a cigarette he had thrown on the ground and walked with a slight limp into the house. He had a dark, tangled beard peppered with grey and caterpillar-like eyebrows that covered his eyelids. His hair was oily and seemed to cling to the stained collar of the vest. He walked into the dingy kitchen that smelled of old garbage, stale cigarettes and booze. Jostling open the refrigerator, whose light had long ago burned out, he grabbed a bottle of beer and slammed the refrigerator door several times before it stayed shut. This ritual was accompanied by a symphony of swear words and snarls. He draped his skinny body over a grease-stained couch that creaked and tilted to one side. The house remained dark, except for the lights from a few cars passing on the street. Dawn was approaching. The dim light revealed the dingy wallpaper stained with water damage from a leak in the upstairs bathroom. The debris from old takeout food and empty beer bottles surrounded the couch and the man lying on the couch. As the morning light pierced the smudged windows, the man rubbed his puffy eyes and wiped the saliva dripping from his mouth on the sleeve of his sweatshirt. After a few choice grumbles, he limped over to a small wooden table near the stairway, opened the top drawer and took out a gun along with a box of bullets. He laid the box on the top of the table. In doing so he knocked a small music box onto the floor. The base cracked, and a few notes exited before his trembling hands picked up the pieces and threw them across the room. For a few seconds "Over the Rainbow" managed to reach his ears. The notes attempted to wrap themselves around his hazy memories of better times. The man he was now was not allowing any good feelings touch him. He had drowned them in the oblivion of a booze induced stupor. He let out a wail so pitiful that it drowned out the last two notes of the song. The box exploded into pieces when he threw it at the wall. He crammed the box of shells into his vest pocket and the gun under the belt of his faded jeans. He limped to the front door, slamming it behind him, and climbed into his rusty truck. The truck rattled down Morrow to Vanguard and headed towards town.

Hal had asked his partner and Jeff to wait for him outside the Intensive Care Unit of the hospital until he went into the unit to check with the staff on Melinda's condition. She had been transferred from the Emergency Room and her cubicle was buzzing with the activity of several nurses, doctors and technicians. A ventilator was controlling her breathing and multiple Intravenous lines, delivering life-saving medications and fluids, dripped into catheters and needles in her arms and upper chest. Hal could barely see Melinda other than some strands of hair lying on the white sheets of the bed. One of the doctors in blue scrubs came out to report that Melinda had suffered a skull fracture with some bleeding into her brain, a partial collapse of the right lung, rib, pelvic and right leg fractures and a spinal contusion. The team was doing all they could to stabilise her, so she could be taken to surgery to perform the repairs needed. At least she was still alive, which the doctors said was a miracle. She had lost a lot of blood from her wounds and the lacerations on her skin from the pavement where she had been run down. Hal never totally became desensitised to the tragedies he encountered working on the streets. He had to mask his feelings, so he could think clearly and objectively. Those buried feelings erupted at the end of his shift and in his dreams. A mind that has witnessed trauma, death, disfigurement, violence and pain repeatedly, suffers post-traumatic stress syndrome that can exhibit itself in many ways. Hal told Jeff that Melinda was being stabilised so she could go to surgery. He offered to have his partner take Jeff home, so he could rest and eat something.

"She will need you more after surgery. Let me get you home. You can leave your number with the nurses. They will not be able to give you much information as you are not a relative. There is very little you can do right now." Hal reasoned.

"I can't leave. I can't even think of eating anything. Has anyone called her family? She has a sister who lives in Indianapolis. I can get someone to take me home when I know Millie has made it out of surgery," Jeff slumped in one of the waiting room chairs. "Her father and mother have both passed away."

Hal took out a notebook. "I'll check to see if anyone has contacted the sister. Is there anyone else who she was close to?"

Jeff paused. "There is an ex-husband but he…he's not a very nice guy. They have been divorced for about one year. I don't think she has even talked to him in a long time. She was afraid of him."

"I'll need to know how to get in touch with him, especially if she was afraid of him. Do you have any idea where he lives?" Hal continued to write in his notebook.

"His name is Ron Sherman. They used to live on 41st Street in Moline but Melinda sold the house after the divorce. He just disappeared. He's older than Millie. I don't know what she ever saw in that guy. He's tall, about six feet three and skinny. I think he had a beard when I last saw him. The last time was when I was helping her move from the house. He pulled up in an old truck and started yelling, calling her all kinds of names. She was so embarrassed. The neighbors were coming out of their houses, he was yelling so loud. He started to run towards her. He was so drunk he tripped on the cement steps. She was upset. I tried to help him up and talk some sense into him. Then he pushed me. I told him we were going to call the cops and he hightailed it out of there."

"Were you intimately involved with Mrs Sherman?" Hal asked as he watched for Jeff's facial expression.

Jeff hesitated. "I love her. I've always loved her. We went to college together. We were good buddies. She didn't seem to feel the same way I did. I…I never told her. I should have told her, but I was afraid it would change our friendship or scare her away. I lost touch when I suffered from some problems just after we graduated. When I came back from two tours with the army before college I was pretty messed up. I had a bad time adjusting. The Veterans' Hospital helped me get back on my feet. After several months, I got a job with a financial consulting firm and that's where I reconnected with Melinda. She came for an interview with my boss. She was even more beautiful than she was in college. We were so happy to see one another. I guess the interview went well, though my boss doesn't interact much with me. Anyhow, Melinda and I got together for dinner and she shared with me the gory details of her marriage. Her husband was an engineer at John Deere and had a problem with alcohol. To make a long story short, he was caught embezzling from the company. He was kiting checks and placing false orders for equipment. He was fired. They did not report him to the police. It was downhill from then on. Melinda tried to get him to seek help for his alcoholism, but he refused. He added drugs to the mixture which made him more difficult to deal with. He got physically abusive and Melinda filed for divorce. She told me he threatened her; that if she left him, she would be sorry. When I saw her three weeks ago, she hadn't heard from him. She hoped he had moved on, perhaps even entered a rehab, but I seriously doubt it. We argued the last time I saw her. I urged her to let the police know he had threatened her. She felt sorry for him and didn't want to stir up any trouble. Melinda changed her phone number and was going to take back her maiden name. Because she was afraid he might see us together, she told me it would be best to part. I called her several times, but she kept telling me to leave her alone. If he… I should have insisted on protecting her. Now look what happened. She might die. If he did this, he should pay!"

Hal took down Melinda's address and phone number, her sister's contact information and anything Jeff could recall about Ron Sherman.

Martin Ballingsford had his qualms about bringing a woman into the firm as a partner. It wasn't that he had anything against women. In fact, he loved them. He sought their companionship and love making frequently. There was something about him that charmed the pants off most women, literally, as well as figuratively. He worked out every day, sometimes twice a day when he could. He could carry on a conversation in a way that made the person he was conversing with feel he had known them for a long time. He could read people; he had the ability to see when they were pretending to be someone they weren't. His photographic memory was advantageous in his business dealings, impressing even the most hesitant client. Most of all Martin was aware of his strengths and weaknesses. No egomaniac here. Martin related to the narcissist as well as the schizophrenic living under a bridge. Another talent he owned was the ability to diffuse an argument. He could usually take the most arduous disagreement and present the pros and cons in a way that he soon had both sides working in concert to reach an agreement. He had his faults. Maintaining any long-term relationship was not his strong suit. Although he was only 5'8" tall, his toned physique and calm manner gave him a dominant presence. When Francesca started making frequent visits to the firm, it seemed innocent enough. The three partners were appreciative of the lunches she would bring. She was a pleasant distraction as she knew how to dress, showing off her tantalising figure with just enough skin oozing from her business suits to entice the testosterone of her male counterparts in JBT as well as in the engineering firm where she worked. She managed to maintain a professional air while utilising her feminine wiles. Even though she was given challenging projects at Compton Engineering its misogynism caused her to seek greater opportunities for positions of power in her husband's rapidly growing consulting firm. She loved Douglas, but there was a part of her that loved having a position of power even more. Many people deal with the battle between good and evil. Evil can be an insidious motivator allowing rationalisation to make a person believe the self-serving path is ethical and right. This fine line can be crossed without the person noticing. If awareness seeps into the consciousness, and the person desires to turn back, the line may have turned into a wall, making turning back almost impossible. Francesca looked at the difference between the minus and plus signs of business profits to be a slash through the middle of the minus sign while bending that line to erect a perfect dollar sign—not a Christian cross.

As JBT Consulting prospered, it moved its main offices to Chicago with satellite offices in several States and the Quad cities. Francesca increased her visits inconspicuously at first. She brought lunches for the partners, filled in for secretaries when they were off, put together power point presentations and re-decorated offices. Martin became increasingly uneasy. Though Francesca pretended to be less interested in the actual business, Martin would observe her going through clients' files and casually interspersing her ideas in meetings. Douglas worshipped her and saw her increased presence as supporting him and JBT overall.

Henri Treacher scrutinised the countless cells of the firm's spreadsheets with the skill of a forensic scientist. He could spot errors and miscalculations in the mountains of data sent to his desk from clients and other consultants under his critical leadership. Investments, business prospectuses, bankruptcy petitions, partnership proposals and tax issues were reviewed and processed by Henri and his staff. Doug and Martin trusted him. Henri trusted the four hand—picked consultants working in his department because he reviewed their work with an eagle eye. All employees were bonded, had thorough background checks, and were not offered established positions in the firm until they had passed his meticulous inspection during a six—month observation period.

Samantha Reynolds observed the owners of JBT as they came and went past the registration desk. She grew to know from their gait, body language and facial expressions, how certain clients and other visitors had affected them. Samantha could tell when Mr Jacob had a difficult day. His gait would change from a lively step to a slow halting one. His usual friendly smile would diminish to a forced unengaging side glance and his eyes would lose their sparkle. Mr Ballingsford was the most difficult to read. He was the charmer. He would wink at her and compliment her on her hairdo or outfit no matter who had visited him that day. The only times he seemed to be less engaging were when Mr Jacob's wife, Francesca, visited. She was becoming more active in the company and that seemed to effect Mr B's demeanor. Then there was that German guy, Mr Treacher. He rarely greeted Samantha, wore dark glassed no matter what the weather and was often engrossed in searching his briefcase for something. She paid less attention to him because he was consistent. His walk, facial expression (or lack thereof) was always the same. Henri would be the one with whom she needed to gain favor. The others would be more easily managed.

Melinda opened her eyes. She couldn't move her head to see what was making a whooshing noise. She remembered parts of conversations—"pressure's dropping. It will be okay. Change that IV. Need more suction. My boyfriend is a jerk." The voices and phrases swirled around her hazy consciousness. None of it made sense.

Who are these people? Where am I? I need to get to my job! Her thoughts were scattered and scary. The lights were so bright, and her right leg and hip felt like someone was squeezing them. She tried to call out but there was something in her throat. She tried to scream—to swallow. Nothing! Then she felt like she was falling into a dark pit. She heard voices but could not make out what they were saying as the sounds pulled her into a tunnel of forced sleep. Three days had passed since she was brought to the ICU. Doctors had placed pins in her fractured leg, immobilised her crushed pelvis, placed chest tubes between her ribs into her chest cavity to re-inflate her collapsed lung and had performed a craniotomy to remove bone fragments and a blood clot from her brain. Her left kidney had been fractured and was removed. The team of trauma doctors and nurses worked feverishly to keep Melinda alive and were constantly on the watch for infections that often occurred when people were injured in car accidents. The cold weather had been both a curse and a blessing. The hypothermia, her body temperature falling below normal, reduced the amount of bleeding and lowered the oxygen requirements to her tissues. The risk of frostbite to her skin would complicate the healing process. She had been placed on a ventilator to assist her breathing and to keep her in a sedated state. By the fifth day the doctors felt they could begin to wean her from the ventilator hoping she would be able to breath on her own. The staff and physicians were relieved when Melinda responded appropriately to some simple commands. Raise your right hand, blink your eyes. Correct "yes" and "no" responses all were signs that her brain function appeared to be intact.

Melinda's sister, Phyllis, had arrived at the hospital as soon as she was notified of the accident and could leave her work. Phyllis was ten years older than Melinda. She worked at a law firm in Indianapolis as a corporate lawyer and hadn't seen her sister for about a year. Her work was her life. She couldn't understand why Melinda had married that crude bully of a man. Jeff came to visit Melinda every day that he could. He had obtained permission to see her from the police and the ICU supervisor until her sister arrived. Phyllis met Jeff in the waiting room when she arrived on the second day after the accident. He briefly recounted the details of the accident and his relationship with Millie. Phyllis offered little about herself other than they were sisters and her displeasure with Millie's choices in men. Jeff and Phyllis talked briefly before visiting Melinda.

Jeff had initiated the conversation with Phyllis. "Millie and I went to the same college. We lost touch when I had some issues I needed to attend to. We did not reconnect until several months ago." I am so glad to meet you. She spoke of you often." Phyllis seemed distracted as they entered Millie's cubicle in the ICU.

Jeff gently touched Millie's hand. Phyllis could barely look at Millie. She whispered to Jeff. "I'm surprised she mentioned me at all. We sort of lost touch over the past several years. I guess that is because I am married to my job. It pretty much owns my life." She raised her voice when she glanced at the machinery and tubes entering various portions of Millie's pale body. "Have there been any leads on who might have done this? The bastard! Probably that low-life ex-husband of hers. She never should have married him." Phyllis forgot the warning from the nurses that even though Millie was heavily sedated she could still hear every word they said. Melinda's pulse rate increased, and her blood pressure rose. Alarms went off and the nurses rushed in, ushering Jeff and Phyllis out of the ICU and into the waiting room. Jeff visited each day. Phyllis came back to visit the day the breathing tube was to be removed. She wandered how Millie felt about the hiatus in their relationship.

"Ms Strigow and Mr Collins, we will be out to talk with you after the breathing tube is removed. The doctors feel she will be able to breath on her own. Melinda will be exhausted, so we can only promise a very short visit afterwards. Her throat will be sore, and she will be quite hoarse for a few days. She also may be somewhat confused. Please refrain from discussing anything that might upset her. I'll keep you posted." The nurse smiled and returned to the ICU. Phyllis took a chair some distance from where Jeff sat. She took a folder from a brown leather briefcase and began to leaf through the papers. Jeff got up and went to pour some coffee asking Phyllis if she would like a cup.

"What? Oh, no thank you. I've had quite a bit more than I should have since I arrived." She returned her focus to the paperwork in her lap.

"I know this is very upsetting for you." Jeff sat in a chair next to Phyllis who sighed.

"How was it that you were on the bus near her home when Melinda was found?" She asked with just a glance towards Jeff.

Jeff looked at his hands and pushed his tousled hair out of his eyes. "I was coming to see her at her apartment that morning. We hadn't talked for a few weeks. She was concerned that her ex might see us together and mess with me. I wanted to report him to the cops, but she wouldn't let me. I can't think of anyone else who would want to hurt her. All her friends loved her. She was about to start a new job at JBT Consultants the day she was injured. That's where I work as a technician in the accounting department. Millie had interviewed for a job a couple of months ago. When her husband found out she had applied for work he was furious. As far as he was concerned, she was to stay home and be there to do his bidding. By then Millie had enough of his abusive behavior and told him she was leaving him. She filed for a divorce and found an apartment. She knew that he drank too much. She also found out why he was let go from his job at John Deere. He was falsifying invoices for equipment and writing bad checks. When he found out it was our consulting firm that uncovered the discrepancies, he was livid and began harassing Millie. She and I had begun seeing each other again. She had told me about Ron and their volcanic marriage. One day I was helping her move the last of her furniture out of the house she and Ron had together, and he pulled up in his truck. He jumped out and started screaming at her. When he raised his hand to hit her, I tackled him, and we wrestled until he pulled out a knife. Melinda begged him to leave. I told him I was going to call the police. John Deere hadn't filed charges against him, but the police were aware that he needed to be watched. He ran towards his truck rather than face the cops. He was yelling every swear word he could get out. Millie was so embarrassed. The neighbors had come out of their houses and witnessed the entire encounter. I went in the house to call the cops, but Millie wouldn't let me. She said she didn't want any more of a scene and that she wasn't afraid of him. She was going to apply at JBT again and wanted to make sure that history with him wouldn't interfere with her getting the job this time. Look where that got her." Jeff held his head in his hands.

Phyllis was entirely different from her sister. She never let anyone, especially a man, push her around. She had been the pride and joy of her father, John Strigow. When she was a little girl, she went to ball games and on fishing excursions with him. She accompanied him to work at his construction company and loved the way he would tease her and her friends. Everyone was welcome in the Strigow home. She worshiped John Strigow. When she was ten years old a dark cloud settled over her father for a period and their lives changed. One thing she and her mother loved to do was to go fishing with him in their small boat. They would pack some sandwiches, grab a bunch of shiners from the marina store and head out to Lake Branson. Rain or shine they would head out and cast their lines, laughing as they all bartered for the biggest catch of the day. Phyllis remembers one day when it had rained in the morning, the clouds had parted, and the rain ceased about noon. A beautiful rainbow arched across the sky. It seemed as if they could reach up and touch the colors it was so bright. John was quieter than usual that day. He seemed to be just going through the motions without his usual teasing and chatter. Phyllis's mother seemed pre-occupied. Phyllis chortled away, interspersed with OOO's and AHHHH's over the amazing rainbow. When Phyllis asked, "What's the matter with Daddy?" her mother hugged her harder than she normally would have. Her father was the more affectionate of the two. Her father sat facing the stern of the boat not seeming to notice the beautiful rainbow.

“Daddy look at the rainbow! I wonder if we keep going towards the part where it touches the shore, we will find a pot of gold! Daddy, do you see it?”

John turned slightly and looked at his daughter. Her eyes glistened with excitement. His heart felt heavy in his chest. His voice was hoarse and came in almost a whisper, “There isn’t a pot of gold, precious. Those are vapors that look like they touch the earth. Some things in life aren’t always what they seem to be.” He turned and faced the back of the boat again. His shoulders drooped. His line lay idle in the water. Droplets of water, like teardrops, glistened in the sunlight as they hung from the line.

“What’s wrong with Daddy, Mom? He is sad. You should hug him instead of me.”

“He has a lot on his mind,” her voice cracked, and she rubbed her eyes under her sunglasses. “Your father has some things to deal with from work. Don’t worry, honey, he loves us very much.”

A few clouds covered the rainbow.

John Strigow was a hard worker and one of the most respected and honest men around the Quad cities. Ask anyone and they will say, “Good old John. You can trust him with your life”; “That Strigow guy is a saint. He never charged me for the repairs he did on my roof when the tree hit it last year in a big windstorm.”; “John Strigow—he’s a peach. The kids love him. He always has a pocket full of candy to hand out to them.”

John owned a construction company that had been started in his father’s barn. It had grown into a large firm due to its spotless reputation, safe and solid construction of his buildings and affordable prices. Hank Baldoni was John’s partner before John’s father passed away. Hank and John had grown up together. They went to the same grade school and high school, played the same pranks boys will play and learned the building trade from John’s father from the time they were old enough to hold a hammer. Hank always had trouble hanging on to his money. He liked to buy flashy cars, to shower his female companions with gifts which eventually lead him to the gambling tables. Casinos had become legal in Illinois and Hank made a point of blessing them with his presence. Hank also had been in on some shady business ventures with the mob and was trying to extricate himself from those. John had the opposite personality. His frugal practices allowed him to have a reasonable cushion in the bank to make sure he could cover rainy day expenses. Hank often got himself so deep in debt that he would play on John's kindness and their friendship to bail him out. John had several "come to Jesus" talks with Hank and had recently threatened to dissolve their partnership if things didn't change. Hank's addiction to the gambling scene was more about the ambiance than the winning or losing. He had streaks of luck when he gathered in chips lavishly then spent them to give him that "big man" image. This got him in hock with some very shady and unforgiving bookies and loan sharks, as well as the Casino banks that loaned him thousands, because he drew a crowd of potential naïve marks.

Strigow & Baldoni Construction had been hired to build a restaurant/bar/club on stilts on the top floor of a hotel on one of the small islands in the Mississippi River. The distance from the mainland and the nearest town was about three miles. The location they picked was at the point where the river was quite wide and deep. It would be tricky to drive support pilings into the muddy bottom strong enough to keep the structure intact and safe as well as withstand the current caused by a bend in the river at that point. John was working with a crew on a new stadium in Moline, so he gave the project to Hank. Hank always loved a challenge, and this certainly was one.

"Hank, we probably will spend more than usual on this one since the deck that surrounds the restaurant and bar needs to be well reinforced. It is on the top floor of the hotel, five stories up, and the patio /deck hangs out over the water at least fourteen feet. People will probably be dancing on that deck and God knows what else they'll be doing if they get juiced up." John pulled out the plans and laid them on the desk in front of Hank.

"Huh…what… Oh yeah," Hank mumbled as he looked absently at the diagram of the hotel and restaurant. His mind was on the second threat he had received in a phone call that morning from some syndicate thugs that ran the casinos in the area. They told him in no uncertain terms to pay up or they would make sure he was checking out for good. Hank and his crew began to work on construction of the hotel and patio deck outside the restaurant. Within two months the hotel was completed other than some finishing cosmetic work. The framework for the patio was in its early phase of construction. John met with Hank in between working on the stadium. John looked at his friend and noticed the dark circles under his eyes. Hank hadn't been himself the past few days. Usually he was full of energy and excited to be working on a challenging project. He always kidded with the crew and made sure they heard about his winnings and descriptions of the ladies he took to his bedroom.

"Hank, what's going on. You seem out of it the past week or so. Are you in trouble again?" John asked.

Hank straightened his drooping shoulders and put on a charming smile. "Now, Johnnie boy, not to worry. I'm just having a little row with my latest squeeze. Let's go over these plans and what kind of supports we need for this crazy porch."

John wanted to believe Hank. They had been friends since grade school and had worked very hard to build their business. They had strayed apart at times during the past year because of Hank's compulsive gambling and womanising. John still loved him like a brother. Despite Hank's defects his work had been almost impeccable. Phyllis and Alicia considered Hank part of the family. He teased Phyllis incessantly and he managed to pat Alicia on the bottom just to hear her squeal. They nick named him "Hanky Panky". He fit that name well.

Hank's attention wasn't totally on the details John was pointing out. Transporting of building materials and workers from the mainland had to be arranged on barges. They had to make sure they minimised the number of trips as it could hold up work. If the bid was off, the cost would be prohibitive. The beams that would extend from the main Hotel building to the deck surrounding the restaurant and bar were made of high-grade steel. Twenty-two beams in all would be placed under the structure at pie shaped intervals then connected to the main building at the edge of the river. The weight of the deck floor constructed of 4x6 oak cuts locked together with steel braces had to be calculated exactly so that the amount of steel reinforcements could be added to the connections to the main building as an added safety feature. A decorative wrought iron railing with a lattice design was attached to the floor and to the supports under the deck. Hank was responsible for making any changes to the design, ordering materials, shipping schedules, scheduling crews and making sure the structure would be safe. The maximum load of people was calculated at thirty, each weighing not more than two-hundred pounds. Warning signs would be placed in plain sight across from each of the glass doors leading from the restaurant. He was going to request additional funds to place support pilings from several areas of the porch into cement footers sunk into the bed of the river to insure the deck would not collapse in a bad storm or flood as well as overloading of patrons, despite the company giving warnings to the owners.

Hank's brain was paralysed by fear that any moment a bullet might find its mark, or he would be strapped to a cement block and thrown into the river. John didn't see Hank much during the months they were working on the two large projects. He didn't notice the weight loss, trembling hands and irritability affecting his partner. The construction of the stadium was moving along ahead of schedule. The main structure had been completed. They were waiting for the stands to be inserted, the artificial turf to be laid, and the concession stands and restrooms to be added. The project would be completed in time for another company to surface the parking lot. Hank's hotel and restaurant were nearly completed a little past schedule due to rain and some materials on back order. He wanted to get this project out of the way, so he could think of a way to get the money he owed the syndicate. He vowed, for the tenth time, that he would stop gambling and spending his money frivolously. As he stood on the deck and looked down at the water below, he felt guilty for not insisting on the additional supports. He jumped up and down on the deck and it felt solid. He had used the best and strongest materials and they might still take a loss from the original bid. The crystal chandeliers and furnishings were being installed in the restaurant and hotel. At night when the lights were on the building it looked like it was suspended in the water. The reflection of the lights in the water combined with the reflection from the stars overhead and the other businesses was breathtaking. The deck railing was decorated with tiny blinking lights. It looked like a beautiful necklace encircling the building.

Hank tried to focus on the final details of the project. He found himself panicking every time the door to the work trailer opened. Beads of sweat dripped onto the paperwork on his desk and he looked like a deer in the headlights to anyone entering. The crew members who knew Hank were very worried. They had voiced their concerns to John.

Bud Hartwig was a big man. His huge shoulders almost touched the door frame. He had to duck whenever he came in the trailer.

"Hey, Hank, gotta ask you somthin' about those support beams." Hank almost spilled his coffee as he spun his chair around to face the door. "Hank, what's eatin' you lately? You look like a guy who's seen a ghost!"

"Nothing. You just startled me. I was concentrating on this God-awful paperwork. What about the supports?" Hank grabbed his cold coffee and took a swig holding on to it to hide his trembling hands.

"I'm wondering if we shouldn't connect the support beams with 4x6's since we didn't put in an additional footer. I'm feelin' creepy about the distance between the cross bars running from the hotel to the porch." Bud plopped in a chair across from the desk where Hank was sitting. Hank stared at the schematics without seeing them. His mind was tortured by the threats from the guys he owed money to—more money than he had. Even if his friends were willing to help once again, he couldn't possibly raise enough by the deadline tomorrow. He had begged John to help him with a loan from the company, but John had been down that route before. Hank swore that he was done after the last two sprees. John didn't know that these guys had threatened Hank.

"Earth to Hank," Bud repeated as he shook Hank's shoulder. What's goin' on, buddy?"

"Bud don't worry about the supports. I'll take care of it. I'm just tired. Go back to work. I'm okay."

Bud hesitated, "You're sure there isn't anything I…"

"I said get back to work!" Hank shouted as he stood and glared at his friend. "Nothing's getting done with you hanging around here." Bud squinted at his boss. Hank had never yelled at anyone. This was a different Hank.

"Okay, okay, I'll go. Just order the damn supports!" Bud slammed the door behind him so hard that a picture of Hank and John when they first started the company fell off the wall and hit the floor hard enough for the glass to shatter. The first dollar they had earned had been placed with the picture and it flew across the room landing under the desk. Hank bent down to pick up the shattered frame and picture. He stared at the two young, smiling men, their eyes lit with excitement and hope for the future. Tears burned his eyes and he held the picture to his chest as he sobbed. He jumped up when the phone rang and wiped his eyes on his sleeve.

"Strigow Construction… Hank speaking," he said hoarsely.

"Meet me at the railroad yard at 9 pm tonight with the cash or you won't see another sunrise. Kapeesh?" A gravelly voice whispered.

"Wait! Wait!" The click of the phone felt like a bullet already barreling through his brain. He was nauseated and felt like he was going to heave as he fumbled with the combination to the safe. He reached in, his heart thumping so hard he could hear it in his ears and grabbed three large envelopes of cash—all that was in the safe. He stuffed them in a leather briefcase. His mouth was dry, and his stomach burned. *John…I'm so sorry. I'll pay you back. God, help me!* he could hardly stand his legs were so weak. He looked around at the trailer they hauled around so many sites …so many great jobs…so many great times. The door closed behind him.

The railroad yard was six miles west of the main part of town. Hank's red truck needed shocks. It hammered in and out of the potholes on US 24. The rugged ride only added a headache to his fried nerves and queasy stomach. Hank had been instructed to leave his truck outside the metal gates and walk between the railroad cars until he came to the Yard Master's Station. Then he was to drop the cash into a covered seat outside the building that contained tools used when there were problems with the train cars or tracks. The chain on the gate had been moved so that there was space enough for one moderately built person to squeeze through. In the distance, a train whistle grabbed the warm breeze with a mournful aria. His boots crunched into the gravel mixed with the screeching of frogs anxious to mate. There are points in peoples' lives where a choice to take a step forward or backward makes all the difference, that nanosecond when the choice between right and wrong resets the direction of a person's life. Hank felt the weight of that decision pulling him back towards his truck. The fear of consequences he would suffer, probably death, if he did not go through the gate and leave the money pulled him forward. The thought of his best friend and partner finding he had taken the company's money, the remorse and shame for the lifestyle that had led him to this point turned him around and he started to run back to the gate. Something hit him in the back so hard that he fell to the ground a few feet from the gate and the safety of his truck. As he started to run the bullet pierced his left side and the air in his left lung seeped into his chest cavity collapsing his lung. He gasped as he fought to keep moving but it seemed like his efforts were reduced to slow motion. Every breath sent a searing pain into his chest and back. The gravel scraped his skin as he was unable to break his fall. A hazy light shone on the ground near his head.

Muffled voices faded as he felt himself being dragged along the rocky ground. The blackness closed around him as he lost consciousness. The briefcase carrying the money from the construction business was ripped from his hand and his truck keys wrenched from his weakening grasp. Two men scanned the yard, their eyes eerily peering out through dark face masks. They dragged Hank's lifeless body over stones to a freight car, threw him into the dark opening and slid the door shut. The two men who had dumped Hank took some branches from a nearby tree and swept the ground where Hank had fallen and the area where his truck tires had made marks. One of the men slid into the driver's seat of Hank's red truck and drove it slowly onto the road outside of the railroad yard. The headlights did not come on until the truck was headed west towards a swampy area several miles from the yard. Hanover swamp was named after a young boy who had gone missing while catching frogs near the swamp many years ago. The hills near what was a small lake had been stripped of trees and brush by prospectors in the 1800's looking for opals. Whether true or just a tall tale, it was rumored that a large opal had been found in that area. With little attention to the ecosystem, greedy men raped the hillsides searching for a similar treasure. Rain undressed the injured damsel land further and her tears of mud slid into the lake rendering it a murky brown the consistency of melted peanut butter. Rodney Hanover was never found but his ghost was reported to be seen hovering over the lake in the early morning and late evening. The small box he had fashioned from a shoebox was found lying frog-less near the swamp.

The man driving Hank's truck stopped at the edge of Hanover swamp and moved the shifter into drive position. He wiped away any trace of his prints even though he was wearing gloves. He jumped from the truck as it slowly headed towards the swamp. The swamp mud oozed around the truck, broke the windows and crept into the cab. The only part of the truck that wasn't enveloped in mud was the antenna and the roof of the cab. An owl watched the mud gobble the truck like a hungry monster. His sad call followed the waning footsteps as the hooded man ran towards a black sedan.

The freight train awaited the tall chute preparing to empty coal into the cars. It was scheduled to take its load to Pennsylvania.

John came over to the construction company trailer to see if Hank needed any help with plans to reinforce the porch attached to the hotel. He did not see Hank's truck. He hoped that Hank had gone to the restaurant site rather than to the gambling tables. He was surprised to find the door unlocked. Cautiously, he opened the door. It made a groaning noise as John entered the room. He peered around the corner, behind the door and peeked under the bed and chairs before he spoke.

"Hank… Hey Hank! Where are you, man?" he looked at the cluttered desk, the empty chairs and half empty coffee pot. The floor was littered with glass. He picked up the shattered picture and dollar bill he and Hank had earned when they started their business. As he moved closer to the desk, he could see that the safe door was open. Almost leaping over the desk, he stared into the empty safe his heart pumping "no, no, no" in his ears. The safe had contained three-thousand dollars in cash for incidentals for the restaurant project. Hank and John were always careful to lock the work trailer whenever they left the site. John was about to call the police when he noticed the plans for the hotel/restaurant open on the desk. Part of the additional support beams had been penciled into the schematic. John thought, *Hank probably went into town to the lumber yard to purchase the beams and forgot to close the safe after he took the money.* He breathed a little easier. Hank had been distraught lately, for sure. John felt bad that he refused to give Hank money to pay off some gambling debt, but it was time that Hank faced his addiction and sought help.

Bud ran as fast as he could towards the work trailer when he saw John's truck parked nearby. Bud burst through the door almost sacrificing the hinges. His face was red, and his massive chest heaved as he tried to force the words out, "John… Hank's truck… They…they found it buried in the Hanover Swamp's mud! Hank wasn't in the cab and they have not found him! They are searching the area around the railroad yard and between that and the swamp! Geez! What the hell was he doing out there? He lives on the other side of town." The burly carpenter plopped into the sagging couch. He bent over and rubbed his greying hair with large, calloused hands.

"Bud, slow down. Where did you hear this?

"On the radio when I was on my way to work. They suspect foul play. Damn right there is somethin' foul about this. Hank babied that truck like he'd given birth to it. He would never leave it in gear with it running let alone near a hill and a swamp. Some creep did this. Probably one of those McQuade boys. They're always lookin' for trouble. Just last week…"

"Hank wasn't here when I got here. The safe door was left open and I assumed he took the money to go to the lumber yard for extra beams and forgot to lock it. If his truck was found in the swamp maybe someone followed him and robbed him. I… I don't know. I better call the Sheriff and tell him about the unlocked safe. I sure hope he's okay. He's been down and agitated these past couple of weeks." John picked up the phone and started to dial the Sheriff's office. *I sure hope Hank wasn't that desperate for cash that he would rob his own company. No… It's just not like him.* John quickly erased that thought and concentrated on reporting the open safe to the authorities. *I know he was worried about money he owed somebody. I wouldn't give him another loan. Figured it was about time he got help for his gambling problem.* "Um, hello. This is John Strigow from Strigow Construction. I'd like to report a possible robbery and a miss…um at our work trailer. We are located on a lot on Plankard Rd. several miles from the railroad yard. There is a crossroad about twenty yards from the site called Archibold Rd. Yes, Sir. I'm not sure that anyone was here but $3000 is gone from the safe and I can't imagine any of our guys leaving it open. Yes, Sir, I will be here." John turned to Bud, "Bud, did Hank say anything to you about using cash to purchase support beams for his hotel project?"

Bud scratched his head, "I remember he said he was going to put in a work order. Gosh, I hope he's okay."

Hank did not come to work the next two days. John went to his apartment, called him several times but heard nothing. A missing persons' report was filed. John contacted all the suppliers the company used to obtain materials for their projects. No one had heard from Hank since a week prior when he was ordering goods for the hotel project. The stadium project was completed. John focused on the restaurant project. The police searched Hank's apartment for any clues to his whereabouts. It seemed like he had disappeared. They dragged the entire swamp for several days without any results except furniture and other debris. Hank's truck was examined for fingerprints—even Hank's own prints were not found on the steering wheel leading them to believe someone had wiped it clean. The keys were in the ignition and the gear was in drive. After two weeks, the search was suspended. It was assumed Hank had crawled out of the truck window, had not been able to get to shore and been swallowed up by the muddy ooze of the swamp. John begged the sheriff to keep having the search team drag the swamp.

"John, I know that Hank was a good friend and your partner. Believe me, we will continue to put out APB's to other counties to see if he turns up anywhere. We've done all we can do, and more, to locate his body…I mean him."

"Don't say "body! I know that Hank used to go to Chicago to some of the casino's there. He mentioned he had met a girl there and she was special to him. I'm going to go there and see if I can find her. Maybe she might have seen him or knows something about him we don't. I think he was mixed up with some shady characters because of gambling. Maybe he was running from them." John rubbed his calloused hands over his forehead.

"That is not something you should be doing, John. If you can give me the name and location of this lady, we will check it out."

"I'm sure these people won't be happy to talk to the cops. The woman he was friendly with, well…she doesn't have the best reputation. She absolutely would run if she saw or heard a cop!"

"Promise me if you find out anything you will let us follow up. If he was involved with the gambling syndicate, they are very dangerous. You need to give us anything you know."

"Hank had promised he would come back for her. Maybe that is what he did. I will stay away from the casinos and just focus on her." John meant that he would keep them in the loop, but the loop kept getting wider and wider.

John shared his concerns with his wife about Hank's involvement with some less than reputable characters and Hank had asked John for money before his disappearance. He did not tell her that money was missing from the safe at the office nor the real reason he was going to Chicago. He told Alicia that he needed to meet with some contractors in the area. Perhaps he could find a temporary replacement for Hank. Alicia rarely saw John depressed. She suggested he take her and Phyllis for a short fishing trip before he left.

Even the beautiful rainbow and fishing with the two women he loved dearly couldn't take his mind of Hank. If Hank had taken money from the safe to pay off his gambling debts John could forgive him. He was worried that Hank might have been beaten or killed by these thugs.

Sally Thatcher lived in a run—down apartment building on the lower east side of Gary Indiana. Everything seemed to be covered with a dingy grey film from the factories surrounding the neighborhood. Even the air was a smoky grey color covering the sun. Sally, known as Sal, had a job. It paid for the rent, food, cigarettes and cheap booze. The men she "entertained" had to wear a condom as they used her body on the squeaky beds at Madam Olivia's Gentlemen's Club. The sickening smell of vanilla candles burning helped Sal to close her eyes and mind to the grunts and groans of men using her for their pleasure. It had become such a routine part of her life that she could ignore the pain of their aggressive thrusts, the biting the nipples of her breasts and the trashy words they growled. They were faceless instruments in the job she had been forced to do since she was thirteen years old. She had no other skills. Even if she wanted to get out of the streets littered with garbage, both human and inanimate, she couldn't. The few times she tried to escape her owners beat her and threatened to kill her. At times, she thought death would be the better option. One of her clients had treated her like a human being. That man did not force himself on her. He had talked to her and gently made love to her in a way she had never experienced. The fourth time he came to her he said he was in love with her and promised to take her away from the hell in which she existed. But, like all the other men, he hadn't shown up for almost a month. Hank had said that he had some business to take care of at the Casino and then he would work out a plan to help her escape. Sal had made a mistake believing Hank. They had made love, not just sex, really made love-passionate, tender love without condoms; without vanilla candles; without Madam Olivia's or her pimp's oversight. They had explored each other's bodies with real feelings, with a respectfulness that Sally had never known since her life had been taken from her when she was very young, sold to anyone who would pay and thrown into the gutter with the rest of the prostitutes.

When John Strigow knocked on Sally's door, she was just about to inject herself with enough street drug to end her life and the baby growing inside her. She felt it would be better to end it this way rather than being beaten to death by her pimp and his henchmen. Getting pregnant meant termination in the true sense of the word; not in her job description. Sal hid the syringe in the toilet tank when she heard the knock on her door. God must have been watching over her and urging her to answer John's persistent pounding. The chain on the door allowed only a small portion of the tiny woman's face to show as she cautiously opened it. Her eyes were deep blue, and her eyelashes blinked as the daylight hit her face. There were dark circles under her eyes. Her face was childlike, and her ivory skin had no blemishes other than a tiny scar over her upper lip.

"Yeah, what do you want," she whispered.

" My name is John Strigow. I'm Hank Baldoni's friend. Are you Sally Thatcher?"

The man standing outside her door had kind eyes and a pleasant voice. He appeared to be much different from the men she was used to meeting. Anyhow, her pimp would have arranged to meet a client at Madam Olivia's, not at her apartment. She drew in a breath and her heart rate quickened at the sound of Hank's name. *Hank never came back. He's like all the rest. I thought he was different. Now I have this kid inside me.* She slammed the door shut and locked it as she yelled, "Go to hell!" Tears filled her eyes as she leaned against the door. She hadn't cried in years—not even when they beat her, not even when the men ravaged her body, not even afterwards when the humiliation, the pain and feeling like a piece of shit hit her like a hurricane. She was crying because the prison walls of non-feeling she had built to survive had been breached.

John knocked on the door again. She could hear his muffled pleas. "Please, Ms Thatcher, open the door. We can't find Hank. We think someone was after him and might have hurt or killed him!" Sally's heart skipped a couple of beats when she heard Hank might be dead. She unlocked the door and removed the chain as she pulled John into the dismal entrance.

"Follow me." Sal walked down a dreary hallway. The paint was peeling off the walls and the carpet was threadbare.

She's just a child, for God's sake. John thought as he followed her slim body down the hall into her apartment. She pointed to a chair with torn covers on the sagging arm rests. The rest of the apartment was shabby, but neat. There was a three—legged table with a yellowed lace doily under a picture of a woman, a cot covered with a quilt made of patches of faded material, a microwave with some dials missing and a small dresser. There was a room to the left of the hallway that appeared to be a bathroom.

"You think Hank is in trouble? Do you think he is…? Dead?" She sat across from him on a wooden chair wringing her hands.

"We haven't seen or heard from him in three weeks. The police found his truck in a swampy lake but no sign of him. He told me about you Ms Thatcher."

"You can call me Sally."

"He wanted to help you get out of… I mean, help you move near him. He really cares about you. I thought maybe he may have told you about anyone that was looking for him or if he was going somewhere."

"I don't know anything. I only saw him a few times. He was nice to me." She folded her arms around her chest. She was wearing tight jeans with holes in the knees, a loose-fitting green sweater that did a poor job of hiding a shapely figure. Her hair was blond with dark roots showing through a part. The bright red lipstick and dark eye shadow covered a face that looked young, but her eyes looked like that of a much older woman. Perhaps they had seen much more of the dark world than they should have. John felt sorry for her as he thought about his daughter, Phyllis. Sally couldn't be much older than eighteen or nineteen.

"Did he tell you about anyone he might owe money to?"

"We didn't have much time to talk. I'm only supposed to spend one hour with a client. I mean a date." She began to cry holding her head in her hands. John didn't know if he should console her.

"Sally, I'm so sorry I made you upset. Is there anything I can do?"

"I'm pregnant."

John leaned towards her. "What? You think it is Hank's!"

"Yes, I'm sure it is his. We didn't use protection the last two times. I feel so stupid. They will kill me!" Her shoulders shook.

John walked over to her and put his hand on her shoulder. "Who will hurt you?"

"The people who own me run the casino. If they find out I was seeing someone here and I am pregnant they will kill me and the baby! I was going to do it myself…then you knocked, and I don't know why I answered it." She sobbed, and her body trembled.

"We have got to get you out of here, for God's sake."

"There is nowhere for me to go! I have no money. I have nothing."

"You are alive now and we will find a safe place for you to stay and a way to take care of you and the baby."

"It's too dangerous. These men are horrible! You don't even know me."

"Hank saw something in you, and he would want me to do this. Now, get together any of your things you want to take. We won't be coming back here." John was trembling. He didn't know what he was going to do with a pregnant call girl. Sal grabbed a duffel bag and stuffed some clothes from the closet and the dresser into it. John took the bag and began to go down the hallway.

"Wait! The pictures! I have to take the pictures." John waited while Sally put the two pictures that were on the three—legged table tenderly into her bag. He helped her into his truck. It was getting dark. He looked both ways and saw no-one on the street as he jumped into the driver's seat and sped away from the curb. He passed people standing or lying in doorways and on benches. They were faceless in the few streetlights that were working. Several people standing on a corner started to walk towards the truck. John looked quickly for cars coming across the intersection and ran the red light before they reached the truck. Sally hunched in her seat so that she could not be seen in the window. Beads of sweat trickled down John's face and armpits as he tried to keep to the speed limit, so he wouldn't be stopped by a cop. It started to rain, and the wind blew garbage lining the curbs in front of the truck. Neither spoke until they were safely out of the ghetto and on the highway headed towards Moline.

"Sally, I am taking you to our house until we can work out a plan. My wife, Alicia, is very kind. You will like her. I have a ten—year-old daughter named Phyllis. She is always asking questions about everything. Don't let that bother you. I'll do my best to put a reign on her. We will do our best to keep you safe." John wasn't sure what to do with a frightened, pregnant girl who had led a terrible life. Hank was missing, and John wasn't sure that he was the father of Sally's baby. "Are you hungry?" John could see Sally's skinny arms. She hardly had any fat on her. She didn't look pregnant, but her belly was covered by the oversized sweater she wore.

"I guess," she murmured staring at the truck window. "I suppose I should eat for the baby."

John pulled the truck into a fast food restaurant and ordered a chicken sandwich, some fries and a milkshake at the drive thru. It probably wasn't the best food for an expectant mother, but it was nourishment just the same. They drove on while she picked at the meal. The rain stopped, and the night sky unfolded its tapestry of stars.

"Sally, can you think of anyone Hank might he owed money to?"

"There was this guy that came to see my p… er, boss one day. I overheard the guy say Hank's name, so I hid behind a door and heard him say he was going to find Hank and make him pay up. When I saw Hank about a month ago (she began to cry) he…he shook his head and told me to stay away from that guy and forget about it. He promised me he would come and get me. I didn't know I was pregnant then. When he didn't come back, I was so pissed off…but now I am so scared that he is hurt or dead! What am I going to do with a baby? I can barely take care of myself." Her tears dripped on to her half—eaten sandwich. John gripped the steering wheel harder.

"It will be okay. We will find him. Hank is a survivor." John's voice was shaking. They spoke very little as John headed home.

The lights were on in John's house when they arrived. Sally was hesitant to come out of the truck, but John finally convinced her. She hid behind the big man as he hugged and kissed Alicia.

"Who have we here?" Alicia smiled as she peered around her husband.

"Alicia, this is Sally, Hanks girlfriend from Gary. I brought her here to stay with us for a while. I hope it is okay with you. I can explain more later. She is exhausted and so am I. Could she stay in our spare bedroom? Is Phyl still awake?" John stared at Alicia trying to burn his request into her giving heart.

Alicia loved John so much that she held her questions and put her arm gently around the girl. "Phyllis is upstairs waiting for you to tuck her in. Come on upstairs with me, Sally. We can get you a nice warm bath and some pajamas. I have some leftover meatloaf for some sandwiches. I'm sure you are very tired and hungry." Alicia guided Sally through a cheerful kitchen that smelled like apples, through a dining room and living room with cozy furniture without holes. They passed a fireplace and a TV.

"My name is Sally Thatcher. People call me Sal." Sally said as Alicia guided her up a stairway and into a bathroom. Alicia went to a cupboard and brought out fluffy blue towels, a matching washcloth, a toothbrush and toothpaste. Sally's eyes were wide, and she smiled thinking of wrapping herself in the towels. The walls in the bathroom were painted with whales and dolphins jumping into foaming waves. They looked so real that Sally wanted to touch them. They were free and even seemed to smile at her.

"Sally…Sal, feel free to take a shower or bath. I'll bring in some pajamas for you. When you are done, I will introduce you to Phyllis. There is soap and shampoo on the ledge in the shower. Let me show you your room first. It was hard to pull the tiny girl away from her mesmerised state staring at the whales and dolphins. Alicia guided Sal to a room not far from the bathroom. Phyllis heard voices outside her bedroom. She slipped out of her warm covers and tiptoed into the hallway.

"Where is Daddy?" she asked as she glanced at Sal who was trying to hide behind Alicia.

"He is downstairs, honey. He will be up soon to tuck you in. Phyl, this is Sally Thatcher, Sal for short. She is a friend of Hanks and your father has brought her here for a while. Sal, this is our daughter, Phyllis. She likes to be called Phyl. Sal is very tired and hungry so let's hold our questions until she gets a good night's sleep. Okay honey?" Alicia looked at Phyl who appeared to be holding back a bevy of questions.

"Hi Sal, I hope you like it here. I'm ten years old in a few days. I am so sorry we haven't heard from Hank. He is like a member of our family. I…"

"Honey let Sal here get a shower or bath and we can hold the questions until tomorrow. Please go back to bed and your father will be up soon to tuck you in."

The spare bedroom looked like the Taj Mahal to Sally. She sunk into the plush brown carpet and gazed at the puffy bedspread with birds in various poses flying about on the material. There was a small dresser and a dressing table with a mirror that wasn't cracked and smeared with cigarette smoke haze.

John came upstairs calling, "Phyl, Phyl, my little pill - where is my beautiful daughter?"?

"Daddy…Daddy! I missed you so much. Did you find Hanky Panky? Did you meet Sally? She is going to stay with us for a while. Right?" Phyllis asked questions while she ran to her father and hugged him tightly. Sally had retreated to the bathroom and shut the door.

"Where are you, Sal? Are you hiding? Playing a game of hide and seek? I love games!" John picked up his chatterbox daughter carrying her into her bedroom. She giggled and wriggled pretending to try and get out of his arms. John gently laid her on her bed and pulled the covers up to her chin.

"We haven't given up looking for Hank, honey. Please try not to worry. We will find him. Sally has had a very difficult life. We are going to help her because it is the right thing to do." He gently pushed her hair away from her forehead and gave her a kiss.

"Sal looks sad, Daddy. Is she sad because we haven't found Hank?"

"Yes, I'm sure she is worried. You go to sleep, now, and we will talk more in the morning, honey." John kissed her again and winked at her as he walked towards her door.

"I'll say a prayer for Sal and Hank, Daddy."

"That's my girl." John felt proud of his only child and sad for the young woman he had rescued.

Sally sat on the fuzzy blue toilet seat that was so different from the cold, cracked seat at her apartment. She stared at the wallpaper and imagined how wonderful it would be to jump in and out of the water like the whales imprinted on the paper. Her life since she had been abducted from her family had taught her to trust no-one. She had already allowed herself to be taken by a stranger from a world she had forgotten, a home with pleasant furnishings and soft spoken, kind people. She was sure she was pregnant with Hank's baby and that he was probably like all the other men she knew. She had trusted Hank and allowed herself to believe that her really loved her and would do right by his promise to come for her and love her. At least in her world she knew what each day would be like. She had pills to wash away any feelings, so she could continue to robotically do her job. Her body was a cheap bauble dangled by her abusive pimp. Her hands were shaking as she sat motionless, unable to face a world foreign to her.

There was a soft knock on the door, "Sally, may I come in? I'm sure this is all overwhelming. This is Alicia. Please let me help you." Alicia waited for a good five minutes before Sally opened the bathroom door slightly. Her big, brown eyes stared through the opening.

"I promise I will not ask any more questions. There is a bedroom across the hall. I laid a pair of my pajamas on the bed for you. Feel free to take a shower or bath. There are more clean towels and washcloths in the cupboard in the bathroom. Try to get some sleep, dear. I will have breakfast for you in the morning and you can ask me any question. I'm sure you are exhausted and anxious. Let me know if you need anything. I will be in the room down the hall for a while before going to bed. That is my sewing room. I love to sew. Good night. Sleep as late as you want." Sally stared at Alicia through the crack in the door until she turned and walked to her sewing room. Alicia was sure those big brown eyes had seen more of life than they should have.

Sally closed the door and filled the tub with hot water and some pink liquid that smelled like flowers. As soon as the liquid hit the hot water it rose into bubbles. The light turned the bubbles into tiny rainbows. She was so mesmerised by them that they began to ooze over the edge of the tub onto the floor. Sally quickly turned off the water and took her shabby clothes off. When she stepped into the tub the bubbles popped as her body seemed to melt into the hot, flowery bath. She closed her eyes and smiled as the bubbles enveloped her thin body. It was amazing. She had not had a hot bath or shower in so long. Any place her owner kept her always smelled like old cigarettes and garbage. The apartments rarely had a tub or even a poor excuse for a shower. She often had to wash herself from a filthy sink with tepid water. She always felt unclean. She filled her washcloth with the suds and scrubbed her face, her arms, her legs—every part of her. Wishing she could scrub away the horrible life she had been forced to live, she stayed in the tub until the bubbles had disappeared and the water was no longer warm. She scrubbed her hair bending under the faucet. The towel was soft and thicker than any she had used. When she had dried herself, she wrapped the towel around her hair like a turban. She looked in the mirror and was surprised to see how young she looked without the gaudy make-up she caked on before she met her clients. She felt like the painting of her face was the mask she had to wear to block the sadness inside. She couldn't wash away the bruises and scars on her arms and chest from the beatings her pimp doled out on a regular basis. He seemed to take pleasure in watching her cower in a corner as he called her a "cunt" and several other humiliating titles. She hated and feared him. When she ran away from home seven years ago, she had only meant to go a couple of blocks with her small pink suitcase. She wanted to teach her babysitter, Monica, a lesson. Monica made it very clear to Sally and her brother she really didn't like kids though she put on a good act for Sally's parents. That creepy girl could be sweet and syrupy when the parents were around, pretending to hug and cuddle the kids. As soon as the parents left for work, she would ignore her charges, plop on the couch to watch TV or talk on the phone with her friends. The only lunch she knew how to make was peanut butter smeared on a single piece of bread. Sally was a difficult child. She fought rules from the time she was a toddler. Her parents had even taken her to a counselor a couple of times. They both worked in menial jobs and couldn't afford the prescription the counselor ordered for Sally's passive-aggressive behavior. They were good people and tried to bring up their children the best they knew how.

Sal figured she could hide if Monica even cared enough to notice she was gone. She would teach that lazy girl to treat her brother and her like they were invisible. Monica was busy talking on the phone with her latest squeeze. She had sent Sally to her room for some reason and Sally's brother, Ben, was busy emptying a cupboard of its pots and pans and banging them with a spoon. When their parents came home from work, Ben was asleep on the kitchen floor and Sally was not in her room. Monica made up some story about playing hide and seek. She even called Sally's name to come out from her hiding place. The Thatchers were livid as they searched the house and yard for their daughter, put Ben in his crib and fired Monica.

The white truck with "Harbor Electric" painted on the sides drove West towards Chicago. In the back, behind the drivers, was a pink suitcase, a teddy bear with one eye missing and a drugged twelve-year-old girl whose life, as she knew it, would drastically change.

Sally dried herself with a soft blue towel, brushed her teeth and stared at her image in the mirror. She was only nineteen. Without the gaudy make-up, she was used to wearing she appeared to be about fourteen years old. Her hair was wavy and used to be auburn. She pulled aside the bleached part of her hair to look at the dark roots. Tears welled up in her eyes as suppressed memories of a life she had almost forgotten surfaced. *I'll let my hair grow out. Maybe I can grow into a better person, a better life. Please, God, help me.* She wiped away her tears, wrapped the blue towel around her after breathing a deep breath into it. She tiptoed into the bedroom across the hall. The nightgown Mrs Strigow had laid on the bed was too long, but she loved the feel of it on her skin. After she folded the towel neatly and placed it on a table, she slid under the crisp, yellow sheets and warm comforter. She felt safe, clean and warm for the first time in many years. She slept and dreamed of sailboats and smiling whales jumping high in the air and diving into a sea of pink and blue bubbles.

Melinda felt the thing in her throat that kept her from talking being removed. She coughed and gagged while someone kept telling her everything was okay, just relax, we know this is hard. Just work with us. Melinda felt like part of her throat was being pulled out along with the tube. Mucus filled her throat. The person put something in her mouth that reminded her of when she went to the dentist to have her teeth cleaned. The suction tube was removed, and a mask was placed over her mouth and nose. Cool, moist air entered her airway. She was instructed to take slow, deep breaths. Every part of her body ached. She couldn't move her arms or legs. They seemed to be tied down. Melinda tried to speak but only a tiny squeak came out. She was so confused. Where was she? Why were all these strangers hovering around her? Why were her legs and arms tied down? She couldn't remember her name.

Who am I? Where am I? I am so frightened. I surely am late for work, but I can't remember if, or where I work. Help me! Somebody helps me! She tried to yell for help as she struggled to release an arm, so she could grab the girl who was standing near her bed. Tears burned her eyes.

"Melinda, I am a respiratory therapist. My name is Rachael. Try to relax. We are going to take off the restraints on your arms and legs. You need to promise us that you won't take the mask off your face. This is your nurse, Carey. You were in an accident and are in the hospital in Moline, Illinois."

Carey smiled at Millie and gently removed the restraint from Millie's right arm She held her hand "Melinda, we just took a tube out of your throat that was helping you to breath. I know you are frightened and confused. As soon as your throat feels better, and you can talk we will try to answer your questions." Carey said kindly. Millie looked around at the monitors, the IV lines, the bright lights and her two companions. Her breathing slowed slightly. She tried to make sense of what she had been told.

Hospital? Accident? I don't remember anything.

Carey continued, "You are getting better. The reason we have your arms and legs restrained is that we knew you may not remember some things. It was critical that you not remove the tube we had in your throat because it was helping you to breathe. You had surgery on your right leg, and it is in a cast so that it can heal. The surgeons also removed a blood clot from your brain, so your hair had to be shaved off. Don't try to talk yet. Your voice will get stronger. For now, I am giving you a writing board, so you can tell us what you need and can ask questions. I'm going to moisten your lips with some oil. They are very dry. I can't give you anything to eat or drink until I know you are able to swallow. We are giving special nutrition through the tubes in your veins in your shoulder. It's not steaks but it is giving you nourishment."

Melinda listened to Carey, her eyes wide and terribly frightened. It was difficult to take it all in—the tubes, the lights, the beeping of the monitors and, most of all the strange faces. Carey gently removed one of Melinda's arm restraints instructing her not to reach for or pull on any of the lines attached to her body. Carey handed Melinda the dry erase board and a marking pen. She rolled up the head of the bed, so Melinda was sitting up. Melinda looked around the room and then focused on the board.

Her hands shook as the pen seemed to way several pounds. MY NAME IS MELINDA?

Carey nodded "Yes."

WHAT HAPPENED TO ME?

"Melinda, someone hit you with a car or truck while you were waiting for a bus last week."

I HAVE TO GET TO WORK, BUT I DON'T KNOW WHY ……OR WHERE.

"I'm not sure, Melinda. You have a friend, Jeff Collins, and a sister waiting to see you outside the unit. Do you want me to bring them in? Maybe they can answer some of your questions. Can I get anything for you?"

"NO… SISTER?

"Her name is Phyllis. She has been here since you had your accident."

"WHO IS THE FRIEND?"

"His name is Jeff Collins. He was on a bus when he saw you lying in the street near your house. He has been very worried about you. He really saved your life." Carey smiled. "He realised he knew you. He was on his way to see you when you had your accident. He laid next to you to keep you warm and to keep you from moving until the ambulance came."

"I COULD HAVE DIED?"

"You were hurt quite badly. The doctors had to do surgery to fix your injuries. Melinda, do you remember anything?"

"NO, ONLY SOMETHING ABOUT WORK." Melinda closed her eyes and tried to remember.

"If you aren't too tired, I can have Phyllis and Jeff come in to see you. Only for a few minutes though." Carey touched Melinda's hand gently. Melinda shook her head "yes".

Carey went out to the waiting room to speak with Phyllis and Jeff. Phyllis had closed her eyes, her paperwork falling to the floor. Jeff sat with his head resting against the wall. His eyes were closed, but he could not sleep.

"Mr Collins…Jeff." Jeff jumped up from his chair towering over the five-foot-one Carey. "I'm sorry to wake you." Carey smiled as she looked towards Phyllis. Phyllis opened her eyes and stared blankly at Jeff and Carey. She remembered where she was.

"Oh, dear! Is there something wrong?"

"The breathing tube has been removed and Melinda is breathing well on her own. That is a good sign. She has an oxygen mask on, and her throat is very sore, so it is difficult for her to talk. She doesn't seem to remember anything other than something about work. She has a dry erase—board so she can write questions and answers. She didn't remember her name either." Carey addressed both with a sympathetic tone.

"Oh, my God! Was it from the head injury? Poor Millie." Jeff slumped in the chair holding his head.

"Hopefully, this is temporary," Carey sat between both Phyllis and Jeff. "after a traumatic experience or surgery some amnesia can occur. I want to talk to you, Ms Strigow, privately unless you agree to have Jeff involved. We need your permission to share information about Melinda and to have Jeff visit her as well. Before the accident, did she prefer to be called Millie?" Jeff started to answer. He thought better of it and waited for Phyllis to answer.

Phyllis stood and picked up her paperwork, arranged them neatly and placed them back in the briefcase before answering. "Can we see Melinda?" she asked, her voice emphasising "Melinda" instead of answering Carey's question. Carey stood facing Phyllis. There appeared to be something very icy about Melinda's sister.

"You can see her for just a few minutes. I caution you to introduce yourselves and your relationship to Melinda. She may not recognise either of you. Please keep any questions very brief. Allow her to ask you questions. If you would, see if she responds to being called Millie. Try to be as positive as you can be. I know this is difficult. Ms Strigow, would you give your permission for Mr Collins to see Melinda, and receive information about her condition?" Carey waited as Phyllis looked disapprovingly at Jeff.

After an uncomfortable silence, Phyllis agreed to Jeff being involved in Melinda's care and to visit her. Carey took Phyllis into the Intensive Care Unit first. Jeff filled a cup of day-old coffee, set it on a small table without drinking it. Jeff wanted to see Millie and tell her that he loved her-that he always had loved her from the day they met in college. He was going to Millie's apartment that awful day of the accident to tell her how he felt about her. He wanted to protect her.

The walk down the hall to the double doors that led to the Intensive Care Unit gave Phyllis time to formulate how she was going to approach Melinda. *If she was still on the ventilator and sedated, it would be easier,* she thought. It had been over a year since she had contact with her sister. She had distanced herself from Melinda to advance her career and to try to run from the nagging realisation that she would someday have to tell her sister the secrets hidden from her all these past twenty years. Phyllis had been the big sis, the protector and the buddy to Melinda since she was born. When Phyllis's father had told her the truth before he died, she started to pull away from Melinda.

Phyllis felt as though she hardly knew the person lying in the hospital bed. She looked like a little girl with her shaved head, intravenous lines pouring fluids into her thin arms and lights flashing, monitors beeping all around her. A suture line on the right side of her head looked like the smiles painted on the doll Melinda had received one Christmas. Tiny hairs sprouted from her shaved head. Phyllis wondered if Melinda's hair would grow back in the soft auburn curls she had when she was a child.

She still is a child. I can't do this! Melinda's lips were dry and cracked. She looked like an angel. She had several scrapes and lacerations on the right side of her face. She looked so much like her… Phyllis almost knocked Carey over as she attempted to run from the cubicle—run from the secrets and memories that flooded her heart.

Carey had extensive experience during her nursing career. She had worked in the Emergency Room and the Intensive Care Units for over twenty-six years. Her ability to read people and to observe subtle changes had been refined with her experiences. The Phyllis that came into the Unit to see Millie was not the aloof, composed Phyllis that she encountered in the Waiting Room. Millie's sister's face became drawn and tears filled her eyes when she entered Millie's cubicle. Carey was puzzled but her focus was on her patient. She checked for new orders from the physicians, settings on Intravenous fluids and nutritional fluids, medications to be given and monitor results and adjustments. After Phyllis's abrupt departure she wanted Millie to rest. Millie was exhausted after the removal of the breathing apparatus and the trauma of realising she was in a strange place without her memory intact.

Phyllis had grabbed her briefcase and ran towards the elevator. Upon seeing her hasty departure, Jeff became frightened that Millie had taken a turn for the worse. He jumped up calling after Phyllis and spilling his coffee on the floor of the Waiting Room. Ignoring the spill, he got to the elevator Phyllis had entered just as the doors were closing. Phyllis didn't want to talk to him or anyone. She cowered at the back of the elevator behind the other passengers. A man holding a plantar of flowers pressed back into the elevator to let Jeff in. The old man had a protruding belly that hung over his belt, faded blue jeans and a checked flannel shirt. His baseball cap sported a dismal pennant of the Cleveland Indians above a ribbon of stain from too many wearings or too much Brill Cream. Next to the man was a rather portly woman with a low—cut shirt exposing mountainous breasts. The embroidery on the shirt read "Women Rule". She inspected Jeff like a sergeant would inspect his platoon. She smiled at him with a lilaceous look in her eyes as she applied dark red lipstick to her lips. Tarantula eyelashes batted at Jeff who was attempting to get Phyllis's attention, not the flirty woman's. The ride from the ninth floor to the ground floor seemed to take forever. The elevator stopped on the fifth floor to let the elderly man with the flowers off. "Women Rule" pressed against Jeff more than necessary to allow the man to exit. Phyllis had to chuckle as she noted the visible crack in the woman's butt when she bent forward to snuggle up to Jeff who was trying to plaster himself against the side of the elevator. A man and woman in matching business suits, perfectly coiffed hair and rolling suitcases pushed into the elevator past Jeff and his new "girlfriend". They both wore badges identifying them as sales-reps for a pharmaceutical company. On the fourth floor a man or boy in a black "hoody", drooping pants dangling precariously on his hips and grubby tennis shoes joined the passengers. He held a lit cigarette cupped in his hand, the smoke traveling up the sleeve of his sweatshirt. He kept shifting his weight from one foot to another and humming. The flirty "Women Rule" lady shifted her attention away from Jeff when she smelled the smoke from the cigarette.

"Hey, can't you read? There is no smoking on elevators." She shouted as she pointed to the no smoking sign.

"Shut the fuck up!" the hooded gentleman shouted at her.

"Creep!" she snarled as she pressed against Jeff with her backsidc.

The bell chimed for the first floor and the elevator doors opened just before round one of a fight ensued. Phyllis had seen her opportunity to inch her way towards the elevator door opposite Jeff who was trapped by the woman and hooded man. She darted between the half-open doors into the lobby, between people in wheelchairs, security guards and visitors. She pushed through the revolving doors and hopped into a cab that was waiting at the curb. Jeff watched the taillights of the cab and turned back towards the elevators. He took the stairs two at a time to the ninth floor, hesitant to take another elevator adventure. He rang the buzzer at the entrance to the Intensive Care Unit as he tried to catch his breath. He was in pretty good shape for a thirty-year-old. He tried to work out at the gym several times a week. When there was no answer to the buzzer, he returned to the Waiting Room and tried to clean up the spilled coffee stain he had left. He used the phone to ring the ICU and waited for an answer.

"This is Jeff Collins and I was wondering if I could speak to Melinda Sherman's nurse, Carey." He tried to steady his breathing though his heart was still pounding rapidly.

"I'll see if she can come to the phone, Mr Collins. Can I put you on hold?" the pleasant Clerk answered.

Jeff waited, tapping his foot nervously. “This is Ms Fernier. Is this Mr Collins?” he recognised Carey’s voice.

“Yes…yes, Carey, I mean Ms Fernier, can I see Millie? I tried to catch her sister, but she was in a rush. Is Millie okay?”

“You can call me Carey, Jeff. Millie is resting. She is doing well. She still does not remember much of anything. I think her sister got nervous seeing her without the ventilator. This equipment and the patient’s appearance can be a shock to family members and friends. If you wait about ten minutes I will see if she feels up to having a visitor.” Jazz music played softly on the phone. Jeff felt like he was waiting forever. He was puzzled by Phyllis’s weird actions. Why would she run from him? Why did she leave without spending some time with her sister? Strange, but the whole episode was strange. Why would anyone want to hurt Millie? She was the sweetest, kindest woman he had ever met.

“Jeff, I am so sorry I took so long. There was another one of my patients that I needed to care for.” Carey explained. “Millie is awake and says she does wish to see you. Just come through the double doors and I will meet you to update you on her condition.”

Jeff hung up the phone and grabbed his jacket that he had left when he rushed to try to catch Phyllis. He mopped up the coffee he had spilled with a wet paper towel. He hurried down the hall and through the double doors to the ICU. It seemed like he entered an alien world with beeping sounds, the whooshing of the ventilators, the staff clothed in blue scrubs or white lab coats, the hushed conversations of doctors, therapists and nurses. Carey waved Jeff to an area near a supply room, away from the patient cubicles.

“Jeff, Ms Strigow, Millie’s sister, has given permission to speak with you about Millie’s condition. She is breathing well without the vent, but we need to keep an oxygen mask on her for several hours as a precaution. She is alert and very hoarse. She can use a white board to write on if it is too hard for her to speak. Try not to ask her too many questions. She may have lots of questions to ask you, though. Jeff, she doesn’t remember anything about herself, family and friends nor what happened to her. She keeps saying that she had to go to work but doesn't know why that keeps coming to mind. It will take time. The doctors feel she will regain most of her memory." Jeff looked so concerned and weary; Carey reminded him to take care of himself. He seemed to have a calming effect on her patient.

Millie was awake when Jeff entered her cubicle. The mask over her nose and mouth delivered a fine mist of moistened oxygen. Droplets and fog formed on the inside of the mask with each breath. She was beautiful despite her thick dark hair missing where the surgeons had operated. There were IV poles surrounding the upper half of her bed. Her long, black eyelashes half covered her sleepy eyes as she stared at the television hanging on a platform in the corner of the cubicle. Jeff smiled as he thought of her a sleeping beauty lying in the middle of a forest of poles. He hoped he could be the prince that rescued her. Millie's left arm was loosely holding a small dry erase board with a pen attached with a Velcro strap. Jeff wanted to hold her, lay next to her—protect and comfort her. He stood there hoping she would remember something—anything. He hoped she would turn and see him, smile and reach for him with her tiny hand.

A Respiratory Therapist, Al Major, nodded to Jeff and walked to the bed. Millie turned to see who was next to her.

"Hi Melinda. I'm Al, the Respiratory Therapist. I'm just going to adjust the straps on your oxygen mask so that you get the full benefit of the air in there. Do you remember me? I usually work nights, but I just switched to afternoons."

Jeff watched transfixed as Millie's lips parted and it appeared, she said something because the mask became cloudy. Al leaned close to Millie's face and whispered something. Mille closed her eyes. Jeff moved so cautiously towards her bed that Al did not hear him approach until Jeff was directly behind him. Sensing someone Al turned so abruptly he almost knocked Jeff over.

"Oh, I am so sorry. I didn't see you." Al steadied Jell.

Millie opened her eyes to see both men facing her. She knew the man in the white lab coat must be Al. He had just whispered to her that she was going to be okay. Al's shaving cream or soap perfume had whisked by her nose before he adjusted the mask. She knew she had seen the other man before but had no idea who he was or where he belonged in her life. It was upsetting not being able to remember her own name or anything about herself. There was this voice in her head that kept telling her she was late for work. What work? Where? Why was that the only memory that kept occurring? Melinda stared at Jeff. He was blinking back tears as he reached for Millie's hand. Millie smiled and tried to say something but only a squeak echoed from the mask. Jeff looked at Al who was moving dials on a machine located close to bed. Al looked at Jeff and seemed to be telling Jeff *not to push it* with his gaze.

Jeff bent close to Millie's face. He whispered "Melinda… Millie, I'm a friend. You may not remember me right now, but I want you to know I have been a friend for a long time. I will always be here for you." Jeff watched Millie's face. Her forehead wrinkled as she tried to remember this man. Deep down in the recesses of her brain she felt safe with him. His eyes looked at her with such kindness and his touch so warm she shook her head "yes" when he asked if he could continue to visit.

Millie reached for the dry erase board. *Thank you. So* sorry I can't remember you. Please come back.

Jeff nodded, yes. He wanted to take her in his arms. He knew he couldn't. He kissed her gently on the cheek and turned towards the door so she couldn't see the tears brimming in his eyes.

Chapter V
Miracles

Miracles happen for a reason. Perhaps it is because all the planets are aligned or there is a God that has a plan for us. Who knows? Hank should have been eliminated---done----finished—caput. His right lung had collapsed when the bullet hit his chest and exited under his arm pit. He was barely breathing and unconscious when the train lurched forward and sped down the tracks. Hank started to regain consciousness when he felt the train slow several hours later. Suddenly, a door at the top of the car slid open. Coal began pouring onto his limp body. He barely had enough strength to crawl over to a crate near the door of the car. The air in the freight car was filled with coal dust. He covered his mouth with his blood—soaked shirt. With every breath, he coughed, sending knifelike pains through his chest. He pushed the crate as close as he could to the door of the freight car as the coal began to push against the door. Reaching the lever of the door, he pulled as hard as he could. The pain was excruciating. He gritted his teeth as blood filled his mouth. The door gave way just enough that Hank could fall onto the ground. He rolled down an embankment near the tracks landing in some brush several feet from what would have been his coffin. He laid there burying his mouth and nose into his shirt to stifle his cough. Hank had no idea where he was. He was alive-barely alive. What gave him the strength to stand and stumble away from the train, he would question for years. He weaved through the darkness around trees and over uneven ground, falling several times. He stopped often to allow the dizziness to pass. After about an hour, he started to crawl towards some lights coming from a building beyond an open field. Fear of being seen out in the open, even in the darkness, played a dim second to his will to survive.

Steve Packard had put off doing his least favorite chore as long as he could. His mother, Mary Packard, had dropped a hint for the third time so Steve reluctantly left his erector set creation. The set was a gift from his father two Christmases ago. Assembling bridges and buildings helped Steve to feel close to the man he had worshiped. Gregg Packard was a big man with an even bigger heart. He was an iron worker. Each day he would walk the tightropes of steel as casually as if he was walking on land. He forged together the skeletons of buildings high above the ground. He didn't smoke or drink. He was tough with sinewy arms that lifted many times his weight without even grunting. He loved his wife and son. When he came home from work, he would put his arms around his wife's tiny waist, pull aside her long dark hair and kiss her neck. Steve would run and jump on his father's back. They would wrestle until Mary would threaten to break them up with her wooden spoon. She loved watching them together-the two men in her life that she treasured with all her being. Gregg Packard had died suddenly from a heart attack about a year ago. He had taken the tractor and was plowing a large piece of land preparing to plant a crop of corn. Mary worried when Gregg didn't come to dinner. He was a big man and ate heartily. He always complimented his wife on her cooking. Mary had called their neighbor and asked him to ride out to the field to check on Gregg. When Vern arrived at the field, he found Gregg slumped over the steering wheel of his tractor. Vern attempted to resuscitate Gregg, but it was too late. Steve held his tears to comfort his mother. He went to his room after the funeral and sobbed into his pillow. From that day forward, he became the man of the house. He seeded the field, fed the horses and pigs, attempted to fix anything that was broken. The only thing he couldn't fix was his broken heart.

Steve whistled as he stepped off the porch and headed towards the garbage cans at the side of the house. He stopped suddenly when he heard a noise coming from the woods surrounding the house. Peering into the darkness chills ran up his back when he saw something moving slowly several yards away from where he was standing. The figure was low to the ground. There were lots of critters roaming about at night. Steve was used to the sounds they made and usually ignored them. This sound was different. A low moan like the sound a cow made when it was delivering a calf came from the figure. He had brought all their cows into the barn before dusk. He stood very still. There it was again; a moan, then a cough-a human cough. Steve wasn't sure if he should chance moving towards the figure, which seemed to be lying on the ground, not moving. He cautiously placed the trash into one of the cans, tiptoed onto the porch and slithered inside the house. The screen door creaked. Mary called from the living room.

"Is that you, Steve? "

"Mom, where is a flashlight? There is something alive outside near the woods. It sounds like a person." Steve was rummaging through the kitchen drawers. His mother walked quietly to one of the drawers near the stove and took out her husband's handgun.

"You are not going out there alone! Let me go ahead of you."

"No, Mom. Stay behind me. I found the flashlight. Let's see what it is before we go shooting." Mary followed Steve onto the porch. The flashlight's beam pierced the darkness.

Hank had passed out but was still breathing. He had coughed up some blood. Steve and his mother approached the figure.

"Don't move! Wh—who are you? I have a gun!" Steve shouted. Hank did not move. Steve poked the person's shoulder—no movement. Mary stood next to her son pointing the gun at the figure. When Steve reached for Hank's shoulder, he felt the wetness. Shining the flashlight and turning Hank onto his back, Steve saw Hank's ashen face. Blood ran from his mouth down his torn shirt and onto the ground.

"Oh my God! Who…? What!" Mary dropped the gun.

"Mom… call 911! I think he is still breathing." Steve put his head close to Hank's. Mary ran into the house, grabbed the phone and dialed 911. Someone answered after a few rings. "This is the Emergency Response Service. Please state your name and emergency, please."

"This is Mary Packard at 151 South County Road B in Gettysburg. There is a man lying on the ground near our woods. My son, Steve, is with him. He is breathing but does not appear conscious. There is blood on his shirt and around his body. Please come as fast as you can. Should I cover him with a blanket? We will not move him. Please……"

"Mrs Packard, yes, cover him with a blanket and do not move him. If he regains consciousness before we arrive, try to keep him still. Ask him if he can give you his name and where is he having pain. We will be there within 20 minutes. Talk to him even if he is not conscious. Stay by the phone after you hang up and I will call you back right away to confirm your emergency. Do you have a portable phone?"

"Yes, I do. I'll take it out near the person." Mary's voice was hoarse and shaky. The memory of the last time they had to call 911 wrapped itself around her. One year ago, she had called praying they could save her wonderful husband. The contact person hung up and called Mary back as she walked out of the house with a blanket." Steve was still crouched near the Hank's head. The flashlight beam plus the full moon cast an eerie shadow over the two men. Dried blood circled Hank's lips and cheeks. His skin was pale. His eyes were closed. Steve held the lower jaw forward to keep Hank's airway open, remembering his CPR training at school.

The operator from 911 service complimented Steve for his efforts, "Steve, can you tell me what his breathing sounds like?"

Mary bent down near Hank's mouth. She heard grunting noises with each shallow breath and there was frothy blood coming from his mouth when he exhaled.

"Can you feel a pulse at the side of his neck or at his wrist. Use your two middle fingers and press lightly. Count for a minute. Have your son count slowly to sixty while you count the pulse. Mary felt a very faint irregular pulse on Hank's wrist and reported it to the operator. "You both are doing great. Help should be there shortly. Without moving him, can you see anything in his pockets that might identify him?" In the distance a siren could be heard. Mary cautiously tried to search a shirt pocket and one pants pocket. There was nothing in either pocket.

The Packard house was several miles east of the town of Gettysburg. The EMT's rushed Hank to St. Peter's Hospital in the city. The staff and physicians were amazed that this man had survived a bullet in his chest that missed his heart by just a few millimeters, a collapsed lung, another bullet wound with an exit wound under his armpit, loss of blood and a concussion. After surgery for removal of the bullet, reinflation of his lung and easing of the headaches and dizziness from the concussion, Hank was sent to the rehabilitation center attached to the hospital for two weeks. Mary Packard insisted Hank stay with them until he was healed and regained his strength. Hank had grown a beard, lost thirty pounds and gave his name as Jack Turner, a railroad man from Chicago who had been shot be two men attempting to confiscate some cartons filled with chemicals. Hank told everyone he didn't remember what happened until he regained consciousness in a boxcar filling with coal, rolled out of a small opening between the doors and crawled through the woods to the Packard's house. Part of the story was true. Hank decided he would go as far away from Iowa as he could. Mary and Steve were wonderful to him They loaned him some money and clothes that they had saved from Tom to tide him over until he could get settled. Hank was afraid that the mob would hurt John and his family if they found out Hank was still alive. He knew enough about the Balpar investment scheme that he could rat on them, putting a lot of the mob in prison. He could be charged with fraud as well. The Packards didn't pressure him to give them more information. They assured the police that he hadn't changed his story when he stayed with them and that what he told the police was the same as he had told the them. Hank Baldoni was put to rest. Losing himself would be the only way to protect the Strigow family that he loved like his own.

Chapter VI
The Invisible Line

Francesca loved Douglas. The sex was terrific, and she enjoyed having intelligent conversations with him. As JBT & Associates became successful, and the profits afforded her a luxurious lifestyle, greed began to transform the love of her husband to the love of money and power. Francesca was approaching that invisible line from ethical goals to a hunger for more intangible pursuits. The odd thing about this transition is that the person believes that he or she is still the same. They rationalise the actions they take and the human debris that collects as they trample anything in their way to the "top". They feel that collateral damage is a necessary evil in order to insure the growth and success of the company. A wall of deceit begins to grow behind them so that turning back behind the line becomes impossible.

Samantha had sent her application for a position at JBT to Human Resources. Now that she had a sense of the personalities of the partners and she was taking classes to obtain a degree in finance and marketing, she hoped to begin her quest by establishing a relationship with the partner that seemed the most vulnerable. Martin Balingsford liked woman. Samantha could see that the first time she met him. His eyes scanned her body like a periscope on a submarine looking for enemy ships. She was taller than Martin and could use this to her advantage. He had a "love 'em and leave 'em" reputation. That eased her fear of any firm romantic entanglements. It was Friday and the rumor mill buzzed with the news of a vacancy in the finance department of JBT. The vacancy had occurred when a girl who was supposed to start several weeks ago had gotten into an accident. One of the technicians in the department knew the girl and was taking time off to help her. The vacancy needed to be filled ASAP.

Monday morning Samantha was contacted to set up an interview with Henri Treacher. Samantha smiled as she sat in the waiting area of HR. She straightened her grey suit making sure the jacket was buttoned to highlight her tiny waist. She had pulled her auburn hair into a twist; made sure her make-up was fresh and not too bold. The eye shadow accented her emerald green eyes. After signing some paperwork giving permission to contact references and do a background check, Samantha was directed to the ninth floor and the office of Henri Treacher.

After greeting Mr Treacher's secretary she sat demurely, with her ankles crossed for several minutes. The man who rarely gave her a glance when he passed her desk on the ground floor walked in and handed several files to his secretary. She was a sour-faced woman in her early 40's. Her dress was a dull powder blue, her generous figure filling it out quite well.

She said, "Good morning, Mr Treacher," without looking at him. He grunted a reply and pointed to the files he had handed to her.

"I will need follow-up on these cases, Ms Scribner. Any questions just send me an e-mail." Samantha looked at Henri. He glanced her way unsmilingly and walked into his office. Samantha wondered if she could ever break his icy shell. She needed to get a position at JBT, and Henri seemed to be the partner she could impress with her intelligence rather than her womanly charms.

"Ms Reynolds," the secretary called out without looking up from the files on her desk. Samantha stood and walked to the desk.

Clearing her throat, she answered in a confident tone, "I am Samantha Reynolds." In her mind she envisioned a spacious office with her name and "Vice-President" in gold lettering on the door. Ms Scribner pointed to a set of double doors.

"Mr Treacher will see you now, Ms Reynolds." She glanced up as Samantha walked through the doors.

"Thank you." Samantha smiled as she walked through the doors and closed them quietly behind her. She stood a few feet into the pristine office and scanned the room. Henri stood in front of a massive dark mahogany desk. The room was sparsely but tastefully furnished. There were two leather chairs facing the front of the desk and large dark file cabinets flanking it. The desk was perfectly centered in front of large, floor to ceiling windows with blinds partially drawn. Henri Treacher stood in front of the desk with his arms folded across his chest. He observed the woman standing in front of the doors evaluating her posture, her body language and her outfit. Samantha did not feel it was appropriate to speak first. A grandfather clock ticked away the seconds which seemed to her like hours.

"Have a seat, please, Ms Reynolds." Henri motioned to one of the leather chairs facing his desk. He moved slowly, standing beside his desk chair until Samantha was seated. Another silence broken only by the ticking of the clock assured Samantha that her heartbeat easily overshadowed the clocks incessant pulse.

"I see you are interested in working with short-term investments in this company. Do you know what a short-term investment is, Ms Reynolds?" the sober-faced man asked her.

Samantha made sure she took a moment to respond and looked directly into Henri's eyes when she spoke. "Mr Treacher, I believe that type of investment is also known as a temporary investment plan or marketable security plan. It is a debt free or equity security that is usually sold or converted into cash within a one to three—month period." Samantha used the "business tone" she practiced each night in front of the mirror as soon as she realised being a receptionist was only a steppingstone to the pinnacle of success she deserved. Henri seemed unimpressed.

"What do you feel is the difference between a short and long-term investment?" Henri uncrossed his arms and leaned forward on his massive desktop.

"Sir, long-term investments are those accounts on the asset side of a company's balance sheet." Samantha's eyes lit up and she leaned forward in her chair. "They represent the company's investments—stocks, bonds, real estate, cash—that the company intends to hold on to for more than one year. An investor can see how much the company is investing in its operations compared to its activities." Samantha pushed back in her chair as she reprimanded herself for getting too enthusiastic and verbose. *Just answer the question-don't give a lecture!*

The tiniest smile lifted the corners of Henri's mouth. He seldom saw enthusiasm for finance in others that he felt himself. "Can you name some long-term assets, Sam… I mean, Ms Reynolds?"

"Most long-term assets are depreciable—they tend to amortise such as property, plant and equipment expense, furniture, land, vehicles…"

Henri held up his hand to interrupt her, "My, you have been studying, haven't you? That is rhetorical. You needn't expound." Henri stood and moved to the front of his desk. He stood over her—and imposing figure.

"Mr Treacher…I…" Samantha could almost smell his aftershave from this venue.

"You can call me Henri since I see you every day when I pass the reception desk."

"Sir, I don't call you Henri there and I prefer to call you Mr Treacher. It would be professional, (ahem) Sir."

"Very well. Name types of liquid assets, Ms Reynolds." Henri folded his arms and leaned on his desk but remained looming above her.

"Liquid assets are the result of transactions. Cash, AR-accounts receivables, inventory, pre-paid insurance, trademarks and customer lists purchased from another company are examples." Samantha vowed to remain cool and in control even though she wished he would put the desk in between them once again. She had been pretty sure she had him pegged as an iceberg until he smiled and stood over her. She braced herself for another onslaught of questions.

"Ms Reynolds, you can relax. There is only one more question I have to ask." Henri helped by moving back behind the desk but continued to stand. "Why do you think you are qualified for this position?"

I'll bet he is counting how long I take to answer that one. "I have a Bachelors' degree in business with a major in finance. I am proficient in accounting and am presently studying at Chicago University for a Masters' in Marketing and Business Administration." Samantha crossed her legs just enough to show their shapeliness then resumed crossing at the ankles demurely. She prayed her deodorant was continuing to work as perspiration gathered in her armpits.

"Ms Reynolds, I asked why you believe you are qualified for this position, not your education."

"Mr Treacher, I do not have access to the JBT job description. I am aware that education is usually a pre-requisite for positions in similar departments of investment counseling. I have always been intrigued by finance and mathematics since I was very young. The world has its foundation in financial transactions. It excites me and I want to learn from the best, giving the best that I can give." *Sam, that was a little too mushy for this piece of ice!* Henri smiled and uncrossed his arms, leaning on his desk.

"Thank you, Ms Reynolds. We will be getting back to you by the end of the week." He moved towards the door. Samantha's legs felt like rubber as she walked towards him. She looked into those piercing blue eyes and a chill ran down her back as he touched her arm and ushered her through the door. She barely had time to say "thank you" before he began to close the door.

"Thank you, sir, for your time."

"You are welcome. Stop calling me "Sir." Henri did not smile but there was a slight change in the tone of his voice. That shift lifted Samantha's spirits as she walked out of his office. She wanted to shout "YES!" as she moved past his secretary's desk. Samantha could feel the secretary's intense stare piercing her back as she exited. *I'll bet she plastered her ear to his office door. I wonder if he asks her opinion on the candidates. He asked me to stop calling him "Sir". I don't think he would ask me to do that if he weren't considering me for the position. He's a perfectionist and probably micro-manages. He might be difficult to work for, but I always like a challenge.* The elevator arrived. Samantha smiled and nodded when she saw Francesca—the only passenger. Francesca barely noticed Samantha. She had more pressing issues on her mind.

Chapter VII
Metamorphosis

Millie could finally talk above a whisper, interspersed with coughs and squeaks. She had graduated from using the embarrassing bedside commode for elimination to being escorted to the bathroom; from those awful patient gowns that left little to the imagination to pajamas with bears cavorting in several positions. That nice young man, Jeff, had bought them for her. Though she could not recall their connection, she did feel safe when he came to visit. He was cute too. Her sister, Phyllis, came to visit several times, but never stayed long. Millie wanted to remember something, anything. The Psychiatrist brought music, pictures of family and friends and flash cards attempting to pull the memories out of the deep regions of her brain. Very little came through except for an occasional, brief flash of sadness or memory of an event related to a song or a picture. Her dreams consisted of milliseconds filled with the flash of a scarf blowing in the wind, an ice—cold sensation on the side of her face or someone singing a lullaby. If there were people in her dream, they were faceless. Phyllis told Millie their parents had passed away several years ago. She told Millie that their Mom and Dad had loved them both very much.

Phyllis's voice had an edge to it. "Can't you remember how good they were to you?" She stood to leave.

"I'm so sorry. I am trying to remember…Philli." Millie sighed.

Phyllis stopped suddenly and turned, "You remembered! You remembered!" She moved towards the bed and grabbed Millie's hand. "You hated the name "Phyllis" because it sounded like an old maid schoolteacher's name. You called me Phylli." Phyllis sat down next to the bed.

Millie smiled." Maybe that is a sign that my memory is finally coming back. Did our mom sing a special lullaby to us? I keep dreaming about a soft voice singing. It sounds like a lullaby. I can't see the face of the person—they are always in the shadows." Phyllis wiped a tear away from her eye before Millie saw it.

"Of course, she is in the shadows. She was an Au Pere' who lived with us when we were children." Phyllis squeezed Millie's hand. Her voice was shaking. "She used to sing *Over the Rainbow* before she tucked us in. Her name was Sally. She… she got really sick and died." Phyllis watched Millie's face intently. Millie closed her eyes tightly and her brow wrinkled as she tried hard to remember this person. When she opened them, Phyllis was no longer in the room.

Hank, alias Jack Turner, left the Packard farm promising to keep in touch. He wasn't good at keeping promises. He had promised John Strigow, his partner, that he would mend his gambling and philandering ways and then stole from him. He had promised to reinforce the restaurant patio but had taken the money to pay off his gambling debts. He had promised to rescue Sally from her prostitution prison, but he couldn't risk being followed, plus putting her in danger. He was good at making promises but sucked at keeping them.

Jack Turner traveled to the docks along Lake Michigan and joined the Merchant Marine Corps. No one knew Hank Baldoni, alias Jack Turner. He lost himself for five years traveling around the Great Lakes. His skin became dark and leathery in the sun and blistering winds of winter. He rarely went into the cities and towns with the rest of the crew. He kept to himself most of the time.

It was November. Lake Erie wrestled with frostbitten winds that molded into waves over ten feet. The *Mariner,* a huge ship hauling grain from Toledo, Ohio to Toronto,

Canada, rocked against the pilings as the grain towers emptied their contents into the hold of the ship.

"Captain, this storm is picking up. The Coast Guard had issued a warning to all ships to remain in port until the storm moves eastward." The Mariner's first mate reported to his captain, Scott Paulsen. Captain Paulsen had challenged the Lakes. He called them "those damned unpredictable women" for over forty years.

"We've got to get this cargo to Toronto in three days or we take a cut in our payment. I'll wait for an hour to see if it settles down a little, but then we have to head out." Paulsen chewed on his wad of tobacco and stared out at the pounding surf. "Those uniforms are sometimes squeamish—more for the smaller ships than for our big bastards." The First Mate, Carl Smogalski, shook his head and stepped out of the way before the captain's partially chewed wad of tobacco hit him.

"Hee, Hee—almost got you, son!" He stared out of the frosted window at the white caps glistening in the beam of the searchlights piercing the darkness from shore. Carl left the bridge to tell the crew to sit tight—no land passes.

"The Captain thinks we might have a window to set out if the storm doesn't reach forty or fifty knots. That old fart spit that tobacco wad at me again. I hope he'll change his mind. Batten down everything that could possible move."

"He's a tough old bird! He reads those waters better than a blind man feeling up a whore!" Someone yelled from the back of the group. The crew laughed at that one. They mumbled carefully chosen swear words as they returned to their posts and battening down the hatches.

At 9 pm the clouds shut out the moon. The waves slapped the sides of the Mariner like an angry mom using a switch on a child. The wind had diminished to twenty-four knots (twenty-eight miles per hour). The waves were now six to eight feet high. Captain Paulsen radioed the Coast Guard and the Marina staff that he was heading out at 9:30 pm. Jack Turner pulled the levers to rev up the massive engines. He loved the sound of those monsters hammering away. It somehow drowned out the memories that haunted him. The crew atop ship fought the wind and rain hammering their faces as they reeled in the huge lines holding the ship to the dock. The ship lights cut through the darkness outlining the crew's desperate attempts to gain a foothold on the lurching vessel.

By 12:30 am the wind suddenly changed from Northeast to Northwest. The Mariner had traveled aggressively with the wind to approximately sixteen miles from the port of Cleveland, through the Welland Canal. Captain Paulsen fought the ship's battle to turn in the funnel caused by the sudden switch in wind direction. Yelling orders to the crew down below to adjust the engines to allow the ship to slowly head towards the eastern port, the wheel spun out of his hands and he fell against the wall of the wheelhouse. The winds increased to over sixty miles per hour. The port side of the ship dipped into a dangerous angle below the waves. The pitch of the ship made it almost impossible for the crew that was topside to regain a foothold. When the Mariner careened onto its side, the grain in the hold shifted. The starboard deck teetered straight into the air. Crewmen clung to anything they could grab in order to save themselves from the clutches of the waves engulfing the drowning ship. Screams of the drowning men mingled with those of the wind and slashing of waves against the steel side of the ship. Captain Paulsen grabbed the wheel and hollered for all port engines full speed ahead in a vain attempt to control the ship. Men in the engine room fought through the water entering the hatches to try to help the drowning men topside. Jack and Ben Boswell were the only members of the crew not yet smashed into metal posts and equipment in the engine room. Torrents of water gushed through the seams as the ship reached the point of no return. Jack grabbed Ben who had a large gash at the back of his head having been hit by a part of a turbine. With all the strength he could muster, Jack dragged himself and Ben through the ever—rising water. He managed to grab hold of a ladder and fight the onslaught of water pouring into the hatch. How he had the strength to drag the unconscious and water—soaked man topside was a miracle. Unable to see much of anything as Jack was hit with the wind and waves, he felt what seemed to be a rope that was tied to one of the few lifeboats left on the ship. He could barely see the lifeboat swinging by that rope around a partially collapsed pole. Its rope had managed to keep the lifeboat attached to the part of the deck remaining above the angry sea. Jack was able to lift Ben into the lifeboat and pull the rope away from its grasp on the pole. His hands were bleeding and the pounding waves assaulted every breath he took. The up-ended ship dove into the swirling waters. Jack dug his hands into the side of the lifeboat as it was launched into the air. The ship plunged to its grave causing a Tsunami wave that somehow rocketed the lifeboat right side up away from the disappearing ship. Jack garnered his last bit of strength to pull himself into the boat and wrap the rope around his passenger. Both men lay in the bottom of the water filled lifeboat—Ben was unconscious, and Jack passed out from near drowning and exhaustion. It was a miracle that the small vessel was not pulled under by the suction created when the ship dove to the floor of the lake.

Two hours after the ship sunk Jack came to. The flesh on the palms of his hands was torn away. Trickles of blood oozed from the wounds and from multiple lacerations on his body. Barely able to move his arms and legs he crawled over to his lifeless crewman. The gash on Ben's head was deep and ran along his right temple. Jack felt for a pulse at the side of Ben's neck even though his fingers were numb and shaking. Jack thought he felt a pulse. He turned the ashen faced man on his side to see if there were any other injuries. Ben groaned. The waves had calmed slightly rocking the lifeboat from side to side. The rain continued to pour gradually filling the lifeboat. Jack noticed a taught line that seemed to be putting a drag on the progress of the boat. He pulled on the line with the little strength he had left and found it attached to the survival bag. He could not see if it had remained intact but from its weight, he hoped some of the contents were still inside. When he had hauled the bag on board, he found two blankets which he wrapped around himself and Ben. There were also gloves, a first-aid kit, a flashlight, flares, two bottles of water and dehydrated food packages wrapped in heavy plastic. He did his best to bandage Ben's head wound. He checked the reaction of Ben's pupils with the beam from the flashlight. He managed to get him to swallow small sips of water and took a couple of sips himself. Since the Captain was in the process of turning the ship southeast towards the nearest port in Cleveland, Ohio Jack rowed towards the area where he remembered the ship sinking. If he only had the damn moon! He looked up through the dwindling curtain of rain repeating a silent prayer that the moon would peak through the murky sky. Jack had no idea what time it was, where he was and if anyone had been alerted to the ships demise. He vowed to go back to Iowa, if he survived, face his old friend and partner, John, and repay him for the money he had stolen. He wondered if Sally was waiting for him, he would rescue her and spend the rest of his life trying to pay back the debts of his fruitless past. Deep inside the survival bag there was a dented metal box. Jack's swollen fingers pried open the box and laughed when he found a compass. Feelings of fear mixed with pain and the realisation that he must have a guardian angel. He had survived a gunshot wound that should have killed him, almost being buried by tons of coal, and a shipwreck in a deadly storm. His angel probably was putting resume's in with the Big Man for a different assignment. Jack sat Ben against the side of the lifeboat, reinforced the bloody bandage and siphoned drops of water into his mouth with a piece of rubber tubing floating among other debris in the water-logged boat. He took the metal box and began to scoop out the icy water ankle deep in the boat's bottom. Ben wafted in and out of consciousness. Jack told him they were in a lifeboat, that they had a compass and flares and that they were hopefully headed towards the port in Cleveland. He told Ben he was sure the Coast Guard had been alerted to the ship's sinking and would be coming soon to look for survivors, even if he doubted that himself. He tried to assure Ben that they would be okay. Ben's hollow eyes stared at Jack. Tears ran down their faces for the men who were most certainly lost at sea and thankful that they had survived. Jack directed the beam form the flashlight over the water with little hope of finding any other survivors. He turned the boat with the one oar that had remained attached until the compass showed they were heading southeast. The waves settled down and the clouds parted. A sliver of moon shown low in the sky as dawn crept through the horizon. No land, rescue ships or helicopters appeared as daylight pushed the moon away. The two men chewed on the dry morsels of food as though it was a gourmet meal. Jack's eyelids drooped. He talked, whistled and sang trying to keep awake enough to ensure the boat stayed on course. Several hours passed.

Suddenly, Ben shouted, "Lights! Lights!"

Jack turned and saw a group of lights, like a diamond bracelet, in the distance.

Chapter VIII
Transfer

Melinda was doing well. Some vague memories were starting to break through her damaged cortex. Phyllis had returned to her job in Indianapolis. She kept in touch by phone to Millie, Jeff and the doctors and nurses. Jeff continued to visit almost every day. He told her about their friendship, their days in college and that she had been married to Ron. He only told her theirs had been a rocky marriage, leaving out the details. The police had not been able to connect Ron with her accident. His alibi was flimsy but there were no other clues to charge him with anything. No other suspect had been found. The police had a restraining order placed so Ron would not be able to come near Millie. The hospital staff and security were given photos of Ron and instructed to notify them if he attempted to visit her. Visitors were limited to Jeff, the detectives assigned to her case and Phyllis. A complication to her recovery developed when she began to experience headaches that increased in intensity. The doctors feared she may have developed some scarring of the ventricles (structures in the brain tissue that produced the cerebral spinal fluid that bathes the brain and spinal cord) or an aneurysm (distention of a blood vessel) from the injury and surgery that was applying pressure in her brain tissue. A decision was made for Melinda to be transferred to Cleveland Clinic for evaluation and possible placement of a stent. A stent is a tube placed from the ventricles to the kidneys to equalise the pressure against the brain tissue. Cleveland Clinic also would be able to provide the physical and occupational therapy rehabilitation she needed. There were risks to having additional surgical procedures but should either hydrocephalus or an aneurysm be the cause of the headaches it was imperative they be addressed. Melinda was so appreciative of the hospital staff and doctors who saved her life, she trusted the decision to transfer her to Cleveland Clinic and to consent to treatment recommended, despite the risks. She hoped she would regain her memory and be able to return to a normal life. A vague memory of a confrontation between Jeff and her ex-husband had started to seep into her consciousness. Jeff had protected her. She started to have feelings for him that she recalled had started well before her current circumstances. She didn't want him to feel obligated to see her through rehabilitation and possible surgery in another city.

"Jeff, I don't expect you to continue to put your life on hold for me." Millie told him one afternoon when he visited. "I will be fine. They have decided to transfer me to Cleveland Clinic, and I may have to have more surgery, then rehab for some time. I am so thankful for saving my life a month ago. If you hadn't seen me lying in the road, I wouldn't be here. I am realising we had a relationship before the accident. I am starting to get some snippets of feelings …I'm… I just don't know where this is all going. They still haven't found out who or why I was run down. Someone might still be out there looking for me. I can't have anyone in danger because of me. I told Phyllis she needed to keep her distance. I will keep her in the loop as to my progress. I just don't know……"

"Stop right there! You are not going to get rid of me that easily." Jeff grasped her hand. "I almost lost you. I have been in love with you for years. I understand you may not feel the same or even recall what we had. I was headed to see you that awful morning to tell you the same thing I am telling you now. You can try to push me away. I am not going anywhere unless you absolutely sure you never want to see me again." Millie looked into those gorgeous greenish blue eyes. A warm sensation melted over her and she brought his hand to her cheek, then kissed it. He wanted to hold her and have her melt into his arms, to kiss those lips and feel her skin, once again, pressing against him. Jeff had all he could do to hold back from those urges.

"You are just getting some of your memory back. Please let me be there for you while you recover, have surgery…whatever. When all of that is over then you can see how you feel about me, and I will disappear or be a part of your life in any way you wish. I will take a week off when you go to Cleveland and I will see you as much as I can until you are ready to be discharged. Is that okay with you?"

Melinda squeezed his hand. "Oh, Jeff. I don't deserve someone as wonderful as you. I am so sorry I can't bring back memories of us together before the accident." She held her head as the pounding sensation grew more intense. Her vision became blurred. Jeff rang the nurses. Melinda was transferred that day. An emergency CAT scan was performed. The ventricles were dilated (the structures located in the central portion of the upper brain that produce the cerebrospinal fluid that bathes and protects the brain) there was no aneurysm. A stent was placed as an emergency procedure shortly after she arrived at Cleveland Clinic. She was transferred to the Intensive Care Unit. Phyllis and Jeff arrived in the waiting area about the same time. Both of their faces showed the results of the stress they felt not knowing if Millie would survive, let alone be able to fully recover. Phyllis needed to tell Millie the secrets that had been kept locked in the Strigow family's history for years.

Millie recovered quickly from the stent placement and was going to be evaluated by the Physical and Occupational therapists in a few days. She had been transferred to the Rehabilitation Center on the hospital's campus. Jeff had gone back to work. Millie was no longer experiencing headaches and blurred vision. Phyllis had discussed with the doctors the hesitancy to tell Millie about parts of her life of which she had no knowledge. The doctors felt the things she told them should be shared with a Detective on the case. They arranged for Detective Brad Keller to meet with Phyllis to gain the information. Brad Keller was a big man, both in stature and in reputation. He had been with the police force for fifteen years. Ten of those years were spent chasing felons, performing dangerous under cover assignments and gaining the "hard ass" reputation on the streets of Chicago. This last year he had taken the job as the Chief of the Chicago's Homicide Division. He worked out as often as he could so he could keep his forty-something body in tip-top shape. He was a tank. When his six-foot—five-inch-tall frame towered over a person, the smirk that seemed to be always present and his piercing dark blue eyes made one feel like a Lilliputian. He had remained single, though hardly celibate, during his life. As a young boy he had his share of escapades due to an addiction to adventure, risk taking and a keen ability in to "read" people, no matter how they attempted to disguise the truth. He put tabasco sauce on almost everything he ate, including ice cream and loved beer that smelled like a skunk's delivery system. The case had been sent to the Chicago Homicide Division because of a tip from one of the many "snitches" the division employed.

The hospital had set aside a small conference room used by doctors to speak to families about their loved ones' progress, or lack of. Phyllis fidgeted with the necklace she always wore, sliding the locket that contained a picture of her father and mother back and forth along the chain. She had met twice before with this Detective Keller and didn't like the way he made her feel —like he was dissecting her like a coroner would a cadaver. He was a big presence in any room, not just because he was big but in the big way, he seemed to take over the room with confidence and an irritating smirk on his face.

A knock on the door made Phyllis jump. "Yes?" she practically whispered. The door opened and there he was. *I wish he would wipe that smirk off his face. He's quite a hunk and not too shabby in the looks department. Gosh, Phyl, remember you don't like him.*

"Hello, Ms Strigow. Thank you so much for staying in Cleveland. I'm sure you want to get back to work and home. This has certainly been a terrible experience for you." He sat across from her and leaned towards her. Phyllis inched farther back in her chair. Her palms were sweating, and she hoped that she was not doing the same in a more visible area. "The doctors tell me that you have some information you wished to give to Melinda Strigow, your sister, that could be of some assistance with our investigation. This is strictly confidential. I will only share what you tell me with my team in order to help us find the facts.

He reminds me of an old TV show—just the facts, Ma'am. "My mother and father are both deceased. They made me promise I would not tell Millie any of this while they were still alive." Detective Keller did not take out a notebook or a recorder as she thought he would. He just looked into her eyes, barely blinking, and that smirk turning up one corner of his mouth. Phyllis proceeded to tell him about the disappearance of Hank Baldoni, his trouble with the mob and gambling, the missing money from the construction business, her father's appearance one evening with a young lady he said he had rescued from a bad situation, her finding out that her mother had not been pregnant with another child, that it had been Sally, the rescued prostitute turned Nanny and that Melinda was actually Sally's daughter. Sally had died when Melinda was only two years old. She was raised as their child, Phyllis's sister, until the night before her father died. He told her the truth. Phyllis was shocked and angry. She couldn't believe that her parents let her believe Melinda was her actual sister. Feelings of being lied to, confusion, and anger towards Melinda, Sally, her parents and especially Hank choked her. He had abandoned a woman he had promised to rescue, stolen from her father, left an unborn child and deceived her and her parents. Because they never found a body, the police booked his disappearance up as a cold case. It collected dust on the shelves of the government building.

Detective Keller could see Phyllis stiffen and the color of her cheeks glow red as she poured out her story. The catalogue in his brain dropped two more suspects into its files—Phyllis and the missing Mr Baldoni. "Ms Strigow, can I get you some water or coffee? I see this is very difficult for you." *She is really very attractive. A little cold. Not showing much forgiveness. I wonder how mad she is.* He stood and walked out the door to the coffee pot and small refrigerator nearby. When he brought water and coffee with packets of cream and sugar into the conference room for her, she thanked him. Her posture and hardened expression remained intact.

"Thank you." Phyllis began moving the locket back and forth along the chain. She drank a few sips of water and coffee, cleared her throat and tried not to look into his searching eyes.

"Why would you want to tell your sis… Melinda about all of this?" Keller asked.

"I have to tell her. She deserves to know that the woman who took care of her those first two years was her real mother. It had to be hard for Miss Sally holding her own baby but pretending it was my mother's child. The doctors seem to think it will bring back some memories even if they are distorted." *I need to get this over with. I hope this guy is finished. He makes me so jittery.*

She probably should get this off her chest, nice one, too, I must admit. Keller, you dog, behave. "Ms Strigow, do you have any idea whether this Hank Baldoni is alive? Did your father or mother ever find out what happened to him?"

"No, Mr Keller, they found his truck but not him. They searched his apartment but didn't find anything either. He was like an uncle to me when I was a little girl. He always had candy in his pocket, and he teased me… Oh, that isn't important. They never found him after he stole all the money from the safe at my father's business. Sure, had us fooled." A tiny tear formed in the corner of her eye which she quickly whisked away with a napkin Keller had brought with the coffee.

Hmmm. She does have a soft side. I guess I've heard enough. Need to get my hands on the files on that Hank Baldoni missing person case. Still not convinced that Ron character's alibi is solid. "Thank you so much, Ms Strigow for this information. I hope things go well if you bring this up with Melinda. Could you call me when you are back home? Here is my card. I may have some more questions. I appreciate how difficult this is for you." Keller walked out of the door, leaving it ajar. He heard the quiet sobs from the room he just left. *Damn, this job doesn't get any easier.*

Phyllis found Millie sitting in a chair in her room in the Rehab Center. She was writing in a journal the nurses had encouraged her to keep. They told her it would help to put together some of the pieces of the puzzle that were still missing.

"Hi Philli." Millie smiled as Phyllis cautiously entered the room. "Sorry you had to miss work again. Millie pointed to a chair near to her. "You look tired. You really don't have to come all this way. I'll be walking on my own soon. I hope it won't be long before I can get home, wherever that is." She chuckled.

Phyllis stared at Millie as if she had just met her. *I don't know how to tell her all of this. No matter what, I still think of her as my sister. Here goes nothing...or everything.*

"Melinda (Phyllis always used Millie's proper name when she was being serious), I have something to tell you that might bring back some memories. I talked with the doctors and they agreed that it was time to give you some information that might help with the amnesia. I hope this won't upset you. Please remember I love you very much." Millie leaned towards Phyllis.

"Phyl, what is it? Are you sick? Is there something I did or said that offended you?" Millie looked like a young child with her fuzzy hair just starting to grow back, no make-up and the loss of weight. She was wearing her own clothes. The sweatshirt and pants looked like hand-me-downs from a much larger woman.

"Millie, no, you did nothing wrong and I am just fine. When I was ten years old, my… our father got caught up in someone else's issues. He became quite depressed because someone he trusted, someone who was his best friend stole money from him and disappeared. Dad, the police, friends looked for this man for almost a year. They found his truck, but never found him. Dad took a trip to Gary to look for a woman who this man supposedly had a… ahem…relationship with, to see if she might know where he was. When Dad came back from Gary, he brought the woman with him. This woman had been part of an "escort" service.

"Oh, dear. I can't imagine Dad cheating on Mom! He wasn't, was he?" Millie already looked distressed. Phyllis took Millie's hand.

"No, no Millie. Not like that. This man…this friend, his name was…is Hank Baldoni. Hank, we even called him Uncle Hank, had a problem with gambling and womanising. Long story, short, he took all the money Dad had in the safe at their construction company and disappeared. Our father found out that Hank had fallen in love with this woman who worked in the Chicago area. She was abused by men who had abducted her when she was almost thirteen years old. They made her do things she hated. Hank had promised her he would come for her and get her out of that nightmare. She waited for him, but he never came. She realised she was pregnant. She never had a chance to tell Hank that she was carrying his baby. Our Dad felt so sorry for her, especially when she told him the men that ruled over her would kill her if they found out she was pregnant.

Millie looked out her window remembering her mother and father. They were such great parents. They were strict with both she and Phyllis, but in a loving way. Her mother loved rainbows and her father took them fishing as often as he could. She was puzzled about this tale Phyllis was speaking about. She looked back at her sister, "Phyl, what do these people have to do with me? What am I supposed to remember?"

Phyllis grasped Millie's hand tighter. She was trembling. She couldn't end the story without telling Millie the truth. "Millie, the woman Dad rescued, Hank's woman was Sally…our Nanny…our sweet, kind Nanny."

"S… S…Sally was a prostitute? She…what happened to her baby?" Millie had tears in her eyes.

"Millie, oh Millie… you are that baby. Sally was your real mother!" Phyllis was sobbing. "I'm so sorry. Dad told me the day before he died. I wanted to tell you…I was going to tell you but the accident…"

Millie sat with her mouth open, tears streaming down her face. "What…what! I'm not mom and dad's daughter…I'm not really your sister! Sally… she was my mother? I… I…how did she keep that from me? Why would she…why would you…they do that?" Millie tore her hand away from Phyllis's. She pulled her legs up into the chair and sobbed. Phyllis tried to put her arms around her. Millie pushed her away. "Go away!

"No, I won't go away. I am still your sister and Mom and Dad raised you from the day you were born as their child. They loved you and I love you. You need to hear the whole story. It might help the police find who wanted you dead! Millie, I am so sorry, but you need to hear me out!" Millie looked at Phyllis. Both of their eyes were puffy and red from crying. Millie turned, blew her nose.

"Okay…finish." She stared out the window while Phyllis cleared her throat and continued.

"Do you need something to—"

"No! Just finish!" Millie yelled.

"Millie, our father… still your father, was warned by the police to stop looking for Hank because of his connections to the mob in Chicago. Dad was more worried that Hank had been beaten or killed than about recovering the money Hank stole. Dad found out where Sally lived by looking in Hank's desk drawer at work. She lived in a less than desirable neighborhood near Gary, Indiana. He told me that he was nervous when he saw the streets littered with garbage, store fronts boarded up and homeless people curled up in doorways and alleys. Dad found the poor girl's apartment and convinced her that he wasn't there as a client, nor would he hurt her. She was frightened and malnourished. She closed the door on him several times before she believed that he was there to see if he could find Hank. She was angry and terrified for her life since she found out she was pregnant. When Dad knocked on her door, she was about to take medicine and end it all." Millie continued to stare out the window. She was trying to remember Sally. She had a vision of someone holding her and singing to her, but she couldn't remember her face.

"Sally wasn't able to give Dad very much information about Hank. She knew he owed money to some dangerous people. She knew Hank had to be the father of her child because she used protection with all her clients except him." Millie tried to remember the man and woman who tucked her in bed at night. She remembered their kisses and encouragement when she left for school; when she scraped her knees, when she made the track team. She tried to remember Sally whose smile greeted her every morning; whose sad eyes watched as John and Alicia raised her daughter as theirs. That was the way it had to be. She didn't want Millie to be identified as her child in case the horrible people she was associated with found her and wanted revenge. "Sally begged my mother and father to adopt you and raise you as their own. Sally almost died giving birth to you. It must have been so difficult to watch her own child become someone else's. Sally passed away when you were almost three years old. You may not remember but her last words before she died were "I love you, Melinda." I was only eleven years old when you were born. I believed my mother had you. She had told me Sally had to go away for a while because she was sick. I never suspected that you were her daughter. You were so tiny…only three pounds. I never noticed Sally's belly getting bigger. Mom wore house dressed without a waist. I just thought Sally ate too much pie. She made the most wonderful pies!" Millie managed a tiny smile. "Sally had cancer. She stayed away for about six months in a Cancer Center in DesMoines. Mom helped Dad with the construction business, so when Sally came home, she took care of us a lot. Sally's cancer was in remission for two years after you were born and then it returned with a vengeance. Before Dad passed away, he told me the real story. I was a teen-ager and my ego was huge. I was resentful for many years that you had gotten attention that I thought only I deserved. I am so very sorry that I distanced myself from you. When this accident happened, and I saw you there in the ICU hooked up to all those machines and tubes… I felt horrible. I consider you my sister, no matter where your egg came from. They loved us both."

"Stop… Please stop! Phyl, I'm just remembering a few things about my life that were lost to me after the accident. Then this! Was I a prostitute like my real mother? Why would someone run me over and leave me to die? Am I going to be safe when I don't even know if there are people looking to kill me? Where is…who is my real father? Is this Hank person really my father? What happened to him?" Millie was shaking. Her nurse came in the give her some medication and to check on her. When she saw the state Millie was in, she looked over at Phyllis.

"Melinda, what is the matter? Are you in pain?" The nurse put her hand on Millie's arm and started to take her vital signs. "Ms Strigow, is there something you might have said to upset Millie? She was so excited to be working with PT today."

"I am so sorry. I thought… I'm sorry Millie. I should go." Phyllis ran from the room almost knocking over a nurse.

When animal cubs are threatened, the female animal protects them, her lair and the food she hoards for her cubs to eat. She protects them at any cost, even putting herself in danger. She protects them because instinct directs her to and the more members of her pride, the more chance she has of survival. The mate protects the lair and the cubs while the mother is hunting for food. If the mate injures or kills the cubs, does not protect the lair, the mother might kill him.

Francesca skillfully separated the egg yolks from the whites of the eggs. Every task she performed, even the mundane tasks, had purpose and meticulous planning. The tiramisu would be the encore to Doug's favorite dinner—prime rib cooked just enough to allow some blood to exit the pink meat and mix with the Au Jus, red skin potatoes in a garlic sauce, white wine, melted cheese over braised broccoli. Francesca had set the table with their fine china. Candles sent tiny wisps of light dancing on the walls. Linen napkins engraved with her initials were folded around their elegant table service. There was a part of Francesca that very few people had seen. There was a Mr Hyde that lay dormant, but not asleep. As she sliced the prime rib and watched the blood ooze from tender pink meat, the primitive part of her brain rejected remorse, incited a hunger for power and awakened the evil demon. Her face darkened. Her eyes seemed to burn with a fire sparked with selfish prospects. As quickly as that part of her surfaced, it hid. Doug came home quietly and glanced at the romantic scene awaiting him. His spirits lifted in anticipation as he tiptoed into the kitchen. It had been a difficult day. Henri seemed distracted. There were very few things that could pull Henri's attention away from his numbers. His work was his passion. Doug couldn't explain the uneasy feeling about Henri's new accountant. Samantha met or exceeded all the qualifications for the position. She had presented herself professionally during the interviews, answered their questions appropriately and had always been reserved and efficient at her job as a receptionist in the building. She seemed confident without being pretentious. She also was attractive and well spoken, which rarely played a part in Henri's decisions. He was generally indifferent to women and intimidating to men. Doug and Martin had noticed Henri getting nervous when she was in the same room. He had eventually given her permission to call him by his first name. Perhaps that is why Henri was acting distracted. Perhaps this woman that he had basically ignored when she saw him every day while she was a receptionist had aroused feelings in the staunch German. JBT was growing rapidly. Douglas was in favor of taking on another partner. Despite Martin's and Henri's concerns, Doug felt that Francesca would be the right choice for that position. He said that he and Francesca could separate business and personal issues. He argued that neither would have a problem being honest about business issues even if they were contentious. Francesca's experience in marketing, accounting and negotiating contracts would be a welcome addition to the firm.

Chapter IX
Jack Turner

Hank Baldoni, alias Jack Turner, and Ben were picked up by the Harbor Patrol in Cleveland Harbor. The Coast Guard had received information that the Mariner had capsized during the storm and there were no reports of survivors. The ambulance rushed through the icy streets of the city arriving at the Cleveland Clinic Emergency bay ten days after the ship had reportedly capsized. Hank was in shock, dehydrated and malnourished. His fingers and toes were frostbitten. Large wounds on his back and right shoulder were infected and his kidneys were beginning to fail. He was rushed to surgery. Two of his fingers on his non-dominant hand and three toes on his left foot had to be amputated. His wounds were cleansed and debrided, left open with drains and flushed with antibiotics. He was taken to the Intensive Care Unit and intravenous antibiotics were started along with nutritional support. Ben was also rushed to surgery. There was a collection of blood in his brain in the area of the head wound that the surgeons attempted to evacuate. While on the surgery table, Ben succumbed to a heart attack. The doctors were unable to revive him. He was pronounced dead at 1:10 AM on his birthday. He was only fifty-seven years old. He left a wife and three children. No identification was found on either man. The staff had to wait until Hank (Jack) came out of the anesthetic to obtain any identifying information. Jack became septic despite the IV antibiotics. He was placed on dialysis to support his failing kidney function. It was three days from the day they were picked up in their damaged lifeboat before Jack's fever subsided, he began to respond to the antibiotics and his kidneys began to produce urine. Something inside him fought to stay alive. He decided to continue with a new life if he survived. The past was the past. He promised that he would anonymously send John the money he had stolen. He wanted to forget the mess his life had been when he was consumed with an addiction to gamble that led him to doing business with the mob and had caused him to cheat his best friend. He had also promised that poor young woman, Sally, that he would come back for her and take her away from the horrible life she was forced to live. *She wouldn't be any better off with me. I would have exposed her to the mob, and she might have been killed.* He couldn't live with that Hank Baldoni that had gotten into an illegal business, gambled every penny he had and, worst of all, stolen company money from his friend and business partner. What he didn't know was that he had a child who had almost died, that John and Alicia had both passed away; that Sally had also died from cancer. The construction was closed, and Balpar Industries remained a client of JBT & Associates. When Phyllis left the cocoon of her youth she went to college and dove into her career as a corporate lawyer and auditor. Money and success changed her. She rarely went home to see her family and friends. It was easier to pull away from Melinda, unable to deal with the fact they were not actually sisters. When Melinda married Ron, whom Phyllis disliked and mistrusted, the gap grew into a chasm. John had passed away one year before Alicia died. Their funeral had brought Phyllis and Melinda together for a brief period. Other than a few short conversations on the phone, Phyllis had not seen Melinda until she received the call from the police that Melinda had been in an accident.

It took almost a year for Hank (Jack) to recover. During his rehabilitation he became known for his good humor and that he loved teasing the nurses and the therapists. Other patients in the Rehab Center responded to his chiding, pushing them to performing painful exercises. Jack earned the nickname "Bulldozer" because he had the ability to move people and lift their spirits. One of the doctors encouraged him to consider going to school to obtain a physical therapy degree. He took their advice, graduated from the University with a 3.9 GPA and was accepted to Tennessee University's physical therapy program. Four years after his rescue and recovery, he obtained his certification. He vowed to return to Iowa to make amends to John and Alicia. Each time he was close to contacting them, the ghost of the men who tried to kill him haunted him. Three years after working in the PT Department at the Clinic, his maturity and good humor prompted his supervisors to recommend him for the position of Director of Rehabilitation Services at the Cleveland Clinic.

It was the beginning of the afternoon shift in early-December. Jack had collapsed on a cot in the on-call lounge. He had taken an extra shift because one of Physical Therapists had called in sick. He had splashed cold water on his face. That face sported a short beard scattered with a smattering of grey. His dark eyes still twinkled set in the wrinkling skin of his fifth decade. He stared at his weary face in the mirror. Jack felt he was paying Hank's debt to society by helping others heal, but he needed closure. The only way he could have that was to bite the bullet, take his savings and make a visit to Moline. He didn't know if John and Alicia were still alive. He wanted to try to find Sally. Then there was the danger those visits might generate. Even though it had been years since Hank's disappearance, he knew the mob rarely forgot a vendetta. If they knew Hank somehow had survived being shot and nearly crushed, they would pass on the "debt" to whomever had been associated with him. No one would be safe. Jack had sent a letter to John Strigow. It had returned stamped with "address unknown". He had considered taking a leave of absence from work and making a trip to Moline to find John and Alicia, pay them back the money he had stolen and try to make amends. It had been almost twenty years since that awful day. Hank dried his face and ran a comb through his greying hair. He put on Jack's costume in order to play the part he had chosen; the crooked smile that cheered up the injured; the sense of humor that turned hopelessness into hope and the kindness that helped his patients make it through days filled with pain. Most of the patients receiving therapy as outpatients had left. Jack looked at the schedule. He was relieved to see there were just two new patients from the Rehab Unit he needed to evaluate. Double shifts sucked the life out of him.

Edward McKenzie was a thirty-year-old black male who had been admitted to the Intensive Care Unit two weeks ago following a motorcycle accident. His ten-year-old Harley-Davidson bike had slipped on black ice on the highway, flipped over a guardrail and hit a UPS truck head on. Eddie wound up airborne, landing against a cement retainer wall. The bones in his right arm were shattered. The doctors were unable to save his arm requiring an amputation at the elbow joint. Three of his right ribs were fractured as well as both collarbones. He also suffered multiple lacerations and a concussion. The doctors could not believe he had lived. They operated on his wounds and fractures for over seven hours. Eddie refused to look at his amputated limb. He stared at the floor, slumped in his wheelchair. He wouldn't look at Jack or anyone else in the therapy unit. The nurses had told Jack that Eddie refused to speak to anyone, even his friends who had faithfully visited him every day he was in the ICU on the ventilator and unconscious. When regained consciousness and he was weaned off the ventilator, he refused to take any medication or interact with the staff, doctors and visitors. Jack loved a challenge.

"There he is—the guy that beat the odds and got a chance to live!" Jack patted Eddie on the back Eddie stiffened and scowled, his head bowed to his chest and his good arm limp at the side of the wheelchair. "You know, Eddie, you can sit here staring at the floor for an hour or you can start living again. Some of the other patients, worse off than you are, want my help. For some reason you survived with both legs, a brain, one good arm and another arm that has the chance to recover and be useful. One way or another, I'll be getting paid. How you choose to spend this hour, the rest of your life, is up to you." Jack walked away from Eddie and joined one of the PT Techs who was assisting an elderly man who had suffered a stroke. The left side of his face drooped, saliva dripping from the flaccid corner of his mouth. He mumbled unintelligibly as the Tech moved his paralysed arm and leg through a series of passive exercises. Eddie watched as Jack encouraged the old man to attempt to move any part of his arm or leg. He joked with the Tech and even solicited a grin from the unaffected side of the patient's mouth. Slowly, Eddie moved his wheelchair, using both legs, closer to where Jack was working.

"Maybe I can try a few things." Eddie whispered hoarsely.

"You talking to me?" Jack asked as he turned to look Eddie in his eyes.

"Yeah…maybe."

Jack returned his attention to the patient with the stroke who stared at the man in the wheelchair with part of his arm missing.

"Yes… sir, I am." Eddie lowered his head to his chest once again.

Jack turned halfway towards Eddie and pointed. "There is a machine with a sling hanging from the frame over in that corner. Please wheel over to the machine, Eddie, and I will be with you as soon as we have completed Mr Cleary's exercises. I want you to use your left arm, not your legs, to assist in navigating those thirty feet to the machine. You will need strength in that arm until you are ready for a prosthesis for your right arm. "Jack turned back to Mr Cleary. Eddie remained unmoving. He did raise his head and watched how the Tech and Jack worked gently, but firmly, with their patient.

"Eddie, your hour is almost up. You need to start moving that "Harley" wheelchair or today will be a bust for you." Jack stood over Eddie. Eddie grimaced as he turned his wheelchair with his legs and slowly headed towards the machine Jack had pointed to. "Eddie, use your left arm, not your legs." Eddie slammed his feet onto the foot pedals, swore under his breath and tried to move using his left arm. Jack watched with a crooked grin on his face as Eddie and the wheelchair zig zagged across the room. Eddie realised how weak his arm had become. It took an inordinate amount of strength to try to move forward just using his good arm. He snarled at Jack who raised his eyebrows and continued to smile at Eddie's attempts to get to the equipment. After much grunting and swearing Eddie sat in front of the equipment to which Jack had directed him. Eddie considered standing and walking out of the therapy unit but remembered when he had tried to stand to transfer into his bed his legs were too weak to allow him to even stand and pivot.

Jack walked over to where Eddie sat dejectedly in his wheelchair. "Are you ready to work; to work harder than you have ever worked in your life?" From that day forward Eddie worked tirelessly to strengthen and retrain the muscles in the remaining portion of his right arm and shoulder. The muscles in his left arm and legs grew taught and sinewy. Jack and the other physical and occupational therapists pushed him and encouraged him.

She was late. The bus that transported patients from the Cleveland Clinic Rehabilitation Center to the physician offices in the main hospital campus had difficulty navigating icy streets and slowed traffic. Dr Raphael Coronado was the Neurosurgeon who had placed the stent into Millie's ventricles. He was checking her neurologic status and overall state of her recovery in order to devise a plan for rehabilitation. Millie waited in her wheelchair for over an hour because of missing her original appointment. She was nervous and agitated when her name was finally called to see the doctor.

"Well, Mrs Sherman, I'm sorry you had to wait. How are you feeling?" Dr Coronado's kind eyes searched her unsmiling face. Millie shrugged her shoulders. "Hmmm, in that case let me ask you some questions and test your strength and reflexes." Dr Coronado was known for his quiet presence and pleasant bedside manner. Some surgeons faltered in the bedside manner area but the five-foot three-inch tall, world-famous neurosurgeon rarely raised his voice. His dark brown eyes and thick black hair highlighted a handsome face. Nurses loved assisting him in surgery and when making rounds because he delighted in teaching them, hardly ever corrected them in front of his patients and other staff and took their calls with respect and a soft voice, even in the middle of the night.

After he examined Millie and asked several questions, he remarked, “May I call you Melinda?” Millie nodded yes. “I am sending you to be evaluated by Jack Turner who is the Department Chairman for Physical and Occupational Services at the Rehabilitation Center. I know it is late in the day. I have contacted Mr Turner and he has agreed to stay over to get started on a plan to attain the strength to get you home and back to living your life.”

“How am I supposed to do that? I remember so little about that life before the accident. They still have not found out if someone deliberately ran me down. I just found out that the few memories I have of my parents—of my sister are untrue. I…I feel so lost. Sometimes I wish… I wish I hadn’t survived.” Millie began to sob. She felt comfortable enough with this kind physician to tell him how alone and frightened she was. Dr Coronado put his hands on her shoulders and allowed her to cry for several minutes.

“Melinda, I understand how confused you are. It will take time. The fact that you are regaining memories of your past, have no other complications from your head injury and your other injuries are healing well are very good signs. I would like you to see one of our staff Psychologists who can help you with the anxiety you most deservedly feel. Will you agree to be evaluated today for your physical rehabilitation and I will have Leona schedule an appointment to see Dr Marcia Woodard in the counseling department for some time this week?”

Millie managed to smile and agreed to his suggestions. “There is one more thing I am asking you to do, Melinda. I want you to spend as much time as possible working on starting a new life. The past is the past. Some of the memories may come back distorted or totally out of context. The brain is an amazing organ. We understand very little of how the brain is wired, how it catalogues and recognises events, people and places. As you work to gain strength, continue to heal more memories will present themselves. Try to validate those with people who knew you before the accident and with loved ones. I understand there is a young man who has been in your life before the accident and who continues to support you as you recover. You also have a sister who—"

"She is not my sister!" Millie interrupted.

"Whoa! It was my understanding that Ms Phyllis Strigow is your sister and has been here for you."

"She told me something last week that broke my heart. There were secrets she kept from me. I haven't seen or heard from her since she shared the awful truth." Millie buried her face in her hands.

"I am so very sorry. You don't have to give me the details. I think Dr Woodard can help you through this. Melinda, promise me you will focus on the future, your recovery and let the psychologist help you to deal with the past."

"I'll try." Millie thanked Dr Coronado and wheeled herself out of the exam room.

That poor young lady has such a difficult road ahead of her. I certainly will pray for her, as I do for all my patients. He shook his head and moved on to the next exam room.

Millie arrived back at the Rehab Center. The nurses helped her change into sweatshirt and sweatpants. Her transporter was Ted Farmington. He had worked at the Clinic for twenty-two years moving patients throughout the hospital and in most of the Clinic's satellites. He knew almost every nook and cranny of the vast campus. He loved his job. He went to work every day with a smile on his face, whistling or humming old tunes. Millie liked Ted. He didn't ask her questions or seem in a hurry to deposit her at her various destinations. Her hair was starting to grow back with a mind of its own as to which direction each strand would shoot from her scalp. Ted always told her she looked beautiful no matter how deranged her hair behaved. Millie was starting to experience flashes of memories. Memories of John and Alicia in a boat laughing and hugging her when she caught a fish, Sally singing to her, her sad eyes glistening, smatterings of classes in college, Jeff and her sharing giddy moments. These made her smile. There also were flashes of memories that made her shiver; a cold wind against her skin, headlights blinding her, a warm body next to her as she laid on the cold ground, sirens blaring—falling into a pit of darkness. It was a huge puzzle with pieces seeming to fit together and suddenly pulling apart. A barrage of emotions wrapped around her at times. She wanted to hold on to them but also wanted to push them aside. The nurses, therapists and doctors kept asking the same questions over and over. It was part of their job and she knew that. Jeff visited as often as he could. He allowed her to talk without questioning her scattered thoughts. He was so kind and understanding.

Ted was taking Millie to the physical therapy department to be evaluated. "Ted, do you think the therapists would let you take me to the gift shop one of these trips? I want to get something for Jeff. He has been so helpful and kind."

"Miss Millie, you ask Mr Turner if that would be okay one of these days. I can take you after your session. I can look at the schedule and make sure I am the one to pick you up that day. I'll put extra time in the schedule for your transport." Ted winked at her. "Sure, do know who that Jeff fellow is. He looks at you with a very special look, Miss Millie." He winked at her again. Millie blushed as she thought about Jeff's kind eyes, the scent of his after shave, his cute butt. She was starting to have feelings she didn't want to acknowledge. It wouldn't be fair to him. She didn't know what life would be like, where she left off, what relationship they had before. She had so much that could change once she was discharged.

Jack grabbed the last settlings of coffee from the morning. He looked out the window as the day's sun descended behind gray clouds. It had snowed most of the day, the ground and trees sparkled as tiny rays of sun spread their fingers in between the darkening clouds. Above the horizon a tiny rainbow formed and started to fade as quickly as it had peeked above the clouds.

Jack called Rachael, one of the PT Techs over to the window. "Quick, Rache, look at that—a rainbow, in December! I've never seen that before." Rachael took in a breath as she caught the last faded colors drifting below the horizon.

"Wow! That was beautiful! I think I remember someone telling me that a Winter rainbow meant good luck for anyone who saw it. I think we both could use a little luck. I wish our patients could have seen it." Jack smiled.

Maybe it's a sign telling me it is time to fess up, to do the right thing and go back to Iowa to clean up Hank's mess. Jack walked into his office just as the phone was ringing. *Oh, boy. Please don't let this be a late consult. I am whipped. I must make some plans.* "Physical Therapy Department, Jack Turner speaking." Jack sighed as he awaited the caller to speak.

"Jack, this is Dr Coronado. How are you doing?"

"Hello, Dr C. I'm a little tired but doing okay. How can I help you?"

"I have a very special patient who I just saw to clear her for therapy. I won't go into her entire history. I placed a ventricular/renal shunt for communicating hydrocephalus, complications from a head trauma she experienced this past year from a hit and run automobile accident. She also suffered a fractured pelvis and hip, comminuted fracture of the right femur and multiple superficial injuries. Her right hip replacement and placement of rods and plates in her femur are healing nicely. She was transferred from another hospital several weeks ago. She almost succumbed to her injuries and had residual amnesia that is slowly subsiding. I was hoping you could evaluate her tonight. I know this is a lot to ask, but I am concerned for her mental state and feel that starting therapy, getting her busy with some positive strides, will help her mentally and emotionally. I am faxing over her orders and… I believe she is on her way down to your department." Dr Coronado held his breath realising Jack had to be exhausted.

"No problem, Doc. What is her name? I'll check your orders. Could you have someone bring over her medical records so I can review them after I evaluate her. I probably won't be able to start a regime until I can review everything."

Jack yawned and watched as the fax machine seemed to chuckle as it was printing the orders.

"Her name is Melinda Sherman. Thanks so much, Jack. You are a saint."

Saint, huh! If he only knew the real me. If he knew Hank, he wouldn't think I was very saintly.

Jack watched as Melinda was wheeled into the Physical Therapy Unit. He hadn't had time to review her chart. Dr Coronado's orders were for upper and lower body strengthening, gait training and coordination. Occupational therapy would consist of training in activities of daily living—writing, reading, cooking, dressing, household chores, shopping, etc. The chart summary indicated she had been the victim of a hit and run automobile accident while she was waiting for a bus in Davenport, Iowa in November. She had sustained head trauma with subsequent evacuation of a subdural hematoma (a blood clot). She had begun to experience headaches two weeks ago with dizziness and blurred vision. Dr Coronado had placed a shunt from the ventricles in her brain to the kidney for communicating hydrocephalus when she was transferred to Cleveland Clinic last week. She had also sustained a pelvic fracture, comminuted fracture of her right tibia and fibula, and fracture of her right hip. Pins, screws and plates had been inserted for fixation and repair of the fractures. Her amnesia was gradually subsiding. Dr Coronado had recently recommended Melinda be evaluated by a Psychologist, Dr Woodard, for the amnesia and post-trauma issues. Melinda's auburn hair had started to grow back, and she was eating better. She had lost sixteen pounds since the accident. She was staring at the equipment and a man in a wheelchair who had his arm, or part of an arm in a sling attached to some king of machine. Eddie glanced her way. As soon as their eyes met, he looked away. Melinda felt a twinge of sadness for that man. At least she had all her parts, physical parts that is. The memory and the confusion about who she was, who she really was, had not been repaired. *Maybe it never would be,* she thought.

"Hi Ted. How is everything going?" Jack shook hands with the transporter. "This must be Mrs Sherman." Jack took her hand. "May I call you Melinda? You can call me Jack. You probably will want to call me a few other things while you are here, but that is to be expected. There may be days when you are exhausted and discouraged. Please don't worry about hurting my feelings. I will be asking a lot of you—pushing you. The other therapists and I only do that so you can get back to a normal life. "

Melinda looked at Jack's kind face and his greying hair. She noticed that he was missing two fingers on his hand. "What happened to your hand?"

"Oh, that. I donated them to a guy who lost his in a poker game." Jack said as a crooked grin played on his face.

"That is really sad! Someone must have dealt him a bad hand." Millie shot back. Jack, Ted and Millie started to laugh. The combination of a weary therapist, a seasoned transporter and an anxious patient drove their laughter into loud belly laughs. Even Eddie had to smile—it was infectious.

Jack finally pulled himself together. "I guess you got me on that one, Melinda—okay to call you Melinda?"

Millie composed herself long enough to sputter out a "yes" before she started laughing again. She hadn't laughed like that in a long time. Even before the accident, there had been enough sadness and disappointment in her life that laughter had taken a back seat. Jack assisted Millie to stand and walk a few steps. Her right leg was very weak. Millie leaned on Jack's arm heavily. Jack encouraged her to stand as erect as possible, look ahead rather than at her feet to prepare her to walk between the parallel bars. He asked if she thought she could walk ten steps to the parallel bars. Millie bit her lip and tried to put her weight on her right leg, but her leg would not hold her weight and she started to fall. Jack held Millie and Ted pulled the wheelchair under her so she could sit down.

"Wow, I am really weak! I haven't walked since the accident. I'm sorry I'm not doing very well."

Jack took her hand, “Melinda, you have nothing to be sorry about. The only time you need to be sorry is if you step on my toes. Even then, if you can step on my toes, I would consider it a compliment.”

“Thanks Jack. I want everyone to call me by my maiden name. Sherman is my ex-husband’s name. I have submitted paperwork to change my last name. “

“I didn’t get to read your entire chart. What is your maiden name?” Jack asked.

Millie looked at Jack. “My maiden name is Melinda Strigow.” Jack’s heart skipped a few beats and his throat went dry.

“Did you say your last name was Strigow?” Jack could barely breathe. He did his best to maintain some composure.

“Yes, my parents were Alicia and John Strigow. At least that was what I was told…until…until.” Millie could not hold back the tears as she remembered the last conversation she had with Phyllis.

Jack took hold of Millie’s cold hands. “Melinda, I will… I knew…” Jack (Hank) searched Millie’s face. He couldn’t make sense of this. How did she have the same last name of his friend? Something about her beautiful, tear filled eyes stabbed at the memory of someone he knew long ago. Millie was trying desperately to remember life before the accident.

“Mr Turner, I can’t remember my parents or much of anything about my life. I have dreams of a house with green shutters and a flower wreath on the front door. People without faces move in and out of the house. I call to them, but they don’t seem to know I am there. Phyllis, my sister… I thought she was my sister, but now… I…I don’t know. I am so confused.” Millie let go of Jack’s hands and started to twist the strings on the waist of her sweatpants. Jack could hardly hold back the many questions circling his brain. He knew that anything he said might upset Millie. He remembered Alicia and John trying to have more children, but they had been unsuccessful up to the time he left Iowa. To add to their attempts, Alicia had begun to show signs of menopause despite being only thirty-nine years old. John had confided in

Hank, his best friend at the time. He had brought up adoption several times, but Alicia was hesitant. Jack felt like he had been hit with a heavy brick. He decided to redirect the conversation to Millie's physical therapy evaluation.

Jack avoided looking at Millie, "Did I say something to upset you? You look sad, frightened almost." Mille stared at Jack.

Jack could feel the sweat dripping from his armpits. "Let's focus on your physical therapy, young lady. I'm sure you want to get back home as soon as possible." Jack wanted the same thing for different reasons. "We can talk another time about memories."

Millie swallowed all the feelings swirling around her mind and heart. "Okay, Mr Turner, I am more than ready to get rid of this wheelchair!" Jack began by observing how Millie stood from the wheelchair and balanced herself while holding on to the parallel bars. Her legs were very weak. She was only able to walk a few steps, bearing most of her weight on her arms and shoulders. Jack coached her in placing one foot in front of the other, stepping up to her foot and transferring her weight to her legs. Every step shot pain through her hip and knee. Her knees buckled twice, but she recovered and grew a tiny bit stronger and less frightened with each step. They moved on to an area with barbell weights resting in a large cabinet. After several repetitions of arm lifts and bends Millie was sweating and dark circles outlined her eyes. Millie needed to develop her upper body strength so that she could eventually use a walker or crutches until she was able to walk on her own. Jack predicted she would need at least two months of physical therapy. She would also be evaluated by the Occupational Therapist to determine a program for activities of daily living.

After Millie's therapy session Ted wheeled her to the gift shop. Jack went into his office and collapsed in the chair behind his desk. He gazed out the frosted window at the clouds playing hide and seek with the sun. *Why didn't I contact John sooner? He had another daughter. I wonder if she was adopted. She said something about Phyllis being her sister, but not really her sister. That is strange! She doesn't even remember her life with them. God, my best friend's daughter was almost killed, and I could have been there for her and her family! What a coward I am! I was so afraid that those thugs that tried to kill me would go after them…I should have let them know I was alive. I should have paid back the money I stole and faced the music. Sally, Oh Sally, I abandoned you too! I wonder if she is still alive. I wanted to rescue you, instead I only thought about rescuing myself!* His remorse stabbed at his heart. He couldn't sleep that night. The next morning, he vowed to revive Hank Baldoni from seclusion, help Millie to recall any part of her life he could and return to Davenport to pick up the pieces of his broken past. *Phyllis, I should try to contact her. She was just a little girl when I ran away. We used to go fishing. She called me Uncle "Hanky Panky". I must be sure that my past doesn't remain a threat to them.*

Chapter X
Power Play

Francesca had been given a partnership in JBT despite Martin's misgivings. Henri and Douglas considered the partnership beneficial because of her experience with marketing. She was extremely intelligent and seemed to have the magic touch with high risk stocks and moderate risk commodities. She also was beautiful and able to remain professional without promoting her sexuality. Francesca was surprised when Henri hired Samantha. Francesca had plans. Those plans did not include another woman snooping around or using her feminine whiles to move up in the company. Francesca had friends who enjoyed the rush they got from manipulating others for their own financial gain. These "friends" promised to assist her in rising to a position of power, using any means necessary. They had no qualms eliminating roadblocks to their business deals, gambling casinos and other questionable interests. The police as well as government offices were infiltrated with men and women who were beholding to or threatened by the "mob". Francesca had studied in the same college as Daniel Pironne. They both had graduated at the top of their class, had been on the same debate team and even had a few dates during their college years. Douglas Jacob knew Dan casually. Dan always seemed to be slithering from one shady deal to the next. They rarely talked and didn't see eye to eye on pushing the boundaries on ethical business practices. Daniel Pironne and Francesca shared a malignant passion for power. Daniel chose to follow in his father's footsteps. Victor Pironne was the Godfather of the "mob" that owned most of the Casinos in the Quad-City area and Chicago. Victor was a crook, but he still had a few scruples. He was known to forgive some debts or decrease the amount owed without demanding retribution. Daniel, however, did not inherit one cell of this characteristic. He was cold, and narcissistic. The world revolved around him and his desires. He deemed anyone he felt shortchanged him, or double crossed him should be eradicated. He was convinced that any choice he made, any hit he ordered, any decision to gain the title, position, place he desired was appropriate because he was always right. Narcissistic Personality Disorder is a personality disorder with a long-term pattern of abnormal behavior characterised by exaggerated feelings of self-importance, excessive need for admiration, and a lack of empathy. Those affected often spend much time thinking about achieving power or success, or on their appearance. They often take advantage of the people around them. Dan watched Douglas and his partners build a business that was worth millions. When Francesca married Doug, Dan saw an opportunity to ensure the companies he inherited from his father were protected. He knew that Francesca shared his desire for power and worship of the almighty dollar. When his father was killed, Dan expanded his horizons from simple money laundering to international "pump and dump" schemes. Investors were enticed to take part in development of vineyards and resorts in foreign countries. Elaborate plans for their development with a promise of good returns on these stocks played on the naivete' of investors. Profits were jerry-rigged by owners who were all members of the mafia that hid behind businessmen who had a good reputation. The company had so many layers the stockholders would not be able to dig through them to see that the actual profits were never seen, nor would they be able to locate the actual businesses in which they were supposedly invested. Dan had contacted Francesca, asking her to meet with him. He had a deal to present to her that would fit both their appetites. Dan presumed her success depended on her marriage to someone she could control and dispose of if needed.

Jeff Collins had become impatient with the investigation into Millie's hit and run accident. The police had hit a dead end when they were unable to locate the car and the driver. They also had come up empty handed in finding clues as to why Millie would be a victim of an intentional plan to injure or eliminate her. The only suspect was Millie's former husband, Ron Sherman. He had a vague alibi that he was passed out in a local tavern where he was a regular at the time of the accident. His truck tire marks did not match those at the scene of the accident. There was one witness to his being passed out in the back room of the club between 2 am and 7 am the day of Millie's accident. The owner of the tavern came to work at 7:15 am and found Ron lying on an old cot in the back room. They had brought Ron in for questioning. He was unkept, foul-mouthed and surly. He swore he had no interest in his former wife nor anything concerning her. After checking his truck for signs of an impact and tire impressions as well as confirming his alibi, they did not have enough evidence to charge him. He was released and warned not to leave town. Jeff decided to do a little investigating of his own.

Jack Turner, alias Hank Baldoni, or vis versa dove into the mountain of paper charting that made up Melinda Sherman (Strigow's) medical record. He had requested the entire MR from Moline Hospital. He was looking for contact information for Phyllis, Alicia and John Strigow and any other individuals that could fill in the years since he had disappeared. Phyllis and Jeff's information were available, but John and Alicia were listed as deceased. *Too late! I waited too long to contact John and make amends. God, please forgive me! I am so sorry.* Jack closed his eyes and prayed. He had so many questions. When had Alicia and John passed? Was Millie adopted? What happened to Sally? He had promised to rescue her from her prostitution prison. He had fallen in love with her in just the few times he had been with her. She was twenty-two years old when he met her. Most prostitutes lose their usefulness when they approach their thirties. Many of these poor girls die from sexually transmitted diseases, drug overdose, suicide or are "eliminated". Jack's hands trembled as he wrestled with what he would say when he called Phyllis. Would she hang up on him? Would she call the police? How could he make her trust him?

Francesca was convinced that the origin of the accounts Dan had presented to her were hidden behind a screen of limited international rules and sanctions. She was so adept at manipulating her monthly presentations to her partners and other Board members that she had begun to believe them herself. Daniel Pirrone was the lynchpin to the information given to her. She would edit profit and loss spreadsheets and reports dangling false profit margins as a carrot for investors then manipulating the figures so that side investments in shell corporations appeared to be real. Despite audits by an independent firm the trail of investments did not come into question up to that point. The partners, even Martin, admitted they were impressed with the clients Francesca brought to the firm. Samantha vowed to stay in Francesca's good graces. She made a concerted effort to convince Francesca that she was an ardent cheerleader supporting her efforts to gain validation from her male counterparts. Samantha genuflected to Francesca's request for research required of new clients and investment opportunities. Samantha prepared elaborate flow charts and projections. In Francesca's haste to fulfill her need for power and money, she forgot a cardinal rule she had learned in college. Always check and re-check all information about clients and businesses yourself. Samantha had worked hard, spending many non-paid hours after the office had closed, reviewing the accounts Francesca had indicated. In doing so, she came across several accounts with layers making it difficult to track the validity of the original business model. She dove into lengthy lists of investments where she noticed three names that appeared in several levels of one certain model. Daniel Pirrone, Victor Pirrone and Hank Baldoni could be traced to a company in Italy. Victor Pirrone's name appeared up until 1962 when it no longer was listed after that year. Hank Baldoni appeared as an owner for only one year early in the history of the group. Daniel Pirrone appeared to have sold his interest in the company to Arthur Mason who was a lawyer (and one of the mob's sleuths). That company is in Amalfi Italy. Amalfi is a town nestled in steep cliffs along the southern edge of Italy's Sorrentine Peninsula. The company's prospectus used a jumble of business jargon describing a holding company. This company was created to buy enough shares in other companies to gain control of them. For investors the holding company provides an avenue for obtaining stocks, bonds, mutual funds, art—a wide range of assets, including minority stakes in the principal business. This can be a legitimate model or totally false based on an imaginary investment model. Balpar Industries was invented by Victor Pirrone. Hank was initially one of the primary investors in the company until he realised this might be a cover for Victor's illegal enterprises. When Dan inherited the business, he ramped up the international businesses. Casinos, prostitution groups, drugs and wineries brought in revenue that was illegal, masked as resorts and other businesses. Francesca had talents that were used to enhance the reputation and client base at JBT, but she crossed that invisible line still believing she was doing the right thing. After all, hadn't she given her all to her former job only to go unrecognised, be paid less than the men with equal job descriptions and have the credit given to male employees for the work she had done. Resentments and anger seethed inside coloring her decisions and challenging her ethics. Douglas did not suspect any of Francesca's business dealings were illegitimate. He still was amazed that she had agreed to date him, let alone marry him. Her beauty and intelligence mesmerised him. Her love making left him dazzled and vulnerable. She was able to gain access to the other partners' accounts, moving money in and out of viable investments and those of Balpar Industries. Even

Henri's eagle eye had not questioned the validity of the company's investments.

Samantha did not relay her suspicions to Henri or the other partners. She saw an opportunity to deal with Francesca or to encourage an alliance by exposing her greed. This would open the door to secure a rapid rise to a more powerful position in JBT. When greed and the promise of power become the driving forces behind a person's actions, rungs on the ladder to success and skipped altering the person's ethical balance. Teetering on the compromised ladder increases one's chance of falling. Hank Baldoni, alias Jack Turner had been eliminated and forgotten. Victor was sure his henchmen had taken care of him. He had let Victor know he wanted to pay off his debts and promised to disappear. He managed to do just that though not in the way he had planned. Victor had discovered his "boys" may not have done their jobs. He took care of them in his own special way. When Victor died, Daniel vowed to finish Hank if he still was alive. He also was sure that Hank had something to do with his father's demise. Melinda seemed to be the love child of Hank Baldoni. Dan's evil grin represented a plan that seeped from his black heart.

Chapter XI
Cloud Cover

Henri had always been a stickler for details. His meticulous attention to the accounts was part of the reason JBT was so successful. As the business grew, he delegated management of some of the older accounts to those he hired for his department. Having rigorously reviewed the qualifications and personal history of those he interviewed, only a few had passed the criteria he required. There had been no room for romance in Henri's life. He rarely dated. He had observed the relationships of his partners and his few friends and concluded that women had the ability to numb even the most brilliant minds, gaining selfish control and often leading to disaster. Until Samantha Reynolds walked into his office for her interview, he had managed to keep his testosterone in check and his brain intact. Samantha's confidence, her demeanor and her beauty stirred feelings he usually was able to drown. She wasn't flirtatious, as other women had been. In contrast she appeared somewhat aloof and frosty while remaining respectful and professional. Henri felt slightly weak in the knees as he slowly walked around his desk motioning to Samantha to seat herself in one of the two leather chairs facing him. He remained standing, studying the graceful movements, almost like slow motion, she used to move from the door to the chair. He stared into her green eyes with tiny gold flecks that pulled him physically and mentally into them. He tried to look down at her resume, but it seemed she had cast a spell on him as his wall began to melt. Her voice was steady and softly commanding. Though she covered her thigh quickly after crossing her legs he had seen enough in that instant to cause him to envision his hand caressing her soft, supple skin. *This is ridiculous! I must be tired, not enough coffee. Henri, old boy, pull yourself together.*

"Thank you for allowing me to be interviewed for this position, Mr Treacher. I have a list of references should you wish to review them. "Samantha's voice was steady and confident. Henri was an orderly man. Everything in his life fit into its own cell on his daily spreadsheet. Henri asked several questions about financial investments and accounting, to which Samantha answered correctly. The hands on the clock moved to noon. The clock's hands reminded Henri of a person raising his arms in a position of surrender. One time, long ago, he had allowed someone to make a chink in his heart. Never again, he had vowed. He walked Samantha to the door and watched her fluently move towards the elevators.

"I will be in touch with you, Ms Reynolds." Henri tried to use his commanding voice.

"Thank you for giving me the opportunity to show you what I can offer as an employee of JBT." Samantha smiled as the elevator doors closed. She had accomplished a small, but critical part of her plan. Henri had dropped the icy façade he normally portrayed for just a few minutes. She had researched the company history and an audit had been performed recently by an independent auditing firm. JBT had passed the scrutiny of the auditing firm with very few recommendations for change. That would allow a year of activity without oversight for Samantha to impress Henri and the other partners with her expertise. She might have to use her feminine whiles to obtain information that was not accessible or redacted.

Jack (Hank) had reviewed Millie's chart. He had learned that Phyllis told Millie that her birth mother was a woman John Strigow had brought home after Hank's disappearance. She and Phyllis were told this woman was their governess. She helped raise the girls. John had admitted to Phyllis when he was dying that this governess was really Millie's mother. Sally Thatcher had been romantically involved with Hank and had become pregnant with his child. Because of her past and being abandoned by Hank, she begged John and Alicia to adopt Millie. Jack read Sally's name and his heart skipped a beat. That didn't make sense. How did John find out that Sally and Hank had a relationship? How could Sally have lived in the same house as her own child pretending to be Millie's governess rather than her mother. That would have been so very difficult. Sally had lived a horrible life from the time she was abducted until she met Hank. She opened her heart to him and really believed that he loved her. He had promised to rescue her, but that never happened. Jack held his head in his hands and let the tears fall onto Millie's chart. Was she his daughter? How could he ever be forgiven for abandoning those who loved and trusted him? He was a coward. He knew he had to confirm whether Millie was his flesh and blood. *A DNA test. I must get something from her so I can prove, one way or another, that she is my daughter... Sally...John...Alicia—what have I done?* He certainly couldn't ask Millie for a sample! That would mean he would have to tell her the whole sordid story. Jack read that Millie had been run down by someone and that the authorities had neither discovered a motive, nor any suspects that didn't have an alibi for the day of her accident. He feared that her accident might have something to do with the criminals with whom he had been involved years ago. Since the first day Jack had evaluated Millie, he felt this need to protect her and personally manage her therapy treatments. This left him with a difficult dilemma. He could risk telling Millie about his sordid past, his relationship with John, Alicia and Sally; that he could possibly be her birth father, or he could continue the masquerade. It was about time he cleaned up his side of the street, regardless of the risk. *If I open this door, will I be putting Millie and Phyllis in danger? Suppose the mob has found out I am alive, are they still looking for revenge and using them as a decoy to find me? Either way, I must take responsibility for my mistakes in order to protect those girls.*

When Victor Pironne discovered that one of his best prostitutes had escaped, he was livid. No one interfered with Pironne enterprises; no one lived long enough to tell about any of the family's dealings. His henchmen searched Sally's apartment. They tore it apart looking for any clue that could lead them to her hiding place. Victor made sure the other girls knew what would happen to them if they tried to hide anything. His men savagely beat several of the girls that were close to Sally. They swore they did not know where she was or with whom she might have left. In a wastebasket one of the thugs found a pregnancy test kit that showed positive. One of the girls told the thugs that she had seen Sally with the same guy several times. She didn't know the guy's last name. She thought his first name was Frank or Hank.

"If that Goddam Hank Baldoni is still alive, knocked up one of my "chicks" and took her, he will pay and so will anyone he knows or is related to!" The look in Victor's eyes was filled with evil. He put out the word that he wanted to talk to the two of his men who were supposed to have annihilated Hank. Billie "the shoe" Gillespie and Buster Cornelli came to Victor's mansion thinking the boss had a "job" for them. They had no qualms about torturing or killing, no remorse—no empathy. They robotically carried out horrific crimes, disappeared for a few months after the event and managed to stay out of jail. Billie's nick name, "the shoe" was earned from the steel tipped shoes he used as a weapon to kick and stomp his victims to death. He usually finished them off with a bullet to the head then tossing the gun in the river or lake. Buster Cornelli was Victor's brother-in-law. He earned enough money from his "hits" to keep Marianna, Victor's sister in diamonds and furs. Victor's mansion was in a remote suburb of Chicago. The immaculately groomed grounds surrounded the twenty-six-room castle. The entire complex was surrounded by wrought-iron fencing decorated with barbed wire. Fierce guard dogs and security men patrolled the area. Security cameras, motion detectors and spotlights supplemented the fortification of the complex. Billie and Buster were escorted to the library where Victor sat behind a huge oak desk. Red velvet tapestries hung from the floor to the ceiling in between rows of bookshelves filled with hard bound books. A cigarette burned in a crystal ashtray, the smoke partially masking Victor's handsome face. The son of an alcoholic father who beat his children for no reason and a mother whose beauty suffered over the years she was abused; Victor joined a gang who taught him how to use violence and manipulation to gain power. He needed the power to feed his anger. His father taught him that abuse could keep things under his control. Dark brown eyes that turned a deep purple when his temper flared, coal black hair and Roman features made it easy for him to attract the ladies so he could use them for his pleasure. He had married Anita Fitzpatrick, a gorgeous blond actress, not because he loved her (though he told her that he loved her) but because he wanted a son to carry on with thc empire he was building. After several miscarriages, Anita gave him Daniel. Daniel not only inherited the combination of both Irish and Italian features, but also his father's cunning and lack of caring for any other human. The only living thing Daniel had any feelings for was his pet parrot, Ivan "the terrible". He taught Ivan every swear word and insult he had learned from the guys his father had in his army of henchmen. Ivan also learned to peck the eyes out of a person when Daniel gave the command "Attack!" Anita was so fearful of her husband she would do anything he commanded her to do. That included dancing nude for him and his selected guests, getting close to men on the police force so they could be coerced into looking the other way when people "disappeared "or laws were broken. Life was good for Victor because he didn't worry. He could do anything he wanted. He was the Godfather.

Billie spoke first. "Hey, boss, whatcha got for us?" Victor waved the two thugs to sit in the leather chairs in front of his desk. Billie and Buster sat down and glanced at each other, then at Victor. The grandfather clock ticked the seconds away as they waited for Victor to answer.

"Do you guys recall a two-bit gambler named Hank Baldoni? Victor leaned back in his chair looking at his desk, not at Billie and Buster.

Buster piped up first. "Yeah, he was the punk we shot and dumped in the coal car, right?" Victor leaned forward, his dark eyebrows folding over his eyelids. He licked his lips.

"Yes, that guy." Victor said in a deep, sinister voice. Billie was a little more educated than Buster. An icy chill ran down his spine.

"That guy had to be dead, boss. After we dumped him in the coal car, a ton of coal was released into the car and on top of him. He wasn't breathing when we put him in there…I swear." Both Billie and Buster had been relieved of their "pieces" before they were taken to the Library.

Buster started to argue with Billie who by now was sitting on the edge of his chair. "Shoe, I told you we should have shot the guy in the head to make sure—"

"Shut up!" Victor held his forty-five in between his legs. He had attached a silencer to the weapon before the two were ushered into the room. "When I give you an order to eliminate someone, what is it you don't understand about the meaning of "eliminate"?" Victor's dark eyes had turned purple and they bore through the two men who were fidgeting in their chairs.

"Boss…he…he got crushed by the coal. We, um, saw it filling up. Right Billie…we." Beads of sweat dripped down Buster's face. Billie's eyes looked down at the carpet. His heartbeat so loud it seemed to drown out the ticking of the clock. Victor stood up and fired two shots. One hit Billie in the head and the other hit Buster in the chest, right over his heart.

Victor waited a moment, watching the blood of the two men drip on to the carpet. "That's what eliminate means." He wiped the gun with his handkerchief and placed it carefully in the desk drawer. He pushed a button on his intercom. "Get a couple of guys from Stanton's Cleaning Service here, Marion. There's a little mess in my office that needs cleaning up. Have them bring a couple of extra—large bags. There is some garbage that needs to be disposed of. Thank you, Marion. Tell the kitchen I'm ready to have my lunch now. I'll take it in the sunroom." Marion was used to "messes". She did everything efficiently because she didn't want to become one of the "messes". Victor vowed he would find Hank Baldoni if he was still alive. He had confided in Daniel about Balpar Industries and that he was concerned that Hank had not been eliminated. Hank would be able to expose Balpar for what it really was. Victor also was sure that Hank had taken Sally and he needed to make sure he paid for stealing one of his prostitutes. If Sally had a kid and it was Hank's, Victor could use the kid to draw Hank out of hiding.

For a year Victor and Dan Pironne searched for Hank. Victor ran into a wall trying to locate Hank, but he did find Sally. She was living with the Strigow family since John had rescued her. There were two children in residence that Victor decided would be useful in his pursuit of Hank. He shared the information with Dan. The Pirrone family had an arch enemy —the Michaletti family. Gato Michaletti heard the Pirrones had lost one of their best prostitutes and that Hank Baldoni may not have been eliminated. Gato wanted to leave profitable businesses to his son, Harry. The hierarchy of the mob was very similar to eighteen century rulers in Europe. The Godfather was expected to maintain successful business operations and to make sure anyone or anything that stood in the way of that bastion of power would be silenced. The family was able to keep its powerful standing among the Mafia community by diminishing the credibility of its rival leaders. Gato was in poor health and nearing eighty years old. Harry had not inherited his father's intelligence and ability to make "friends" in high places as well as his father had done, especially with certain persons on the police force with marginal ethics. Gato devised a plan to get Victor out of the picture so he could take over his family's business interests. Prostitution, extortion, drugs, international ghost businesses were extremely profitable. Daniel Pironne was a loose cannon. He often pulled the trigger before thinking through a plan to deal with the aftermath. He had a personality disorder that blended well with his narcissism. His father often had to reign him in when his temper flared and everyone in his path would be mowed down. Victor had shared with Dan his vendetta for Hank Baldoni and his loved ones. Not only had Victor lost "face" with the Mafia community because Hank might not have been properly eliminated, but also Hank had left after been involved in the initial development of Balpar Industries.

Dan's henchmen, disguised as census takers—fake credentials and all, found that John Strigow had died almost a year before they located his address and that Strigow Construction had gone out of business shortly after his death. John's wife and their governess, Sally, had died several years before his death. There were two children. Phyllis was the oldest and had left Moline to attend a Chicago University after her father had passed. The other daughter, Melinda Strigow, was ten years old and was living with a grandmother in Davenport. Though Dan was intent on avenging his father's death, which Dan was sure had been arranged, he also was very busy growing his prostitution business and shuffling the huge deck of holding companies within Balpar Industries. He felt his father's wishes had been satisfied. Hank Baldoni had not been located. Dan assumed he was dead, at least momentarily.

The two Mafia families continued to battle for territories and business interests over the next ten years. In the years between 1965 and 1970 the Chicago police department tightened its net around organised crime. The mayor at the time, made the lives of the Pirrone and Micholetti families miserable. Dan lost sleep trying to think of ways to continue the illicit business within Balpar without being discovered. He turned over his ownership to one of his lawyers, Arthur Mason, though he remained in control of decisions. The "Hank" problem was placed on the back burner while Dan focused on decreasing the members of the Micholetti family and covering his tracks.

The hit and run case of Melinda Strigow had not been solved. Hank Baldoni was living in Cleveland under the assumed name of Jack Turner. Jack was the head of the Physical Therapy Department at Cleveland Clinic. Melinda had been transferred to Cleveland Clinic to have a shunt placed from her brain to her kidney to relieve pressure within her brain. Dan Pirrone was managing the trafficking, racketeering, extortion businesses. Francesca was a partner in JBK Financial Services, Inc. She was responsible for Balpar Industries and ten other prestigious clients. Henri and Martin were not happy with her sudden rise to a powerful position within the company. Douglas, her husband, was also somewhat uneasy with her assent. He rationalised his qualms because he was still distracted by her beauty and his love for her. Insidiously, the magnet of power and money was pulling Francesca over the line. That line divides the process from right to wrong, from ethical practices to unethical practices, from honesty to dishonesty and, worst of all, kindness to evil. This happens to many people when the access to power and money, strange though it seems, delude them into believing they have not crossed the line. They manipulate information and justify their actions, gradually convincing themselves they are still performing with the same attributes they possessed before they crossed the line. Balpar Industries had so many layers that a lay investor would not be able to dig through them to see that the money went back to the owners and was kept in multiple banks in other countries. The owners, the mob, allowed small profits to go to the investors to keep them from becoming suspicious. There were no wineries, no resorts and no land. They resided in ghost companies off—shore. Francesca had talents that could have been used ethically to enhance the profits of JBT. After all, she had worked very hard at her former job. She had not been paid the same as the male employees, many of whom did shoddy work and were lazy. She had worked many late nights, weekends and even most holidays without compensation. Resentments seethed inside and she convinced herself she should be compensated for her past labors. Resentments and anger should be dealt with and put to rest, but many people give them a home deep inside where they can surface and effect circumstances that have nothing to do with their origin. Douglas tried to dispel any of his partners' discomfort with Francesca's a partnership by reminding them she had brought new business to JBT. Her beauty still mesmerised Douglas. Making love to her cast the spell she wove even more. Her partnership allowed accéss to all the other partners' accounts. Moving money in and out of those accounts help to disguise the offshore dealings of Balpar.

Henri had always been meticulous about details. His scrutiny of accounts early in the development of JBT, Inc, was part of the reason the firm had become successful. As the business grew, he had to delegate some of the detail work to those he personally hired for his department. There was no room in Henri's life for romance. He had learned from observing his partners and his few friends that women could numb even the most brilliant men's brains. Until Samantha walked into his office for her interview, his testosterone remained in check and his brain remained intact. Her confidence and demeanor stirred feelings he had been able to drown with sarcasm and a stiff decorum. Samantha wasn't flirtatious as other women had been. In fact, she seemed quite aloof and frosty at the same time respectful and polite. He felt a little weak in the knees while moving around his desk and easing himself into the chair. Try as he might, he couldn't get the vision of those tantalising green eyes with flecks of gold out of his head. Six spreadsheets nestled on the computer screen registering totals in the millions. Normally, those would be all Henri needed to excite and challenge him.

I can't allow myself to have feelings or think about a woman it that way. The clock hands pointed up to 12 0'clock. Her voice steady and softly commanding. Though she quickly covered her thigh when she crossed her legs, for an instant Henri could envision his hand caressing her soft, supple skin. Surrender popped into Henri's mind. Samantha had accomplished a small, but central part of her plan.

I must be overly tired. She is just an employee.

Samantha had heard that JBT had hired an independent accounting firm to audit the books. There had been a few suggestions for review and confirmation. JBT had a year rectify any questionable areas before there could be outside scrutiny. Samantha knew she could impress Henri with her expertise and work ethic. If necessary, she always could use her feminine wiles to gain control. She had heard the company had voluntarily subcontracted and audit and there had been few suggestions for change. That gave her at least a year without outside scrutiny to impress Henri and his partners.

Chapter XII
Pulling the Curtain Aside

Jack (Hank) had reviewed Millie's chart. He learned that Phyllis had told Millie that her birth mother was the woman their father had brought home after Hank's disappearance. Millie knew the woman as Phyllis's and her au 'Pere. After her accident Phyllis told Millie that Sally was her birth mother. When Jack read the name Sally his heart skipped a beat. Had John rescued Sally from the prostitute ring? How was that possible? John couldn't have known that Hank and Sally had fallen in love and that Hank planned to rescue her himself before the thugs had left him for dead in the coal car. Was Millie his daughter? Sally had died when Millie was very young. John and Alicia had raised her as their own. The only way to be sure that Millie was or wasn't Hank's daughter would be to get a sample of her hair or saliva for a DNA test. These tests were becoming available to the general public. Hank wouldn't send the specimens through the hospital's lab. He would have to use an outside service. He couldn't ask Millie for a sample, of course. That would mean he would have to tell her the whole story—his connection to the Strigow's, his stealing from his best friend's company, almost dying, abandoning all responsibilities and adopting another identity. The list of mistakes and failures grew every time Hank vowed to come clean. Abusing Millie's rights as a patient by secretly obtaining a sample would be added to the nightmare filled with lies and abandonment. Sleepless nights and trying to keep his professional demeanor when working with Millie began to take their toll on Hank. He knew Millie's accident had been the result of a hit and run and that the authorities had not uncovered a motive nor a suspect. Hank was sickened with fear that her accident might have something to do with his past. How could that be? Hank Baldoni was no longer alive. He had disappeared nineteen years ago. He stared at the pile of Millie's charts on his desk and decided to comb through them one more time to make sure there wasn't a connection to his lurid past causing Millie to be used as a trap to lure Hank to expose his existence. Since the day Millie came to the Therapy Department, he felt a special need to protect her and personally manage her treatments. The occurred before he found out about the connection with his former partner, and Sally. The whole scenario was uncanny. The more he wrestled with obtaining a sample for a DNA test, the more he knew he had to do it. Opening that door would lead to a chasm filled with lies and falsehoods. He could be involving Millie in an avalanche of consequences and danger. Should he risk finding out if Millie was his child? Should he tell her what he suspected and lose her trust or, even worse, break her heart? Or should he continue the masquerade?

The law firm where Phyllis worked had been contracted to perform the audit for JBK, Inc. Phyllis was assigned as the chief auditor for the review, but she had to delegate that task to Peter Conroy, her partner, as she was taking time off to accompany Millie to Cleveland Clinic to have a shunt implanted. Phyllis worked with Peter for the past five years as they both climbed the ladder towards a partnership. Both Peter and Phyllis were sticklers for detail. They had proven to be valuable assets to their company. They enhanced Randolph & Associates' reputation for uncovering fraud and other impunities in their clients' negotiations, contracting and business involving millions of dollars. Peter placed the audit of JBT on Phyllis's desk. His preliminary audit had not revealed any questionable areas, but he wanted Phyllis to look over a few items that might warrant more intense scrutiny. An audit of such a large firm required review of reams of paperwork as well as references to computerised files. Phyllis returned when she saw Millie making progress in therapy and the doctors were confident the shunt was relieving pressure on Millie's brain. She unpacked, changed into her sweatpants and shirt, plugged in a full pot of coffee and began the task of reviewing Peter's audits. She was satisfied with all the reports Peter had prepared while she was gone. The JBT audit was voluminous. She packed all the paperwork into a suitcase and left a message for her secretary that she would be working at home for a few days.

After a sandwich and several cups of coffee, the pages of the JBT audit began to blur. Phyllis stretched and yawned after reviewing the summary. She was more than ready to call it a night when her gaze fell on a listing of investment companies overseas. For some reason she focused on the initial administrators listed for Balpar Industries. Victor Pironne, Daniel Pironne and Hank Baldoni's names sharpened her attention. Hank was listed as one of the initial owners. Hank was no longer listed after two years. There was no record of a buyout, merger or why he was dropped from any of the documentation about the same time as he disappeared without a trace. Phyllis's father had told her Hank was probably Millie's real father and that Sally was her birth mother. She regretted breaking the news to Millie and leaving shortly after she had told her. Her father had also told her he thought Hank must have been in financial trouble again because money was missing from the safe the same week Hank disappeared. One of the men had noticed Hank acting differently that week as well. It was midnight. Phyllis was fully awake now. She began to track the cascade of Balpar's holdings. Her suspicions grew as she uncovered slight discrepancies in the earnings from several foreign investors. The banknote for the initial loan to start the business had been paid by Victor Pironne fifteen years prior to when he was listed as deceased. Francesca Jacobs was listed as the oversight accountant from JBT for Balpar Industries. Phyllis became more suspicious when explanations for profit and loss balance discrepancies for multi-layered subsidiaries within the company did not equate to yearly summaries. Phyllis marked pages in the report that she needed to review more thoroughly. After a short nap she packed up the files and left her apartment to return to the office.

Victor spent years hiding behind his mob, paid informants, paid public figures and law enforcement who looked the other way. His henchmen had located Sally and Millie, but had no success locating Hank. The Pironne family had an arch enemy in the Micholetti family. Gato Micholetti groomed two of his own mob to infiltrate Victor's closest security ring. These two men performed every task Victor gave them efficiently. Their meticulous attention to every detail of the horrific acts assigned to them, led Victor to trust them as his personal bodyguards over the next several years. Victor's son, Daniel, had been groomed to take over his father's "businesses" when Victor felt it was time to hand over the baton. Victor had shared his suspicion that Hank was still alive and was living under another name. He charged Dan with the task of using Sally and her daughter as bait to draw Hank out of hiding. One of the most lucrative businesses the Pironne family owned was Balpar Industries. Hank had been involved with the initial plan to set up the false holding companies overseas. When he realised the company was a front for illegal dealings, he stole the money to pay off his gambling debts, devised a plan to rescue Sally and to disappear. He was not aware of the venomous characters with whom he had gotten involved, nor that Sally was pregnant.

The Pironne family fought for years to keep their control of Chicago's drug, prostitution, extortion and other criminal activities. Challenged constantly by the Micholetti family, they protected their territory with an iron fist. Gato Michelitti paid the two men he had groomed to gain Victor and his family's trust. Gato charged them with finding Victor's weaknesses so that he could be eliminated. Daniel had not inherited his father's intelligence and business sense. With Victor out of the way, Gato could make sure Daniel would mess up enough to weaken the Pironne family stature in the mob hierarchy.

One of Victor's favorite pastimes was scuba diving. His sixty-two—foot yacht had a crew that were skilled in managing his dives, protecting him and keeping his equipment in tip-top condition and finding exciting areas for diving in the Great Lakes. He was especially interested in locating shipwrecks and their graveyards. The two bodyguards were the only people to do the final check on his diving equipment. He was so paranoid about deceit among even long-term members of the mob and family that only a handful of people in his organisation had gained his trust.

It was one of those Spring days that made the Chicago skyline sparkle. Victor finished up some business deals, talked with Dan about meeting with Francesca Jacob to go over Balpar's financial intricacies and notified his bodyguards and crew that he would be going on a diving jaunt at noon that day. The Lake was calm and inviting and he was growing weary of battling the Micheletti family. Brandon and Lou, the bodyguards performed the final check of the diving equipment. Four other crew members had also checked the gear and the tanks, passing them on to the two bodyguards. Brandon took one of the tanks containing Oxygen and bled out half of the life supporting chemical. He replaced it with nitrous oxide as he had been directed by Gato. On Victor's dive he was elated to find a sunken freighter that might not have been discovered yet. The yacht had dropped anchor about fifteen miles east of Chicago in water's depth of sixty-eight feet. Thirty minutes into the dive Victor switched to the tank that had been filled with nitrous oxide. Dizziness, nausea and a feeling that his lungs were ready to explode caused Victor to thrash his arms and legs trying to reach the yacht. His blood cells burst as the Nitrogen broke through their membranes and replaced Oxygen. By the time the crew pulled his bloated, blue body out of the water they could not save him. The bodyguards performed CPR for over thirty minutes. Exhausted and panicking they decided to put Victor into the cabin. They powered up the boat and docked it in a dilapidated old marina east of Chicago. The docks were broken and covered with dead fish and debris. Each took a vow to disappear. They knew they would be blamed for Victor's demise. They watched as the beautiful yacht and Victor's body burst into flames. Brandon and Lou reported the "accident" to Gato. Both were given a large cash prize plus a trip to an island resort the Micheletties owned. They were "retired" from active duty for following orders.

When the yacht was finally located after a week of searching and Victor's scorched body was identified, Dan Pironne ordered a platoon of henchmen to search for the missing bodyguards and crew. His anger fueled the promise he had made to his father to find Hank and Sally. If they were still alive, they would pay a debt that had tortured his father. His anger, fueled by his twisted sense of loyalty to his mob family, was projected towards Hank and Sally, even though they had nothing to do with Victor's death. Dan's expertise in international trade and business in general paled compared to that of his father. He had little interest in the intricacies of fake companies and investment schemes. Though it was ten years since Hank's disappearance, Dan kept a team of henchmen on the look—out for clues that Hank might have survived the shooting and the grave of coal. They managed to locate the Strigows. Posing as census takers Dan's men learned that Sally and Mrs Strigow had passed away within a year of each other. John was trying to hold the family together and still run his construction business. Raising two young girls was no easy task. He, too, had tried to locate Hank with no results. John had told Phyllis when she was eighteen who Sally really was -that she was Melinda's mother and Hank probably was her father. Phyllis was shocked that Sally had allowed everyone to think Melinda was Mrs Strigow's daughter and Phyllis's sister. When Phyllis left for college in Chicago she rarely went home to visit. Melinda was heartbroken. She couldn't understand why Phyllis pulled away from her entire family. They had grown very close over the years. Melinda loved her bright and beautiful sister. John and Alicia explained that Phyllis was very busy with college and internships but they, too, were devastated. John regretted having shared the big "secret" with her. Hours of back breaking construction work and the stress of raising two teenage girls on his own was affecting John. he was checking the supports holding up the balcony that Hank had designed and worked on before his disappearance. The harness that was holding him underneath the balcony slipped out of its fastener. As he tumbled towards the icy waters of the Mississippi after slamming into one of the large pillars, he lost consciousness. The music poured out of the ornate doors that opened onto the balcony. Couples danced and laughed and drank drowning out the cry for help coming from below. When John did not return to his office or to his house, Melinda got home to an empty house. She called the construction office—no answer. She called her grandmother, Sarah, Alicia's mother. Sarah had been a strong presence in the Strigow family; more so after Alicia and Sally died. Alicia had confided in her about Sally being Melinda's birth mother and why she had agreed to keeping that secret. Sarah was not aware that John had told Phyllis. She treated both girls with the same firm boundaries and extreme love as if they were actually sisters. Dan's twisted mind could not let Victor's vendetta go. He needed bait to draw Hank out of hiding, should he still be alive. Assuming Melinda might be the "cheese" to lure Hank into a trap, he ordered two of his men to follow Melinda. John's construction business had closed about a year after his death. Melinda lived with Alicia's mother until she left for college and married Ron Sherman.

Melinda had been run down by a mysterious vehicle. Hank was in Cleveland posing as Jack Turner. Dan Pironne was being investigated for racketeering, extortion and running a prostitution ring. The vice was tightening around the Pironne family and their dealings. Feeling like an animal caught in a trap he started to formulate a diversion so devastating, the police would look away from him and his family. Francesca felt her burden of managing the Balpar Industries account increase when Dan was busy avoiding jail time and burying anything the prosecution could dig up.

Martin became more uncomfortable with her wielding power in their company. Douglas discounted his uneasiness with her rapid takeover of many of the most prestigious clients. Insidiously, the magnet of money and power was pulling Francesca further over the line. This happens to many people who normally have the best intentions and motives. Once they have crossed the line, they may still believe they are following a legitimate course. Resentment, anger, hate and revenge drive actions and bury positive emotions. *I am resentful because I fear you don't understand what I need. I need to pay you back for what I fear you did to me or are going to do to me. I jump to conclusions because I fear abandonment. I am hateful and angry because I fear of you may stop me from getting my way.*

Chapter XIII
Tangled Webs

The dream repeated itself several nights in a row. Lights were coming towards her. There was a loud thumping noise. Suddenly, she was floating over a house looking in the windows. There was a lady sitting in a leather chair. The lady was crying. Somehow Millie felt she knew the lady. A man without a face was hovering over her. Suddenly the dream showed Millie lying on the ground. The cold wrapped itself around her and she began to shiver. Snowflakes fell on her face. She hazily felt someone's warm breath on her. Everything went dark. A whooshing sound, something beeping, a mobile of brightly colored rainbows spun above her. She tried to speak but no sound came from her icy lips. Another man with beady eyes, an unkept beard and greasy hair moved towards her. Her heart pounded and she struggled to move. The man ripped down the mobile and kept screaming "Wake Up! Wake Up!" Millie awoke shaking. Her nightgown was wet with perspiration. A chill crept over her arms and legs. She pulled the covers up to her neck and waited until her trembling stopped. A nurse came into the room to take Millie's vitals. She was saying something. Millie couldn't seem to extract herself from her dream. The man's screaming receded.

"Millie…Melinda, are you okay? You look as if you have seen a ghost. Your gown is sopping wet. Are you having pain?" The nurse bent close to Millie and pushed the tangled hair away from Millie's face.

Millie tried to focus on anything besides her dream. *Why would I keep dreaming the same dream?* "I am fine, nurse. I shouldn't have eaten pizza before going to bed. Kathryn… your name is Kathryn, right?"

"Dear, you know me pretty well since I have been taking care of you for a few weeks." The nurse smiled and began to take off Millie's drenched nightgown. Sometimes eating before retiring is not a good idea. Let me help you into the bathroom and you can take a shower before going to PT." Millie's head began to clear as she walked slowly to the bathroom with nurse Kathryn holding her arm gently.

"Do you think dreams mean something?" Millie asked and Kathryn turned on the water in the shower and tested it to make sure in wasn't too hot.

"Was it a dream that upset you, dear? I read a book and attended a class a long time ago about dreams and their meaning. It was very interesting. The speaker told us that we dream many times during the night. We don't remember much when we awaken. The dream can be so vivid that we think it is the only dream we think we have. It seems difficult to understand because it is snatches from many dreams we have while we are in REM sleep. That is the level of sleep that is the deepest. Do you want to tell me about your dream?"

"I…I'm not sure I even remember it. I know I felt frightened. It is foggy now. I'll be okay. I'm not in pain. It will feel good to get a nice warm shower." Millie stepped into the shower stall and allowed the water to run over her body. She vowed to have no food after dinner before she went to bed. *It was just a stupid dream.* Kathryn laid out some clothes for Millie, stripped her bed and asked if Millie was strong enough to finish showering alone while Kathryn went to get fresh linens for the bed.

Jack (Hank) decided he couldn't hide behind his lies any longer. He needed the courage to tell Millie he might be her father. He would be taking a risk that she would erase him from her life. She might request a transfer to her hometown rehab. Hank was worried that she might still be in danger since the police suspected foul play connected to her accident. It could be that the mob had somehow found Hank had not been eliminated. If they found out that Millie was his daughter, they would use her to flush him out of hiding. Since they had taken money from him when he was shot and thrown into the coal car, he couldn't figure out a reason for them to be looking for him. What else would they be afraid of? Then Balpar Industries came to him. *That crazy scheme probably isn't around anymore. I left them when I realised the investor's money was hidden in layers of "ghost" companies and buildings overseas. No, that can't be it.*

Millie yawed as she took the elevator down to the second floor. The physical therapy department was located at the back of the large Rehabilitation Center. It overlooked a pond with a geyser in the middle that continued to work, even though the periphery of the pond was frozen. Millie had gained enough strength that she was starting to walk without crutches. Her shunt was working well. She only had occasionally headaches and no seizures. She was sure the job she was heading to on that fateful day was no longer available. Jeff told her that she was supposed to start that day as an accountant in the same department where he worked at JBT. Jeff had come to visit her twice in the four months she had been at Cleveland Clinic. The more they talked; old feelings began to creep into her consciousness. She needed to get her life in order before she could allow their relationship to be more than a friendship. *He is a wonderful guy—so supportive and encouraging. He never pushes his way into my life any more than I let him.* The walls of Millie's room at the Center were plastered with cards from Phyllis and other friends. The police were still investigating the hit and run. The only person of interest was Ron Sherman, Millie's ex-husband. They had checked the tires on his truck to see if they matched the imprints of the vehicle that had hit Millie, but his tires so worn on his beat-up truck they couldn't find a match. Ron had a witness at the bar that said he was there before and after the time Millie was struck down.

Samantha worked late whenever she could. Henri tried to resist his gaze focusing on her when she passed his office or when he passed her cubicle. She rarely looked away from her work when he walked by. The only interaction between them was when she was called into his office to share her reports. Henri never allowed anything to detract from his work or his rigid personal schedule. He rose every day at 6 am, even on his days off. He went to the gym after eating a bowl of oatmeal and drinking black coffee. He caught the bus to the office (rarely spending money on a cab). After working until 1 pm he ate the lunch he packed every morning. The lunch was always the same unless he had a luncheon meeting with his partners or clients. Cut vegetables and a smoothie laced with kale satisfied him until he left the office at 6 pm, took the bus to his apartment and retired at 9:00pm. He was forty-two years old, had never married and had only dated one woman. He was a virgin, wore pajamas to bed, did not have a dog, cat, fish or gerbil to complicate his regime and was miserly with his money. Though he was handsome his icy blue eyes had a sadness that matched his slowness to smile. It was rare to hear him laugh aloud or to join in any of the office gossip. He had not inherited his Arian ancestor's blond hair and fair complexion. His skin had a slight olive cast. Dark brown hair added to his mysterious demeanor. The strenuous daily workouts produced a trim, muscular body. His six-foot-three-inch figure was an intimidating presence. The females in his department had long since given up flirting or trying to impress him. Some whispered that he might be homosexual, but those rumors had even been discounted. Henri was slow to anger, sometimes walking away from confrontations. He was confident and firm in business negotiations and his clients' financial dealings. His one flirtation with romance occurred when he had just moved into the Chicago offices of JBT after becoming a full partner. The rapid rise of information technology programs replacing hard copy spreadsheets and business data required Henri to take a course at the Moline satellite campus of Iowa State University. Henri could see that Information Technology was the rising star among new advances the past three years. JBT had grown exponentially and the partners wanted to make sure they did not fall behind their competitors in technological advances.

She had ash blond hair and soft green eyes. Her figure was well proportioned, and she carried herself with confidence and an air of mystery. Her smile was gentle; her laugh easy and melodic. Henri was too shy to ask her out for coffee let alone allow her to see him staring at her. Long hair framed her porcelain face. Henri watched her luscious lips move when she was asking a question or whispering as she typed with graceful fingers over the computer keyboard. Henri even caught himself envisioning her without the demure clothes she wore to class. He tried to concentrate on the class instructor, the computer screen, the window, his shoelaces but he kept seeing her face no matter where he focused. She wasn't wearing a wedding band or engagement ring. He had noticed when she came to class alone and left in a practical 1968 Ford without anyone either. With only two sessions remaining in the course Henri felt he needed to make a move. He had to try. His stomach was doing somersaults and he was perspiring though it was a cool, Fall evening. He almost tripped as he weaved in between the desks to approach her. He went back to his own desk three or four times before he finally forced himself to stand in front of her desk. That is what he did—stood there—mute—staring at the top of her head as she followed the lesson on the computer screen. Henri jumped when she looked up at him her dark lashes blinking as she refocused from the computer to the trembling human standing in front of her.

"Hi, your… you are Henri, I mean Mr Treacher. Can I help you with something?" she said in the sweetest voice Henri thought he had ever heard.

Henri cleared his throat several times and muttered, "Yes."

She giggled softly, "What can I help you with, Henri. Okay to call you Henri?"

“Okay” He had rehearsed what he was going to say a thousand times but all the came out was, “Coffee…I mean coffee sometime?”

“Are you asking me to go with you for coffee, Henri?” She smiled and the lights seemed to get brighter in the room.

“Yes” he stammered hoarsely.

“I would love to, but class is starting. I’ll talk to you after class.” Her smile made his cheeks glow and his heart pound even faster than it had been since he got the courage up to approach her.

Henri smiled and nodded, turned and almost ran back to his desk. *What a jerk! I didn’t even thank her. She must feel I am a real scatterbrain.* Henri chastised himself as he plunked his sweaty butt into the desk chair and gazed at the computer screen. He barely heard any of the lecture or attempted any of the exercises the instructor presented.

The class seemed to drag on for much more than the usual two hours. Henri was afraid she would leave abruptly or stick out her tongue, reproach for his bungling. He avoided looking towards her desk gazing at his blank computer screen. When he came out of his stupor, he realised everyone was leaving. He stood, stuffed his workbook and papers into his briefcase and headed towards her workstation. She was not there. He scanned the room and the exits. She wasn’t anywhere in the room. *I probably scared her. I was such a robot. Why can’t I loosen up a little?*

“I’m turning off the lights, Mr Treacher. Was there something you needed to ask me?” Henri shook his head and walked past the instructor with his chin on his chest.

“There you are Henri. I tried to get your attention to let you know I was going to the ladies’ room. You must have been really interested in the lesson. You hardly glanced at me the way you usually do. Did you still want to go for coffee?” Her sweet voice was like a waterfall of kindness.

Henri blurted out “Oh, oh, of course I want to go. Do you want to go? Of course, you do…you just said do I… yes, of course let’s go for coffee. That would be peachy!” *Peachy! Did I just say peachy?*

She chuckled and took Henri's arm. The sensation of her touch traveled down his arm, into his chest and groin, exploding into a feeling he couldn't describe nor had ever felt before. They went to a small Bistro near the school and talked for two hours. Her name was Alyssa. She was interesting, intelligent and vibrant. Her beauty was enhanced by an engaging smile and a quirky sense of humor. Henri had not met any woman like her. They went to a small coffee bistro on the corner near the school. Before they realised how late it was, they had talked for two hours. She was interesting, vibrant and beautiful. Henri walked her to her car. That evening was the start of coffee dates after the last three classes. Henri was overcome with the thought of her. When he came to work after their first coffee date, he was glowing. Doug and Martin noticed his clown-like grin and asked him if he was having "gas" pains. He even was heard whistling in his office. The shocked staff overwhelmed the gossip grapevine. Rumors that he had tried some pot or that he had finally found a female robot interested in his "icy" persona.

Before the final class Henri vowed to aske Alyssa on a real date. The play, "Les Misérables", was playing in a theater off Broadway. Henri had purchased two tickets, praying Alyssa would accompany him. After class Henri and Alyssa walked together to the elevator. Alyssa barely smiled at Henri on the ride to the first floor. She glanced at him with her expressive green eyes that seemed to be glistening with tears. They walked silently to the coffee shop; her usual animated conversation limited to "I'm okay" when Henri asked if there was something wrong. She stared into her gradually cooling cup of coffee excusing herself twice to go to the powder room. Henri tried to fill the awkward silence with talk about his work, the news, the weather-anything, trying to illicit a smile or any conversation from this woman to whom he had opened his heart.

"Alyssa." Henri reached for her hand which was cold and trembling. "I have two tickets to the wonderful play, "Les Misérables", for Saturday evening. I would be honored if you would consider attending with me." Alyssa looked up at him.

Tears fell like raindrops from those captivating eyes. “Aly, what is the matter? Have I offended you in any way? If I have, I am so sorry.”

Alyssa drew her hand away from his. “I… I can’t, Henri. I want to go with you—to be with you, but I can’t. I am so sorry I mislead you.” Tears were streaming down her face. Henri reached for a napkin and gently tried to wipe them away. His heart was pounding and his hand trembled as he touched her beautiful face.

” Alyssa, dear, please tell me. I will do anything for you. Are you in trouble?”

“Oh, sweet Henri, I…I am married. I am so, so sorry.” Alyssa’s eyes were filled with fear.

“Married? I thought… I guess I assumed…” Henri felt as though a hammer landed on his chest.

Alyssa reached for Henri’s cold hand. “I don’t know what I was thinking. I…we… my husband and I have been going through a difficult time. I thought if I took some classes and got a better, job opportunities would improve. They didn’t, they haven’t. I am so sorry. I needed a friend and you were standing there. It was so nice to have someone treat me … well, special, with respect. I am so sorry. You must think I am such a terrible person.” Alyssa laid a crumpled five—dollar bill on the table, grabbed her coat and started to leave. Henri hurriedly left enough cash on the table to buy many cups of coffee. He rushed after her despite her muffled requests to let her go. When he caught up with her outside the bistro, he grabbed her arm and made her face him.

“Please, Henri, let me go. My husband is very jealous and has a terrible temper.” She pulled away from his grasp and started to run across the street. The blow to the back of his head knocked Henri over and on to the unforgiving pavement. Hands dug into his arms and dragged him into an alley nearby where his attacker kicked him until he could barely breathe. The tunnel of blackness closed in as he tried to defend himself. When he came to blood trickled down his face from a large cut on his forehead. Every breath he took sent stabbing pains throughout his chest. He attempted to stand. Stumbling out of the alley, he lost consciousness lying on the sidewalk in front of the coffee shop.

The bright fluorescent lights burned his eyes. There were poles with bags of fluid dripping into his body and muffled voices near where he seemed to be lying. When he tried to move tentacles of pain wrenched his body into agonising spasm. He tried to focus his blurred vision. Shadowy forms moved above him.

"There you are, buddy, finally awake. We thought you were taking computer classes, not boxing lessons. You look like you were run over by a train!" Francesca chided sarcastically.

"Oh, you poor dear," Francesca bent close to Henri. He could smell her perfume. "I have never seen you with your hair out of place. What on earth happen to you?"

"Where… am…I? Where is Alyssa?" Henri tried to pull himself up but collapsed back in the bed.

"Mr Treacher, you must lay quietly, "a soft voice spoke from his left side. "You are in St. Peter's Hospital. Someone found you lying on the sidewalk outside a coffee shop and called for an ambulance. My name is Rachael and I am your nurse today.

"Alyssa! I must find her! She is in danger!" Henri began to cough. Fire pierced his lungs like branding irons. The nurse placed a tube into his mouth to clear out mucus gathering there. She placed an oxygen mask over his face as he fought to gain his breath.

"Mr Treacher. Please try to take slow breaths. Try not to talk. Your friends are here. I am giving you some medication that will ease the pain and help you rest. You will be able to ask questions soon." Rachael drew up medication from an ampule and injected it into a port in the IV tubing. The tunnel appeared again as the sedative blanket covered Henri's injured body.

Francesca was asked to go to the waiting room. Doug had just arrived after being questioned by the police. After she told him what Henri kept asking, he queried "What in the hell? Who the heck is Alyssa? I didn't think the old boy even knew any women's first names except his Secretary's." Doug sloshed some coffee into a cup. "I don't know. The cops said it didn't appear to be a robbery. Henri's wallet and briefcase were still with him, money, credit cards, license and all. They questioned the instructor to see if he had noticed anything unusual when Henri was in class, but he couldn't recall any concerns. He did say Henri would talk to a woman in the class on occasion. He didn't think anything of it as many students would discuss the computer exercises on break and after class."

"What was the woman's name? Maybe that was the Alyssa he is asking about." Francesca asked.

"The cops wouldn't tell me her name or anything they had learned about her." Doug said. "They asked a lot of questions about Henri, his work, his friends, what type of person he was. By the way, where is Martin? I left a message that Henri was in the hospital. Henri is such a private guy and certainly not a ladies' man. It just doesn't make sense. I'd love to get know who would do such a thing." Doug shook his head. The nurse came into the waiting room.

"Is there a Douglas Jacob here for Mr Treacher?" Rachael asked the Volunteer at the desk.

"Yes, Ma'am, I'm Mr Jacob. Is Henri all right?"

"He is stable, Mr Jacob. He is a little hazy from the pain medication, but he is asking to see you. I'll take you back." Francesca asked to see him again, but the nurse felt it best that one person at a time visit him. Doug followed the nurse into the ICU. The hushed voices of nurses, doctors and visitors mingled with the beeping and whooshing of machines keeping people alive in the cubicles. Rachael smiled at Doug as he hesitantly approached Henri's bed. Henri's eyes were practically swollen shut. His face was swollen and bruised. A large cut over his right eye was crusted with dried blood and tiny sutures held the wound together. Several fluids dripped from various bags into Henri's arms and near his shoulder. A tube trailed from the side of his chest into a bag hanging on the bed rails. Dark red liquid filled the bag. Another bag collected urine from his bladder.

"He is doing well. He had to be very healthy to withstand the injuries he sustained. You can only stay a few minutes as he needs to use all his strength to recuperate. If you have any questions or need anything, I will be right outside in the nurses' station." Doug nodded. He felt a little weak in the knees. Rachael seemed to have noticed as she pulled a chair next to the bed for Doug to sit.

Henri opened his eyes enough to see Doug sitting next to his bed. "Doug…I have to find Alyssa. She was…is my friend. She seemed to be afraid of her husband. I don't even know where she lives. You must find her. Doug, please."

"Henri, I talked with the police and they have learned what they could about her from your instructor. They wouldn't give me any information. Were you involved with her, Henri, I mean…seeing her? I'm sorry, that is none of my business." Doug wanted to kick himself.

"She and I went out for coffee after the last few classes. Doug, we did nothing wrong. I had feelings for her, for sure. She was so bright and beautiful. I have never been able to feel at ease talking with women, but she was different. I didn't know she was married, or I wouldn't have even asked her out for coffee. I never thought to ask. It wasn't like that. I was the one who pursued her and wanted to move past just coffee. Oh, God, Doug… I'm sure it must have been her husband or someone who he got to beat me up. She let it slip one time that she knew some people in the protection business who were a little west of the law. This is my fault, the reason I stay out of relationships. What if he hurts her or worse!" Henri grabbed Doug's arm. "Please, Doug, don't tell Francesca or Marv. Don't tell anyone except the police. We had coffee and talked about so many things. I had tickets to a play and asked her to go with me. That is when she told me she was married. None of this was her fault. I was the one who wanted it to be more… I fell for her as soon as I saw her in class. I should have known better."

"Henri, you can count on me. We are all here for you. Are you sure you are safe from this guy? I'm telling the police as soon as I leave. I'll make an excuse to the others. Let me know if you need anything, okay?" Doug squeezed his friend's hand and went out to the desk to let the nurses know he was leaving. He left his private contact information with instructions to call him if Henri's condition changed or if he needed him. "I'll be back tomorrow to check on him. He asked me to be his healthcare power of attorney. If you could have someone arrange to meet me here tomorrow with the paperwork, I would appreciate it. I should be here about eleven in the morning." Doug had met the instructor of Henri's class when both were being questioned at the police station. He thought he might be able to get some information about this woman from the instructor. He told Francesca that he had a client he needed to see, that Henri was doing a little better. He asked her to wait and visit Henri after he had rested a bit and that the nurse would let them know when they could visit. Doug looked up the address of the University satellite where Henri had taken classes. Stanley Applebaum had partially balding dull grey hair. His pale complexion and stooped shoulders added to his nerdy persona. Horned rimmed glasses slid down his pointed nose. He had to keep pushing them back in place so he could see his beloved computer screen. His relationship with electronics fared much better than his relationships with people. What he could not tolerate in humans, he was able to patiently accept in his computers, fax machines and printers. If they shut down and couldn't communicate. he would sigh and patiently search for the reasons for the disturbance. Not so with people. He had very little patience if they complained, broke down or made errors. Teaching a class where he felt confident he was wiser and more skilled than any of his students; where he had to give minimal instructions; and could use power point rather than a formal lecture gave him the ability to keep his position at the University. Evening classes were usually small and non-threatening. He was always more anxious when teaching the younger students who would often challenge him with their questions. The younger students were less in awe of his technical skills as were the adult evening students because they had grown up with technology. This was the last class for this group of evening sessions. He had little to do as the exam was programmed into the computers. His part consisted of outlining the rules, timing of the exam and bidding these students good-bye (he really felt "good riddance.) He had turned in the prospectus for the next group of classes and was going about the classroom to verify all computers were running appropriately before the students arrived.

Doug cleared his throat as he entered the classroom. "Ahem, Professor Applebaum?" The Instructor looked up from the computer he was inspecting. "Professor Applebaum? I'm sorry to disturb you before your class arrives. My name is Douglas Jacob. Could I have a word with you?" Doug started to approach the professor.

"I only have about fifteen minutes before class begins. If you want to sign up for a class, the Admissions office is on the second floor." His eyes returned to the computer screen.

"Professor, I am not here to sign up for a class but to ask you a few questions about my friend, Henri Treacher. He was in this class." Doug stood next to the instructor who had to look up in order to see this person interrupting his work.

"If you are with the police, I have told you everything I know. I don't have any more answers for you." Dr Applebaum's cheeks were slightly flushed and he appeared to shrink even smaller as he started to walk back to his desk. He fidgeted with some papers on his desk only looking up at Doug when he stood waiting in front of him.

"I am not with the police, Sir, I am a friend and partner of Henri Treacher who is injured and, in the hospital, as we speak." Shivers went up and down the wilting professor's spine,

"I…I don't know anything about that. I told the police I barely can remember students' names, let alone anything personal about them." Stanley stared at his blank screen, not at Doug. Doug could see he was making this man nervous.

"My friend had become acquainted with a woman in this class. Her name is Alyssa. She apparently was pretty, blond hair and sat in the front row."

"The police asked me the same question. I gave them the same answer I am giving you. There were only two women in my class. One was a black lady who sat at the end of this row. The other lady who sat where you are pointing was not blond nor was she, um, especially attractive. Neither of those women had the first name, Alyssa. The black woman's name was Sharon and the other woman was Linda or Lyla, something like that. I can't help you. You shouldn't be here asking me questions. Go to the police, maybe they can help you." Stanley was perspiring and agitated. A few students started to filter into the classroom. Stanley whispered to Doug. "Please, Sir, Mr Jacob, my students are arriving. I am sorry about Mr Treacher's misfortune, but I can't help you." Professor Applebaum turned to the board behind him and started to write instructions for the exam. Doug shook his head and walked towards the door. He watched as the students began to take their seats. There were several empty chairs in the front row. Doug stood outside the door until Professor Applebaum spoke to the students. No blond, attractive women were among them.

Doug didn't know how to tell Henri what the professor had told him. Either he was not being truthful, or Henri was delusional. Doug had known Henri for many years. Henri was meticulous about everything. Maybe the person or persons who attacked Henri had threatened the professor. He was very anxious when Doug questioned him. After that encounter, Doug needed to get to the police with Henri's suspicions. He entered the precinct. It was about 8 PM. The black car slowed as the doors of the precinct closed behind Doug and the car sped away from the police station.

Within a week Henri had improved enough to move out of the ICU and into a regular unit of the hospital. His chest tube had been removed and his bruises and lacerations were healing well. Doug had reported his encounter with Professor Applebaum. Henri was even more convinced that someone had threatened him. The day he was discharged he went to the University to see Professor Applebaum. He waited outside his classroom avoiding the stares of those passing by. Henri's face was still bruised and the remains of the laceration over his eye was quite evident. When Professor Applebaum saw Henri standing outside his classroom, he turned pale (more than his usual sallow complexion) and turned abruptly to avoid him. Henri spied him and ran down the hall, grabbed his arm and tried to be as gentle as possible.

"Mr…I mean Professor Applebaum, I am not here to hurt you. I believe someone has threatened to harm you if you answer my question or the questions the police have been asking you. I know you lied to my partner, Doug Jacob about the woman with whom I became friends in your computer class."

Stanley Applebaum tried to wrestle his arm away from Henri, but Henri held firmly. "Let me go!" he snarled. "I'll call security. I don't know anything. Go away!"

"I heard you call her by name during class and I know you saw me talking to her. I just need to find out if she is okay." Henri pleaded.

"Listen, if I were you, I'd forget about her. Whoever beat you up is a mean dude. I'm sorry, I just can't help you. Please let me go to my class." Henri let go of Stanley's arm and walked away.

There was no way of finding out what happened to the one woman who had broken down the wall that Henri had constructed to protect his heart. The wall was rebuilt until Samantha Reynolds found the cracks and began to tear it down again. Samantha wasn't like Alyssa. Other than being a very attractive woman, she exuded confidence, a stylish aloofness and seemed to have little interest in socialising. She was pleasant and respectful but rarely initiated conversation other than to conduct business. In fact, her co-workers whispered she was a female copy of Henri. She worked efficiently, was always on time for work or project deadlines and had no problem working overtime when needed. She dressed professionally, wore very little make-up and was not flirtatious. Henri had not experienced feelings of desire in years after his brief "affair" with Alyssa. Samantha's reserved demeanor aroused the dormant emotions Henri had buried.

Francesca was aware of Dan Pirrone's compulsion to find Hank Baldoni if he was still alive. Her only concern with this Hank person was that he had been an original partner in Balpar Investments. He had left shortly after one year with the company. She was sure he had recognised the intricate cascade of investments based on ghost businesses abroad. Francesca had been careful to hide any evidence that connected her to the Pirrone family. She used intricate accounting schemes to disguise the off—shore dealings in prostitution, gambling and protection businesses. Profits allotted to the investors were channeled through stocks and bonds in the States. This way the only time a client would question a profit and loss history was if they withdrew entirely from Balpar Industries expecting to gain a percentage over their original contribution. That is where Francesca's accounting expertise played a critical part in the business. She was able to manipulate reports showing false declines and profits adding up to a tiny percentage of the actual millions of dollars gained in the offshore businesses. The discomfort Francesca felt occasionally would be whisked away by her belief she deserved her accomplishments, payments and position because they had been denied her in the past. If the partners suspected any wrongdoing, they had not questioned her. If she felt they were becoming suspicious, there were ways to silence them.

Phyllis had spent several days and nights going through years of spreadsheets, ownership agreements, contracts and tax information related to Balpar Industries. The deeper she dug, the more she became suspicious the initial investment into hotels, resorts and wine vineyards in Italy may be a cover for less authentic properties and dealings. It would be very difficult to prove her suspicions were valid unless she made a trip to Europe to visit the properties. Someone in the company had to be involved. JBT had always kept a pristine business profile. The company was one of the most respected firms of its kind in the country. She did not want to tell the partners about her suspicions because she had not proof. She needed someone in the company low enough on the totem pole to do some snooping. She didn't want to tip off whoever might be weaving an unscrupulous scheme into a valid company so that they could bury any evidence. Phyllis put the audit aside and shut off her computer. Millie…what as she going to do to try and repair the damage done when she told her about Sally? Millie was doing well according to Jeff's last visit. Phyllis had kept in touch with Jeff after Millie and she had their falling out. He said Millie really liked her Physical Therapist. Jack Turner. Though he was tough and made her work very hard, she knew it was for the best. She felt a special connection to him from the first time she met him. The doctors felt Millie was doing so well that she could be discharged in the next several weeks. Phyllis planned to visit her that weekend and mend fences. She did not want Millie to go back to her apartment. The police had not come any closer to finding who had caused Millie's accident. Phyllis wanted Millie to come live with her until the perpetrators had been found. She knew that Hank was most likely Millie's father. Was Hank alive? If he was, did he know about Millie; that Sally had lived with John and Alicia; that they had raised Millie as their own? Phyllis's father had also told her that Hank had been mixed up with some unsavory people before he disappeared. John told her that Hank might have stolen money from the business, probably to pay off gambling debts. Could there be some connection between Millie's accident and Hank? Maybe someone was using Millie as bait to see if Hank was alive and want to protect his daughter. So many questions. *Phyl, you better get some sleep. You are driving yourself crazy with all these suspicions. One thing for sure, I am going to make things right with my sister.*

Jeff had visited Millie in Cleveland as often as he could get away from work. Millie was progressing well with physical therapy. Even some of her memory was returning. She had snatches of their past together that reinforced her feelings about him. She looked forward to his visits and even got a little tingle when he kissed her on the cheek. He wanted to take her is his arms and give her a kiss that was far from plutonic, but he did not want to push things until she sent messages that she was ready to do so. When he visited last week, her mood had changed drastically. She seemed withdrawn and sad. When he asked her what was causing the change, she kept saying, "ask Phyllis." He was puzzled. He wouldn't know what to ask Phyllis. When he came back to work, he gave Phyllis a call to see if they could get together for coffee and to talk.

Samantha had met Francesca a couple of times. Her "gut feeling" about people had usually been correct. The frosty hello Samantha received or the lack of response whenever the two passed each other told her Francesca considered any female accountant working with the partners was a threat. Sam would have to tiptoe around the Jacobs if she wanted to accomplish her goal. It seemed like Martin and Henri weren't too enamored with Francesca's escalating role in the company. It made it difficult to be open about their concerns with Douglas, despite his confirming the business relationship between he and his wife were kept separate.

Ron Sherman needed money. He wanted to get out of town as soon as the cops lifted their restraining order. *They can't prove nothin'. As far as they know I was sleepin' it off in the back of the bar.* He walked down Market St. and ducked into a doorway to make sure no one was following him. A dimly lit sign hung lopsided over the entrance to the bar. *Marty's* was barely visible. The paint peeled around the letters. Cigarette smoke and the stale stench of booze escaped into the entrance way as Ron opened the door and plopped his skinny ass onto a barstool.

"Gimme a beer." He growled as he wiped his tobacco stained spittle on his grease stained sleeve. His beard was unkept, his bloodshot eyes peered at the cloudy mirror behind the rack of booze against the wall behind the bar.

“That’ll be two bucks.” The surly, obese bartender spat at his customer.

“Two bucks! What is this crap made of… gold?” Ron threw a crumpled dollar bill and some change on the bar. He sloshed down the brew and spat at the bartender as he stood to leave. A hand pulled him back on to the barstool and a deep and gravelly voice whispered close to his ear.

“Don’t look at me or act like you know me. Look straight ahead and don’t talk.” The voice made Ron’s skin crawl. “You didn’t finish the job. You are only getting half of the dough because you screwed it up. This envelope is only half of the money. You won’t like the consequences if you don’t, kapeesh?”

“I… I did what you t—”

“Shut-up! I said, no talking. You finish the job, or we will finish you.” The man squeezed Ron’s arm so hard he left prints in his skin. Ron stared at the cloudy mirror. The bartender stared at Ron and shook his head. Ron opened the envelope, his greasy hands shaking.

“Shit! Asshole! *I’ll finish the job…yeah…but you won’t like my finish!* He stuck the envelope in the ragged pocket of his shirt and slammed the bar door as he walked out.

Jeff watched the clock that seemed to be moving in slow motion. He was anxious to get home, shower and change and leave for Cleveland. His meeting with Phyllis was strange. When he told her Millie seemed depressed when he visited her last week, Phyllis told him about Sally, the Strigows and Hank. Even more strange was her request for him to keep his eyes open at JBT for any suspicious activity he noticed. When he asked her what type of “suspicious activity” all she would say was if anyone asked for files on Balpar Industries that had not asked for them in the past, to let her know. The questions he had about her request were overshadowed by his need to see Millie. It might help her to talk about the information Phyllis had given her.

Millie tried to fix her hair now that is was getting longer. She put on a little lipstick and eye make-up, pinching her cheeks to bring out some color. Instead of the same old sweats she usually wore to physical therapy, she put on some leggings with a bright flowered print and a top that matched the yellow flowers. Jeff was coming to see her that evening. For the first time she was excited to see him and tell him about a picnic she remembered. They had packed a basket with fried chicken, potato salad and cut vegetables, a bottle of wine and chocolate chip cookies she had baked. It was a beautiful day, sunny and seventy-two degrees. She and Jeff were laughing as they spread a blanket in the park on a hill overlooking Davenport. The memories were flashes of moments that appeared in her mind like a slide show. She hoped his memory of that time would confirm hers. Though she still had a long way to go to be completely recovered, she hoped these memories were a positive prediction of a full recovery. The warm, secure feeling she had when Jeff visited her lately was both scary and exciting.

Hank (Jack) greeted Millie with his usual snarky comment. "Well, it's about time you got up. Sleeping beauty is here, everybody," he shouted to the other techs and patients in the rehab unit.

"I was dreaming of you and I just couldn't wake up because you were trapped in a wheelchair and I was your trainer." Millie snapped back with as much seriousness as she could muster.

Hank knew that she was walking with minimal use of a cane. She had discarded her crutches and only needed the cane for balance when her injured leg got shaky. It wouldn't be long before she would be going back to Moline. If he was going to make things right, he had to start now.

"Melinda, you are doing really well. I think you can graduate to walking on your own, without a cane very soon. Has anyone talked to you about a discharge plan?" Hank was perspiring. He could see a trace of Sally's expressions and smile; the way she would wrinkle her forehead when she was concentrating or experiencing pain; the way her lower lip would cover her upper one just before that infective grin would light up her beautiful face. The more he thought about the possibility that Millie was the product of the passionate lovemaking he and Sally experienced, the more he felt the sadness of loss. The loss of his partner and friend, of a chance to have a life with a woman he loved, a chance to share all the milestones of a growing child of his own; most of all, a chance to absolve himself of the guilt he carried like an albatross around his neck for the lies he could no longer bear.

"Millie, come into my office. I need to speak with you about something very important." Millie had never seen Jack Turner look old and with such a somber expression. She wondered if she had done something to upset him. "Have a seat, dear." Tears began to burn his eyes. *I can't cry...not now...not in front of her.*

Millie took a seat across from his desk. "Did I do something wrong? I'm so sorry I told you about that stupid dream. I was just teasing you. I would never hurt you, Jack."

Hank felt those last words stab his heart. "Oh, no. it isn't anything you did or said, Millie. It's me…I…my real name is not Jack Turner; it is Hank Barone." Hank sat down heavily in his chair.

Millie took in a breath and grew pale. "Why…what are you telling me?"

"Years ago, Millie, I wasn't the man I am today. I was selfish and tiptoed around the law. I lived in Moline, Illinois, very close to where you used to live."

"You lived in Moline? Why are you telling me this?" Millie wriggled in her chair.

"I had a gambling problem, among others. I…I even stole from my business partner to pay off gambling debts. Millie, what was your mother's name?" Hank wanted to be Jack, not that awful Hank Baldoni he hid from all these years. He wanted to hold Millie and protect her, console her.

"My mother…why would you…how would you? Her name was Alicia Strigow. At least I knew her as my mother…but Phyllis…she." Millie twisted her new yellow shirt in her hands. Her anguished face was blotchy red. "Phyllis is…was…my sister. She told me our Au Pere was my real mother. Her name was Sally. I am so confused and angry! What are you trying to tell me?" Millie began to cry. She grabbed some tissues from Hank's desk and blew her nose. She stood, trying to balance herself with her cane.

"Millie, please don't leave like this. I might be your father. I was supposed to take Sally away from… from where she lived. I loved her. You have to believe…" Hank stood and tried to help Millie as she stumbled from the room.

"Stop! Stop! Please! This is insane! You are not my father! John Strigow was my father! Alicia was my mother! They loved me!" She grabbed one of the technicians. "Call my transport and have him take me back to my room… Now!" She looked back at Hank as he stood in the door of his office slumped over and sobbing. "You are a mean, mean man, Jack or Hank or whoever you are!" Everyone in the rehab center stood still as Millie slumped into the wheelchair that Ted was holding for her. He patted her trembling shoulder as he wheeled her into the elevator. Hank tried to follow.

"Please, Millie, give me a chance to explain." He begged as the doors began to close.

"Leave me alone! I hate you!" The doors closed as Hank pounded on them. He turned to face the astonished looks of the patients and technicians.

"I'm sorry," was all he could say to the silent patients and technicians as he walked into his office and closed the door.

Samantha needed to get into Francesca's office while she was out of town. It had been several months since Henri had hired her. She could tell she had gained his trust and he was developing feelings for her. The look in his eyes when she passed him was more than just a casual glance. If she would smile at him, he would turn away or shuffle papers on his desk to keep her from catching him scanning her body. She would gently push a strand of hair from her face or lick her luscious lips. Francesca was going to a conference for several days towards the end of the week. Sam needed a reason to have someone unlock the door to Francesca's office. If she could interest Francesca in her project, Sam would have a better chance of getting approval from the other partners and the other members of the Board. Doug would be the easiest to convince that Sam needed information his wife was privy to. Samantha watched Henri, Doug and Francesca enter and exit the office. The only time she saw they brought paperwork with them was on Wednesday, the day before Francesca was to leave. She was attending a seminar in DesMoines from Thursday to Tuesday night. Henri's secretary was at lunch. Samantha knocked softly on Henri's office door.

"Come in," he said without looking up from the work on his desk. He was eating his usual raw vegetable and smoothie lunch. Sam closed the door noiselessly. She was wearing a tan suit that outlined the curves of her body. Her hair caressed her shoulders and the ceiling lights accented the highlights that framed her beautiful face.

"Mr Treacher," she made sure her voice was liquid and sultry. I am sorry to bother you, but I have a project in mind that would be financially beneficial to the company. I wanted to ask your opinion before I researched it any further. It would be especially attractive to our more affluent clients." She slowly approached Henri's desk. "Would you have time to meet with me this afternoon to discuss it?"

Henri looked up at her and his heartbeat quickened. He caught a whiff of her perfume as he motioned her to take a seat in front of his desk. His voice was hoarse as he turned his gaze back to the work on his desk. "I have a few minutes now, Ms Reynolds, if you can give me a brief synopsis of this project." He tried to steady his voice. This woman was pulling at the door to his loneliness, melting his icy heart by her presence alone. He could imagine his hands touching her skin, pulling back her luscious hair and holding her close to his body. *Stop! She is your employee. You cannot let a woman open that door.* He tried to look through her, but it was impossible when she sat and crossed those amazing legs.

"if I could gather information from the last ten years of investments by clients of one million dollars or more, cross reference the productivity of those receiving at least a cumulative average gain of twenty percent, I believe I could develop and algorithm that the company could use to focus on the most advantageous opportunities. This would eliminate investments that were less likely to succeed thus saving time and demonstrating advantages of doing business with JBT over other firms. This also would attract clients with exceptional wealth who are hesitant to invest." Samantha uncrossed her legs and straightened her skirt. She pushed her hair behind one ear. The light made her earring glisten. The enthusiasm in her sparkling green eyes and her enticing smile poured over Henri. He could barely breath. The desire for her lit a fire inside him. She was not only gorgeous but also intelligent.

"Ms Reynolds…Samantha, a very interesting and challenging proposal. I would very much like to discuss the details with you. Would you consider joining me for dinner after work tonight? Do you have an outline of the project you could bring with you?" Henri stood and moved to the front of his desk leaning against it, in front of where Samantha was sitting. She had not noticed how ruggedly handsome her boss was. His broad shoulders and trim body filled out his expensive grey suit perfectly. His hands were strong and manicured. She closed her eyes and imagined them touching her. Sparks of allure moved between them. They both felt it.

"I would be honored to show you the details…of my project." She had to catch her breath as he leaned towards her. The scent of woodsy cologne lifted her off her chair as they stood staring at each other. She looked into his dark blue eyes and at his strong jaw and cheekbones as he gazed into her eyes. All thoughts of her plan to access Francesca's files melted as they drew closer to each other. Henri reached for the hair she had pushed behind her ear, then touched her face with those strong hands. She kissed his hand and he lifted her chin. The space between their lips disappeared as his mouth closed over hers and they tasted the sweetness in each other's mouths. His hands folded around her as he pulled her against his body.

"Samantha, Oh, Sam, you are so beautiful!" His voice was full of desire. His breathing matched hers as he rummaged for a button on his desk locking the office door. He tore off his jacket. She could see the perspiration on the arms of his shirt. He gently helped her remove her jacket and his hands shook as he unbuttoned her blouse. He was gentle and strong at the same time. When he removed his shirt, she caught her breath as she could see how muscular he was. His biceps flexed as he held her to him. He had hidden his masculinity well under conservative suits and an icy decorum. Her heart pounded as he undressed her and himself. Moistness between her legs prepared her for his lifting her and placing her tenderly on top of his desk he had cleared with one swipe of his arm. Her breasts firmed under his touch and her nipples became erect as his tongue outlined them. He hovered above her, his face flushed and his hair, wet with perspiration, fell over his forehead. He gazed at her perfect body as she spread her legs inviting him to enter her. Samantha had never felt such desire, such passion. His breathing matched hers as he pulled her into him. She felt his strength overcome her. The reached a climax that erupted into muffled moans and screams as they both tried to stifle their outcries. He held her in his arms and gently pushed her damp hair away from her glowing face.

"Henri, Mr T…"

"Don't talk," he whispered. "Just let me hold you." Samantha slowly began to return to her surroundings. She stood and allowed him to take in her nakedness, picked up her clothes, dressed and resumed her demure position in the chair she had vacated. He dressed, brushed back his hair and sat in his chair behind the desk after picking up the items that had been carelessly swept aside. He arranged his paperwork in neat piles, clearing his throat several times. The grandfather clock in the corner of the room broke the silence.

"Ms Reynolds, if you still wish to meet and discuss your project tomorrow evening, you can meet me here at 5:15 pm." His voice had returned to its usual austere tone, though his eyes expressed a much kinder expression. A few moments passed before she answered.

"That will be fine, Mr Treacher. I will be here promptly at 5:15 with my proposal." She stood, straightened her skirt and jacket. Ignoring the weakness in her legs, she turned and started to walk to the door.

"Thank you, Samantha… Ms Reynolds." Henri stood and walked her to the office door. She avoided looking at Henri's secretary as she headed towards the elevator. Once she was in the safety of her own office, she stared out the window wondering how she was going to return to a professional relationship and to go forward with her plan to rise in the company having given herself to this man. *I will just have to think about that tomorrow.*

Henri tried to return to the spreadsheets and financial reports which had been interesting until a few moments ago. He had once again opened a part of him that he thought he had buried.

Millie stared at the small suitcase Jeff had brought her. Images flashed into her awakening memory. Alicia, the sweet, kind woman who she had known as her mother; Sally, the shy, quiet, melancholy woman who had bathed her, put band aids on her skinned knees and brushed her hair while softly humming lullabies; John, her father…not her father, that strong, funny man that made her feel safe and loved: Phyllis, her sister…not her sister, independent, bossy but always had her back. Jeff, did he wear a mask hiding his identity like all the others? She felt trapped between the memories that were trying to resurface and the frightening truth that all she might have known of her life before the accident was a lie. Jack or Hank, whoever he was seemed to have verified the awful truth that Phyllis had thrown at her. Was anything real? Was she caught in a dream world between life and death, a breathing machine forcing her lungs to expand and contract, intravenous fluids keeping her body alive as her mind wrestled with memories that were no longer real? She had to get some answers. Millie needed to pull herself together and find out who Melinda Strigow really was so she could move on. The police had not found who had driven the vehicle that cold, Winter night while she was waiting… waiting for a bus they had told her. She shivered as she remembered the wind, the headlights, then blackness, pain, someone lying next to her, whispering "It is okay. I'm here, Millie." Jeff, that wonderful man who she was starting to have a myriad of feelings for. He told her she was on her way to a new job at a financial investment company, the same one where he worked in the accounting department. Her first day, the last day knowing who she was or who she thought she was. Would it be best to leave the past behind? Would she be better off not tied to a past that wasn't real? She blew her nose and looked at the clock—4 pm. Jack (Hank) should still be on duty. She needed to talk to him, to scream at him. Why had he run away and taken on a new identity? In a way they were alike. Millie pushed the button on the nurse call light. Lillian came within a few minutes. She had noticed that Millie was upset after last week's therapy session and had refused to go to the last several. Millie usually loved her therapy. She was going to be discharged soon and was so excited to get back to Moline to restart her life and rekindle old memories. The doctors were hopeful she would regain most of her memory. Some memories might be lost and never return. Time would tell. The shunt would stay in place for a year, at which time she would need to return for a follow up CAT scan and change of the catheter. Hank had regained his composure externally and was working with a patient in the rehab unit. He kept swallowing back the lump in his throat whenever he remembered her screaming, she hated him. She had every right to. He and Phyllis had shattered the returning image of a family, a mother and father, a sister who loved her. His cowardice had allowed him to become the man he never wanted to be. It was all a lie. Millie told Lillian, the nurse, she needed to go back to therapy, now. She told Lillian she needed to meet with Jack to go over her discharge instructions and exercises she should continue at home. Lillian put hold on Millie's dinner tray, called for the transporter to take her to the physical therapy department. Ted wondered why Millie was so quiet as he wheeled her to the elevator and into the hallway outside the PT area.

"I'm good here, Ted. Thank you."

"Millie are you sure you are okay. You seem a little down." Ted patted her on her shoulder.

"It's okay, Ted. I'm just tired and a little anxious, excited, all kinds of feelings about going home." She smiled. "I'll have them call when I'm finished."

"You will be fine. I've never seen anyone work as hard as you to overcome such a tragic set of circumstances. You are very brave." Ted turned to go on to his next transport.

"Thank you, Ted" Millie waved as she wheeled her chair through the doors and into the PT work area. Jack was in the back of the exercise area with Pete who was walking on his own and was also to be discharged soon. Millie watched as Jack guided Pete through the parallel bars, encouraging him, joking with him. She stared at his face and could see some similarities to herself. His slightly turned-up nose, the way one side of his smile was a little higher than the other—like hers. His eyes were crystal blue, like hers.

Hank was congratulating Pete when he looked across the room and saw Millie. His usual MO was to run. Not anymore. He had to know if he was Millie's father. He had to face his past, no matter how frightening it might be. He needed to convince her to have a DNA test. That test was new at the time. He would have to ask someone in the lab to obtain the materials and send the specimens out to one of the few independent centers that performed the analysis. If it proved that Millie was his daughter, he would have to notify the police about his real identity and his past. On the slim chance that there were people still looking for Hank Baldoni they may have somehow found out Millie might be his daughter and ran her down to see if It would ferrate him out. It just made as much sense as Millie winding up at Cleveland Clinic, in his rehab after all these years. God, if there was one, really did work in strange ways. The rainbow he had seen a few weeks ago may have truly been a sign. There was a bond between Millie and Hank from her first visit to the physical therapy unit. She was stubborn, a survivor, and had courage he used to have. He walked towards Millie with tears in his eyes. Millie stood and walked across the room gripping her cane towards Hank with tears in her eyes. Words seemed inappropriate as he led her to his office. The door closed on two lost souls who hoped to find a path to reconciliation.

Chapter XIV
Best Laid Plans

Samantha and Henri spent most of their evening at the swank Italian Restaurant on the strip staring at each other. Each time their fingers touched or there were gaps in their conversation the air between the two of them seemed to sizzle. Sam wore a black dress accented with a pearl necklace and earrings. The dress was conservative yet clung perfectly to the curves of her body. Her shoulder length auburn hair framed her face. She outlined her project, presenting reasons why she needed to access some files from Francesca's office. Henri looked youthful and handsome in a blue sweater over white shirt and tan trousers. Henri agreed to talk with Doug about her request. He probably would have agreed to most anything she wanted. He was smitten.

Francesca decided to take a few extra days off after the conference to meet with Dan Pironne. She needed to work out a strategy to protect Balpar Industries should the audit question its accounting practices. As she stepped farther away from the Francesca who was ethical and loyal, she devised a plan to eliminate the partners and become sole owner of JBT Enterprises. Rationalising her motives, justifying her methods convinced Francesca she was the same person she used to be. Mistaking the turmoil inside her for motivation, she had authorised a more lucrative transfer of funds to the investor's gain columns. Fabricating damages to one of the actual hotels in Amalfi, Italy Balpar owned to veil its illegitimate dealings, the profit and loss statements would appear authentic. Dan used his venomous tactics to intimidate Francesca. Even if she wished to extract herself from Balpar she would be faced with elimination preceded by unsavory torture. Fear drove away any thoughts she might have of stepping back to what she used to be. A wall constructed for self-preservation precluded her from pulling back from a demonic cavern of darkness.

One of Jeff's responsibilities as JBT's technical consultant was editing and installing reports into the new computer system. The financial advisors prepared the written reports and spreadsheets for Board meetings. Jeff copied them and grammatically edited them before installing them into the system, made hard copies and distributed them to the Board members prior to the meetings. He had rarely examined the reports in detail. The veracity of the information was the responsibility of the financial advisors and Board members, which included the partners. He would have time on Monday to look back over the past few month's reports on Balpar Industries as well as prepare the current reports for Thursday's Board meeting.

Francesca slept fitfully. Dreams of lovemaking with Doug, the Unforgettable Moments Ball, drowning in a pool of blood; unable to swim out of it, children without faces reaching for her left her drenched in perspiration and nauseous. She stumbled from her hotel bed to her purse sitting on a table. Those tiny white pills helped to take the edge off the panic that haunted her sleep. Her meeting with the Pironnes had not gone as well as she planned. Dan was surly, barely listening to the reasons she gave for increasing dividends and falsifying reconstruction costs for the hotel in Amalfi. The police he hadn't been able to bribe had turned over the investigation into the dealings of the Pironne family to the FBI. He yelled at his henchmen who he had sent to find Millie and Hank Baldoni. They came back without any progress on finding Hank. They had found out that Millie had been transferred to Cleveland Clinic, but nothing more than that. Francesca knew that Hank had been one of the initial partners in Balpar. She didn't care about some Millie and some Hank. She needed Dan to sign off on the plan she devised to pass the audit.

Samantha stayed after work for two nights. Henri had convinced Doug to allow Sam into Francesca's office to pull some files of clients who were wealthy but had not increased investments for over a year. If she could convince Francesca to allow her to work with those clients interested in her investment planning model, it would be beneficial to JBT and a feather in the cap of both women. Samantha had watched Francesca manipulate the other partners, especially Doug, into complicated financial models that would be too time consuming for them to manage. Francesca ignored Samantha's attempts to engage her in conversation let alone acknowledge she existed. Henri asked her to spend more time outside the office with him, but Sam only had a few days to obtain the information she needed from Francesca's files. If only she could convince Francesca that working together would give credence to a prototype of her project. The only hope she had of presenting it to the Board would be partnering with Francesca. Samantha was puzzled by one company that was included in many of the investor profiles she reviewed. Balpar Industries appeared more often than any other and could be traced back twenty years. The return on investment was erratic. Many of the older financial reports were not available either in the computer or hard copy. She made a note to ask Francesca or Henri if they were archived. Balpar's primary businesses were in other countries, mainly in Italy. The investment model was atypical of the ones the three original partners recommended to more lucrative clients. Henri had told her there had been an audit performed during the last quarter and the accounting firm used was verifying some minor discrepancies though he did not elaborate what those were. Francesca was returning from the conference in two days. Sam didn't know why the woman was so cold to her. Her gaze seemed to look right through other employees. She seemed distracted, even with her husband who seemed to adore his wife.

Hank and Millie spent two hours after the PT department closed to open a twenty-year-old box of secrets. Memories of John and Alicia, her parents, loving her, protecting her, bandaging scraped knees, wiping tears away. Scattered among those the quiet, gentle kindness of Sally, the governess, singing "Over the Rainbow" and rocking her to sleep, hiding she was Millie's real mother. Hank told her wild tales of gambling, stealing money from John's construction company, being beaten and left for dead and assuming a new identity. They both were exhausted when Millie returned to her room. She had agreed to a DNA test. She needed to know. Hank visited her every day after her PT session to answer questions, trying his best to comfort her. He did not verbalise his concern that her accident may have been related to his being her father. If only John, Alicia and Phyllis knew the truth how could anyone outside the family have known or suspected? Phyllis, he needed to talk to her. She hadn't visited Millie since she told her about Sally. Knowing he could not apologise to John, Alicia and Sally, he wrote a letter, praying that somehow their spirits would sense his contrition. He would send a copy to Phyllis even if she agreed to meet with him.

I know this letter will never explain how deeply sorry I am for abandoning, stealing, hiding and running from the best family I ever had. Sally, I left you in a deplorable and dangerous situation in Chicago. My intent was to pay off my debts, come for you and keep you safe with me forever. That dream was taken from me because of my involvement with the same awful people who destroyed your young life. I was a coward. Had I known you were pregnant I would have come for you as soon as I was physically able. I didn't deserve God saving my life. I repaid him by hiding behind another identity, hiding from myself. Millie is a beautiful, courageous, funny, intelligent woman, just like her mother. You would be so proud of her. I pray that someday I will be forgiven for the cowardly person I have become. I promise to do my best to spend the rest of my life compensating for my behavior. If Millie will allow me, I will love and protect her with every fiber of my being.

Sincerely,
Hank

Douglas and Henri sat in the conference room waiting for Martin. They were looking over the agenda for today's Board meeting. Henri gave them a snapshot of Samantha's proposal. They smiled at him because he was not the obdurate person when saying Sam's name. Francesca was hastily putting together the information she wished to present at the meeting. It had taken her quite a while for Danial Pironne's accountants to sign her current Balpar financial summary. The knock on her door was answered with a curt "What!" She had a terrible headache. The two pills she took before she rushed to work were not dulling her pain nor her feeling of losing control. *I must keep it together. There is too much at stake.*

"Come in, for God's sake!" she yelled after the knocking persisted. Samantha entered the room hesitantly. "What is it Ms.… Reynolds, is it?" Francesca glanced away from her paperwork.

"Mrs Jacob. I'm sorry to interrupt. I wanted to speak with you about a project…"

"Stop right there. I don't have time to talk to you now. I have a Board meeting. Make an appointment." She snarled starring fiendishly at Samantha.

"Yes, I am going to present…" Sam tried to explain.

"I really don't care what you are going to do. Now, please leave…Now!"

"But, the information…" Francesca moved away from her desk and started towards Samantha. She stood only inches away from her.

"Did you hear me? I want you to leave!" She pushed Samantha's shoulder. Sam raised her arm to protect herself. "Go ahead! Hit me! You little cunt!" Sam backed out of the office and closed the door. Her legs felt like Jell-O and her heart was beating like a scared rabbit's. She couldn't imagine why Francesca would treat her that way unless she had found out she had been looking through files in her office. The Board meeting was to start in one hour. Henri told her the other partners had given her fifteen minutes to present her project. She tried to look composed as she walked towards the ladies' room past several technicians glancing at her from their cubicles.

"Welcome, everyone to the monthly JBT Board Meeting. You have been given copies of minutes from the last meeting on November 16 for your review. Are there any additions or corrections?" Doug addressed the eleven members present. He had started the meeting twenty minutes late waiting for Martin. "I apologise for starting the meeting after the appointed time. We will proceed without Mr Balingsford attendance. Please note the attendees in the minutes, Miss Campbell." Delores Campbell, Doug's secretary nodded without expression. Doug was surprised Martin did not show or call for the meeting. He was always on time. He especially enjoyed inserting a little levity into the sober tone of the meetings. He would have to give him a call again if he didn't appear. There had been several times Martin had been late recently which was so unlike him. Doug gave the updated profit and loss reports, a list of new clients and the financial planning team assigned to each. He passed the baton to Henri and Francesca. Henri reported the information from his accounting department, answering any questions with his usual confidence and expertise. Francesca was next in line. She was sure that she had covered any loopholes with Balpar Industries the audit might have uncovered.

Chapter XV
Thunder and Lightening

The flashlight opened a triangle of dim light on the floor, the walls and finally settling on the door leading to the dismal office. When this person started, they never imagined this would lead to this. The person's hair hung over the forehead; strings untamed from the damp snow. The left hand shook some as the switch was turned on the dusty desk lamp. The light uncovered the pile of papers shuffled over the top of the desk. In a very short time, the fruits of this tedious project would pour into this person's pockets, enough that one could start a new life…somewhere. The sound of footsteps, heavy footsteps-not ones that belonged to someone who did not want to be detected. The hand switched off the desk lamp, pulled open the right desk drawer cautiously. The right hand felt for the metal as the shadow disappeared behind the desk. The footsteps stopped and the door swung open. The flash exited the weapon as a spray of bullets echoed off the walls. Short gasps slowed into silence. Another spray of bullets. A hand reached for the flashlight that had dropped from the desk to the floor. It shown on a face leaking blood from several wounds. The eyes were still open.

Samantha began her presentation following a glowing introduction from Henri. Doug and the other Board members were surprised at the enthusiasm from the usually indomitable partner. Samantha smiled demurely. She wore a dark blue suit with a light blue sweater under the jacket. Her pearl necklace and earrings complimented the outfit. Her hair was swept back from her face and secured in a bun with a pearl hairpin. She had applied a light foundation and dusky rose lipstick to enhance her green eyes. Standing with confidence she outlined the project which she hoped would impress the Board members. She also felt it would place Francesca in a defensive position that forced her to work with Samantha.

"Thank you for allowing me to present a project I believe you will find commiserate with the goals and high ideals of JBT Enterprises. Mr Treacher has been kind enough to assist me in this endeavor and to request the next several minutes of your time." Her voice was captivating, not only because of its tone but also because of the lack of hesitancy. "I have reviewed the financial imprint of clients who have impacted an average ten percent of our revenue over the past ten years. There was a common factor that caused me to delve deeper into their financial portfolios. I used information from Mrs Jacob's oversight of these accounts with the permission of Mr Treacher. I hope to work closely with Mrs Jacob following this presentation and present her with the details. I performed the cross referencing of these reports after my regular hours so I would not neglect my daily responsibilities." She glanced at Francesca who stared at her folder and tapped a pencil eraser rhythmically on the desk. Doug and the other members leaned forward as Samantha projected spreadsheets on the screen. A yellow highlight traveled from one spreadsheet to another and were eventually grouped together into one column titled **Balpar Industries.** Millions of dollars had been siphoned from each of the top ten percent financially dominate clients' accounts into holding companies under the Balpar Industries umbrella over a period of ten to fifteen years. "Since Balpar appears to be a rather small, internationally layered company, by reviewing each of the elements of this company's investments there is opportunity to move some areas to a more profitable source while developing those within Balpar into less layered subsidiaries, if feasible. With Mrs Jacob's expertise and experience with this company in the past several years I am convinced we can increase our percentage of lucrative investors and enhance

Balpar's profitability and attractiveness for possible mergers." Samantha distributed copies of her proposed project, research and data analysis to each member. She leaned in slightly to the male components so that her delicate perfume could accompany the aura of the session. Francesca's heart was racing. Samantha had spun a web around her so that she either could be eaten alive or would be bound to work with this woman so that her cover would not be blown. If Dan Pirrone found out that there might be a tear in the façade of Balpar, her life might be over. *There would be questions if anything happened to this bitch. I'll have to play along and keep tabs on what she sees. Damn! I must find a way to tie her hands or get rid of her without them suspecting me.*

Jeff looked at the computer screen. He had helped Ms Reynolds prepare a presentation for the JBT Board meeting along with the other parts of the agenda. His mind was not on work. He had visited Millie, but she seemed distracted and unusually quiet. She told him about her conversation with Phyllis. He felt so sorry for her having to deal with the painful information about her real parents besides dealing with her amnesia. He had encouraged her to share this story with the detective who had interviewed Phyllis and her the last time he came to the Clinic. **Balpar Industries** glowed on the screen at the top of one of the spreadsheets. *Balpar Industries. Is that the one Phyllis asked me to watch for?* He printed that page, looking around the office for any eyes that might question what he was doing. He folded the paper and tucked it into his briefcase. He wanted to get home and call Millie to see if she was feeling better. He loved her more every day. Balpar faded as he switched off the computer realising most everyone had left the office. It was getting dark as he walked to his car in the parking lot.

Hank held the envelope from a laboratory in Washington D.C. His hands shook as he tore it open and sighed, closed his eyes and prayed the results would be a gift he felt he never deserved.

To: Mr Henry R. Baldoni
We are informing you of the results of the DNA exam sent to us December 18, 1978.
Henry R. Baldoni, BD August 22, 1931
Melinda L. Strigow (Sherman), BD March 18, 1954
99.45% Match

Hank walked back into the office where Millie sat anxiously fidgeting with her cane and he locket around her neck. He walked to the chair next to her and their eyes met. "Millie, it is a 99.45 % match that I am your father." Tears trickled down both of their faces. Hank stood and bent over Millie as he put his arms around her shaking shoulders. "I am so sorry that I didn't know, Millie. I am so, so sorry." Millie let him hold her as her mind and feelings twirled in a myriad of directions. He released her and stood with his shoulders bent. "I wrote something for you to share with Phyllis. It's my apology. I don't expect either of you to forgive me. I will speak to Phyllis if she will listen to me." He handed Millie two envelopes and walked behind his desk collapsing in his chair. The envelope for Phyllis contained a check for twice the amount Hank had stolen from the construction company. Millie stared at him. The clock ticking on the wall felt like an endless reminder of time that could not be recovered.

"Hank…Jack… Dad, I don't know how to feel right now. I need some time to get settled back home and put some of these pieces to this crazy puzzle together. I'll talk to Phyllis. I need to let her know I love her. We always will be sisters as far as I am concerned. I'm supposed to be discharged on Tuesday. I will let you know how I am doing. Give me some time. I am sorry too." She stood with her cane and walked behind the desk and hugged him. He shook his head letting her know he understood. She closed the door as he laid his head on the desk and sobbed.

Chapter XVI
Storm

Martin couldn't help attempting to follow up on his suspicions that Francesca was not the untainted person Doug defended. He had looked over the accounts she managed, and they seemed to be indisputable. When Henri was at the computer seminar, one year ago, Martin had met with Francesca to pick her brain and see if she seemed to be hiding anything. He met her at a small cafe' not far from the Jacob apartment building. She was sugary sweet and wore much more suggestive clothing than she donned at the office. She even rubbed her bare leg against his calf, excusing herself having done it by mistake. Martin had one very weak character flaw. His libido was easily aroused by the opposite sex, especially if he was getting positive signals from the damsel. *Not my partner and friend's wife, for cripe's sake!* He gulped down the glass of Chardonnay Francesca had ordered. She asked him to come up to her apartment to look at some files she was working with at home. Martin felt kind of woozy. He had only drunk two glasses of wine-not his usual half bottle. Francesca's voice seemed like it was coming from a tunnel as she grasped his hand and led him away from the cafe'. She had someone taking pictures as she undressed and laid beside the drugged, nude body of Doug's partner. The pictures looked as though Martin was raping her. They were explicit and lude. When she threatened to reveal the photos to Doug and tell him she had hired someone to take photos of one of the episodes where Martin had supposedly repeatedly raped her, Martin was livid. He could barely keep from strangling Francesca whenever he was around her. She was a snake. He had to put on a show for the Doug, Henri and the staff when Francesca was around, but he seethed inside. The new accountant Henri had hired had been pleasant to the eyes each day he saw her in the reception area. Now that she was in this new position her demeanor and polish piqued his interest as well as her beauty. Icy women had always been a challenge to him. When he and Doug noticed Henri's softening towards her, Martin sighed and backed off. Samantha was working on a project. Henri had asked Doug and Martin to allow her access to Francesca's office files while she was attending a conference. Doug was a little hesitant, but Henri promised he would review the files she accessed, he felt more comfortable. Samantha hinted that she and Francesca would be working together on the project. She did not tell them that she had not been able to speak with Francesca to confirm her approval. Martin had hired a private detective he had met in the gym where he worked out. When Henri was in the hospital after being attacked Martin missed going to the hospital to see him. His detective buddy had found out that Francesca had meetings with Daniel Pironne. He was being investigated for activities that were mob related. Martin found a remote connection to one of Francesca's accounts, Balpar Industries where the name, Victor Pironne appeared as one of the original owners. He had made an appointment to talk with the administrator of Balpar, a lawyer named Arthur Mason. Two days before the Board Meeting, Martin asked the technician that oversaw installing a new, updated computer system to do him a favor. JBT was in the process of converting paper data to computerised data. It was a harrowing task. Seventeen years of paper files, spreadsheets, reports were being logged into the new system. Computer refinements were escalating in the late seventies. Many companies were still wary of the electronic elephant. Several had been courageous enough to try out the new wave of artificial intelligence, though that rubric had not been well known at the time. Martin had asked Jeff to look up the original owners, or officers of Balpar industries.

Jeff dreamed of Millie being chased by Ron Sherman. He awoke with a start and glanced at the clock. It was 3 AM. He groaned, visited the bathroom and shuffled to the kitchen. The light from the refrigerator shone on his wrinkled pajamas as he drank a swig from a bottle of orange juice. Something else besides Millie and Ron kept him tossing and turning. Then it came to him. Phyllis had asked him to let her know if anyone asked for information on Balpar Industries. Martin Balangsford, Samantha Reynolds and Phyllis had been the most recent requestors. The only person who had routine access to that account was Mrs Jacob. There had not been any special requests from her in the past several months. She was the lead accountant for Balpar and was gradually sending the hard copy files to Jeff's department as were the other employees and officers of JBT. Jeff reported these findings to Phyllis. The day Millie was run down she was supposed to be starting orientation in Jeff's department as one of the accountants working with the new computers. Millie was being discharged in two days. She had agreed to stay with Phyllis for a month while she gained strength. Phyllis and she had some healing to do as well.

Jeff had secretly followed Ron Sherman whenever he could see his truck parked at different bars and at his run-down house not far from Vanguard Blvd. One of Ron's regular haunts was Marti's Bar. Three days before Millie was to be discharged Jeff had followed Ron to Marti's. A well-dressed man entered the bar shortly after Ron slithered in. The man wore dark glasses, a dark suit and a hat slanted over his forehead. He left after about fifteen minutes and walked to a black sedan parked half a block down the street. The sedan left after Ron stumbled to his truck, evidently quite inebriated. Jeff watched until he noticed the sedan slow, turn and follow Ron's truck down towards the highway. Jeff had to get back to work. He was sure Ron had something to do with Millie's accident. Now he was even more sure. There was someone else following that creep. Jeff felt he should report the recent events to the police, but he needed a little more evidence.

Martin' detective hid in the woods outside a group of abandoned office buildings. He had followed Francesca from her apartment to an office building near the river in downtown Gary. He carried a briefcase and wore a business suit like many entering the building. She took the elevator to the fourteenth floor. He took another set of elevators to the same floor and arrived just in time to see her enter double glass doors with Mason, Murray and Thompson, LLC etched in the glass. He moved into a Men's restroom and changed into a maintenance coverall. Beckman Industrial Cleaners was embroidered on the back of the coverall. He stuffed the suit into the briefcase, donned a baseball cap and put the briefcase in the trash bag. He moved out of the restroom and peered in a wastebasket near the glass doorway at the same time glancing into the room on the inside where he saw Francesca talking with Dan Pironne. He recognised Dan from photos he had seen at the police station. They never seemed to be able to catch the guy even though he was a suspect in many investigations. Francesca seemed to be arguing with Dan. He smirked at her and started to walk away. She tried to follow him but was stopped by a very large, dark haired man with muscles that threatened to burst the seams of his suit. Larry Hudson feigned emptying the small wastebasket into the larger garbage bag as Francesca marched through the doors and pounded the elevator button. Her face was red, and she tapped her foot impatiently as the elevator arrived and she entered. The muscular man followed Francesca into the elevator. Larry took the stairs near the elevator. In the stairwell he scanned the staircases up and down. Seeing no one, he stripped off the coveralls, stuffed them into the bag. He flipped the hood of his running outfit to cover his head and ran down the stairs to the parking garage. The muscle had a firm grasp on Francesca's arm. She looked frightened as he pushed her into her car, then moved behind the wheel and started the car. Larry ran to the van parked in the alley. Francesca's car entered the Skyway and headed out of town. Martin had hired Larry to keep an eye on Francesca and let him know if there were any strange developments. He warned him, though, to keep well hidden. Dan Pironne was no person to confront or even be in the same room with. Martin had heard Doug talk about Dan's escapades in college. He had heard rumors that the police and FBI were trying to get evidence he had taken his father's place in the mob.

The brush was dense as the person ran away from the dilapidated building, the flashlight's erratic beam scaring racoons and rabbits into the brambles. Breaths came heavily between an occasional cough muffled by their arm. Another figure followed the first person. The road finally appeared in the darkness as the figure ducked behind the frozen ditch until headlights disappeared. The second figure dove onto the first. There was the popping sound and then one figure ran across the road and around the bend. The figure grabbed the handle of the blue Ford, yanked open the door and jumped inside. The tires squealed and gravel flew behind them as the car sped towards the quad cities.

In the basement of One Prudential Plaza the roar of machinery running the heating and air conditioning of the huge skyscraper drowned out the hasty footsteps of the two men from Harbor Power and Air Conditioning, Inc. They walked up the stairs and out to the alley where the dark blue van with the same lettering on the sides as on the men's outfits waited with the motor running. The clock ticked each second in red digital numbers on the apparatus the men had attached to the pipes running along the wall. The van exited, turned towards the Skyway and sped across the bridge.

Jeff laid unconscious on the dirty floor. Blood ran from the bullet that had grazed his skull down across his shoulder. It trickled past the bullet hole and powder marks in his upper chest. A hand laid across his right arm. It was cold and pale, its fingertips blue. The darkness was impenetrable. Suddenly, there were footsteps running towards the broken door to the room. Larry stumbled over something as his size sixteen gumshoes connected with the bodies. He tried to get up, blinking, wildly trying to adjust his eyesight to the darkness. He fumbled for the matches in his pocket, found them and bent several attempting to light one. The flame was brief but enough to see two bodies lying next to one another. After burning his fingertips, sweat dripping on the persons lying beneath him, he managed to light another and saw a desk lamp dangling by its cord over the front of the desk. He grabbed the neck of the lamp and felt the base for the switch. Dismal light shone on the macabre scene. One body was that of a woman. She was barely recognisable. Part of her face and skull had been blown away. Blood and brain tissue oozed from the huge wound. The rest of her blood—soaked body was riddled with bullets. Larry's stomach lurched. He almost hurled his last meal of coffee and a sub sandwich. The woman's pale hand laid across the barely moving chest of the man next to her on the floor. His face was streaked with blood. Larry couldn't detect any entry or exit bullet wounds. He put his head as close to the man's nose and mouth as he could to see if there were any breath sounds. The smell of blood and gunshot residue filled his nostrils and he vomited onto the floor. He had seen some awful crime scenes and war scenes. This seemed somehow more personal. There seemed to be some air coming from the guy's mouth. There were gurgling sounds. Larry tore off a part of the woman's dress and held it over what appeared to be a bullet hole in the other victim's chest. What he could see from the dim light of the desk lamp, the room was riddled with bullets. It looked like some of the homes he had hid in and destroyed during his stint in the war. He had to get help. He wrapped his belt around the chest and piece of dress to hold it over the man's wound. He stood, felt kind of woozy. He grabbed onto the desk. There was a phone. He grabbed the receiver not expecting to hear a dial tone. There was one. He dialed 911. Before the operator could finish her greeting. he growled, "Get me the police! Hurry! It's an emergency. There has been a murder, a couple of them!" He steadied himself once more and gave the approximate location to the operator. 911 services had been established in 1967.

"Marty, I'm at Memorial Hospital in Chicago."

"What! Are you okay? I told you to be careful. Did you tangle with the Pironne fellow?"

"No…no, I followed Francesca. I thought it was Francesca from her apartment. She went to this Pirrone guys house. What a house! It's a mansion… a castle, with a barbed wire…"

"Hey, Larry. Slow down. Are you okay, man?"

"Yeh, a little shaky, but I'm okay. Anyhow, I followed Mrs J. She was in there a while. She came out with another big guy, but not Pironne as far as I could see. It was getting dark."

"Where did they go?"

"Way back off the highway before you get to Gary, to an abandoned office building on…um… Town River Rd. It was spooky, I tell you."

"Why are you in the hospital?" Martin locked and chained his apartment door.

"Well. The two of them went into that building and, in a few minutes, after they stepped in there were shots, like from an automatic rifle…rifles, I mean. Man, I ducked onto the ground behind some bushes."

"Geesh, shots! What the hell?" Martin grabbed a glass and poured himself a scotch.

"I waited. In the dark it was hard to see. It looked like two people came out of the building after the gunshots. Then somebody ran past where I was hiding, into the bushes and towards the highway. I froze. A few minutes later another person ran towards the highway"

"Was it a man or woman who ran out of the building?" Martin was reaching for his car keys and throwing on a coat as he questioned Larry.

"It was so dark, and I had ducked into the bushes that I couldn't tell. I waited until I couldn't hear any more sounds and no one else came from the building. It had to be twenty minutes of more. There had been a light coming from a window at the side of the building and it had gone out when the bullets started. I decided to go into the place. Maybe the other person, Francesca or the big guy were dead."

"Gosh, Lar, that was really dangerous. Did you have a gun?" Martin wanted to get to the hospital to see Larry in person.

"Marti, there is a guy that is alive with a bullet in his chest. They took him to surgery. Yes, I always have my piece with me. He was not the big guy I saw go in the building with Francesca, if it was her. When I got in there and could find a light there was a dead woman on the floor and this guy lying next to her with a blood on his face and a hole in his chest. I didn't think I should search for an ID since the cops wouldn't want the scene to be disturbed. They are waiting to ask me more questions. They want me to know why I was there and who I was working for, but I told them it was confidential. They may press for that info. I'll hold out as long as I can."

"I'll be there as fast as I can. Maybe I can identify one or both. This is really getting creepy!" Martin hung up and rushed down the stairs into the parking garage and took off towards the hospital. *What is Francesca doing out in the middle of nowhere with a big man; probably Pironne's muscle? I'm sure Doug doesn't know anything about this craziness. God, I hope the woman who was killed wasn't Francesca!*

The surgeon had removed the bullet that had nicked Jeff's second rib, tore into the right upper portion of his lung and lodged in the soft tissue not far from his heart. The lung had collapsed. A tube had been placed into the chest cavity to reflate his lung. He had been transferred to the Intensive Care Unit following surgery. Larry paced back and forth trying to remember anything about the people that had run from the building through the woods towards the highway. The police asked him to remain available so they could ask more questions. Martin ran into the hospital and went up to the waiting room outside the ICU. He tried to think of how he would explain why he had hired Larry and how the detective wound up at a murder scene.

The dim lighting in the morgue shone on the body covered with a white sheet. The tag attached to her foot read *DOA,* Dead on Arrival. The red nail polish on her toenails were in stark contrast to her blanched skin. The police pathologist had examined the body to look for any identifying scars, tattoos and birthmarks. Fingerprints were obtained and sent to headquarters to identify the body. She appeared to be about forty years old. What was left of her hair and face revealed an ash blonde female with green eyes. There were multiple bullet wounds in her chest, one leg, half of her skull and face had been blown away and a portion of her left arm. Two of the bullets matched the one removed from Jeff's chest wound. It appeared to be from a rapid fire 45 caliber shotgun. Another finding lead the investigating policeman to the conclusion she had been beaten recently from the bruises on her arms and back. She had rope burns on her wrists that looked to be recent. Her dress was made of expensive material and was stylish. Her jewelry was high end also and she had a diamond wedding band and engagement ring on her left hand which lead them to believe she was married. There were no other identifying marks. No purse or keys were found at the scene. The man who had survived had a wallet and car keys in his coat pocket. He was Jeffrey Collins. Two credit cards, a driver's license and a key card for JBT & Associates, LLC was found in his wallet. There was a twenty-dollar bill and some change along with a visitor's pass with room 232 stamped on it from Cleveland Clinic in the billfold. A police guard was stationed outside Jeff's cubicle in the ICU and outside the morgue.

Doug couldn't understand why Francesca hadn't arrived home or called. It was 9:30 pm. He was worried because Martin hadn't shown up for the Board meeting nor had he called. Francesca had left hurriedly after the meeting. Phyllis

Strigow had called him that afternoon and was concerned with some things her assistant had found during the audit. She had reviewed the areas he questioned. She wanted to set up a meeting with him and the partners early next week. All this, together with Samantha's review of Balpar Industries for her project questioning some of the investments in the tiers of that company added to his level of anxiety. Douglas loved Francesca with all his being, but there had also been an undercurrent of fear; one he couldn't understand. He would sweep it out of his conscience as soon as it slithered into their relationship.

Millie packed her clothes. She was being discharged in the morning. Back to a life she barely remembered. Phyllis, who she had always believed to be her sister, was picking her up and having her stay with her in Indiana until she could adjust and gain strength. Her whole existence had been broken like the bones in her body. The father and mother she knew all her life were not her real father and mother. Her governess was her real mother and her physical therapist turned out to be her real father. She was in the midst of a divorce from a man she didn't remember and that everyone, even the police seemed to suspect as her attempted killer. There was Jeff, the kind, supportive man who said he loved her, had loved her for years. She hugged the teddy bear he had given her, plopped into the chair and stared at the hospital bed. She felt safe in the hospital. Would she be safe out there in the new world she was about to enter?

Jeff opened his eyes and gazed at the bright florescent lights. There were unfamiliar beeping sounds, a whooshing sound close to him and hushed voices coming and going nearby. He tried to speak but something was covering his mouth. Where was he? All he could remember was hiding in the dark. Banging noises and a scream, so terrifying, that he shuddered just thinking about it. A man and woman in white coats came into view.

"Hello, Mr Collins, I am Dave from respiratory therapy. This is Rebecca, one of the nurses taking care of you. You are in Chicago General Hospital. I know you must be confused and upset. We are working on taking the tube out of your throat. It is attached to a machine that is helping with your breathing. You were injured by a bullet and the surgeons removed it. You have a chest tube in to help inflate your lung that was injured. Try to relax and we will have this tube out soon so you can ask the many questions you must have." Dave moved out of Jeff's line of vision. The nurse, Rebecca, leaned towards him.

"Mr Collins, Dave is working with the ventilator that is helping with your breathing. I am going to assist him when he is ready to wean you off that machine. You may feel uncomfortable as we take out the tube in your throat. I have a suction tube to make sure you don't breathe in any of the secretions…mucus that may gather there. We will talk you through every step we take. You will be hoarse for a couple of days, so we want you to rest your voice as much as possible. I know you have lots of questions. We will give you a dry erase board to write on as soon as we can after we remove the tube. We have medication for pain and to help with other discomfort you might have." Rebecca smiled and went over to talk to Dave.

Millie… you felt like this. Am I dreaming that I took her place? My chest feels like someone put clamps on it. The gunshots! The woman …her face…it was gone! Jeff closed his eyes trying to block the horrific scene of a woman collapsing near him with part of her face and head splattered on the floor. After several minutes feeling like his throat was being torn out, frightened that he would drown, he was able to breathe on his own. A cannula in his nostrils was forcing humidified oxygen into his respiratory track. He looked around at all the intravenous poles, bags and tubing, the monitors displaying his vital signs across a screen and a tube leading from the side of his chest to a bag filled with dark reddish—brown liquid.

Millie. He started to remember why he had wound up in a deserted building outside of Gary. It was for Millie. He hadn't been convinced Ron Sherman didn't have anything to do with Millie's accident. Before she came home, he needed to follow the creep to see if there were any clues the police had not uncovered. The police had warned him not to involve himself in their investigation, especially when Jeff voiced his belief that Sherman's alibi was a scam.

Jeff tried to talk. The only sound that came out was a rattily squeak. Rebecca came into his cubicle. "Mr Collins try not to talk right now. Your throat is tender from the tube we removed. Here is the board and a marker. I will try to answer your questions.

HOW DID I GET TO THE HOSPITAL? WHO FOUND ME? WHO IS THAT WOMAN THAT WAS SHOT? IS SHE ALIVE? IT WAS SO HORRIBLE. Jeff wrote on the board. His hands shook and his heart pounded. An alarm went off on his monitor because of his rapid heart rate. Rebecca reached up and turned it off.

"I believe there was a gentleman who had found you in a deserted building outside of the city, not far from the highway. He called 911 and an ambulance brought you here. You were unconscious. Your lung was collapsed from the bullet wound and you had lost a lot of blood. The surgeons took you to surgery soon after you arrived. I don't know the name of the man that called 911. The police have asked him to stay in the hospital. They have lots of questions also. They want to talk with you as soon as the doctors feel you are well enough to meet with them. I don't believe the other victim they brought in an ambulance survived. I am not sure. You would have to ask the police any questions you have about her. I am so sorry you had to go through such an awful experience." Rebecca patted his arm. He thought of Millie and suddenly realised he didn't know what day it was.

WHAT DAY IS THIS? He tried to recall the day he had made the big mistake following Ron Sherman.

"Mr Collins, it is Thursday, January 3, 1978." She pointed to a whiteboard across the room that had the date written on it along with names of doctors and nurses caring for him.

Jeff's face turned ashen. Alarms started to go off once again. He struggled to get the words out. "Millie! She…getting out today! Can't…come… (cough, cough) back! Dangerous!" Two nurses and a doctor rushed into the cubicle. Rebecca was administering a clear liquid into one of the ports on an IV. Jeff was pulling at his tubes and IV's trying to get out of bed.

"Mr Collins, Jeff, please calm down. You cannot go anywhere. We will get help from the police if you feel there is danger to this person. You won't be any help to her if you injure yourself by trying to leave." Rebecca said calmly. She gave an order to one of the nurses and turned up the oxygen level. Jeff began to sink into a dark hole. He could hear voices, but they were becoming more distant.

Martin and Larry were ushered into a small room adjacent to the ICU waiting room. The police detective, Hal Putnam, had been briefed at the station about the shooting near Gary. When he saw Jeff Collins' name in the report, he asked permission to go to the hospital to see him because of his involvement with the Strigow hit and run case. He was frustrated that they had been unable to find the person or persons who had run her down and any motive for the crime. When he arrived at the hospital he was introduced to Larry Hudson, the private detective working for Martin. Good old Larry Hudson. Hal had known him from his early days on the police force. Larry had been an excellent policeman. He had been injured several times during his investigations into and confrontations with the mob. When he left the force, he started a private agency vowing to continue to do what he could to clean up the city. Hal had looked up to Larry, though his reputation was that of a "wild man" taking dangerous risks and pushing the rule's page far beyond the tolerance of his superiors.

Hal and Larry greeted each other like old pals with pats on the back and bear hugs. "What in the hell are you doing mixed up in a murder?" Hal quizzed his friend. "I thought you were lying on a beach in Florida or getting info on deviant millionaires for their diamond studded wives." Hal laughed.

"Well, Hal, old boy, I thought you retired a long time ago. Didn't know they kept grumpy old guys like you in the force after they turned eighty!" The detective from the Chicago police just stared at the two with a grim look on his face as he motioned them to sit. Martin sat looking at his big hands and shuffling his feet. He was sure he would be fired from JBT if Doug ever found out he had hired a private eye to follow Francesca.

The Chicago detective assigned to the case was Brad Keller. He looked at some paperwork resting on a table next to where he sat. Some of the information in a folder caught his eye. The name of Dan Pironne had been mentioned by Mr Hudson, he private detective Martin had hired. One of the nurses from the ICU taking care of Jeff Collins reported to him that Jeff was concerned for a Melinda Strigow, that she was in danger. Brad had interviewed the sister of a Melinda Sherman whose name was Phyllis Strigow. He had gone to Cleveland Clinic to follow up on a tip he received while investigating Daniel Pironne's connections to the mob. The informant told Brad that Dan wanted to get the scoop on a Hank Baldoni's whereabouts. He ordered the informant to pose as a census taker in the neighborhood where the Strigow's lived. The informant had gotten information on a Sally Thatcher who was a governess for the Strigow's and there were two kids, Phyllis and Melinda. When the snitch came back with what he had learned, Dan started throwing things around the room and screaming that he would find that Baldoni creep and make him pay. Dan was not aware that the guy he sent on that mission was an informant for the Chicago Police Department.

"I'm Brad Keller, Chief Detective, Division of Homicide, Chicago Police. Thank you for your patience and for agreeing to allow me to ask you some questions. Mr Balingsford, I understand you hired Mr Hudson to perform a service for you. Mr Hudson was present at the murder scene and called 911 after finding two victims inside an old storefront that appeared to be abandoned. Can you tell me why you hired a private detective and why he might have been at the crime scene?

Martin was perspiring. He knew it would make him and Hudson look more suspicious if he refused to give his reason or to lie about it. "Mr Keller, I hired Mr Hudson to follow one of the members of JBT, Jacob, Balingsford & Treacher & Associates." Martin looked at the floor and Mr Hudson. Larry nodded for Martin to proceed. "I had suspected some unusual activity with one of our larger accounts that was being managed by Francesca Jacob. She is the wife of Douglas Jacob who is one of my partners in JBT. She recently was made a partner." He stood and paced back and forth in the small room. Detective Keller and Hal watched him closely. "I… there had been an audit of the company's books, which is routinely done each year by an independent company. The preliminary results revealed the same questions about this large account. The principle auditor is finalising a report to be presented next week." Martin collapsed in the chair.

"Thank you, Mr Balingsford. Mr Hudson, was this Mrs Jacob who you were following one of the persons who entered the building at the crime scene? Please describe in detail your actions related to Mr Balingsford's request. "

Larry loosened his tie and scooted forward in his chair, took out a dogeared notebook and cleared his throat. "On January 2, 1978 I followed Mrs Francesca Jacob at approximately 2 pm to 106 Madison Square Rd, the Oxford Building in Gary, Indiana. She parked her car, a 1977 White Cadillac Sedan, nice wheels, in the underground parking garage of the building. At 2:26 pm she took the elevator to the fourteenth floor and entered the offices of Martin, Murray & Thompson, LLC. She was taken to an office door by the Receptionist. I was disguised as a member of a cleaning service and was emptying wastebaskets so that I could observe Mrs Jacob through the glass doors of the main office entrance. At 3:45 pm Mrs Jacob was seen talking with a man in the reception area of the MM&T office. The subject appeared to be arguing with the man who I identified as Daniel Pironne. Mr Pironne seemed to be ignoring her conversation. He stood grinning at her for several minutes, shook his head and walked away from Mrs Jacob. When she tried to follow Mr Pironne, a tall, stocky man took Mrs Jacob's arm and walked with her to the elevator. I took the stairs and exited on the main floor just in time to see Mrs Jacob and the man get off the elevator and walk down the exit stairs to the underground garage. I discarded the coveralls and ran to a van parked in the alley near the entrance and exit ramps of the garage. Mrs Jacob with the man in the driver's seat exited in her Cadillac, turned onto the highway and headed east. I followed at a safe distance. It was now 4:30 pm." Larry looked up at the other men in the room.

"Please proceed, Mr Hudson." Detective Keller said as he turned the page on the notes he was taking.

"Excuse me, Larry, are you sure it was Daniel Pironne Mrs Jacob met with? That is strange. I am working on a hit and run case, possible attempted murder of a woman from Moline. Daniel Pironne's name came up in the investigation. It seems that he and his late father, Victor Pironne, had a vendetta against this woman's real father. We have very few leads. There is a remote possibility the Pironne family suspected the father was Hank Baldoni and he was still alive. Victor had thought the man was dead. We have no evidence that Victor ordered him killed, nor that the man is alive. He has been missing for almost nineteen years. It is not clear why they pursed him for so many years. We are wondering if this Pironne fellow had found out about this Melinda possibly being Hank's daughter and used her to try to bring him out of hiding, if he was. I 'm sorry to interrupt you, Larry, but it seemed important that Daniel Pironne came up in both cases." Hal scratched his head. "I need to make a call, Brad. Is it okay that I leave for a minute? Hal went to the waiting room where there was a telephone and dialed.

Brad Keller transferred his notes to a blackboard. He started to draw lines from Jeff Collins (shot), Daniel Pironne, Francesca Jacob, Hank Baldoni, Melinda Sherman, an unidentified female (shot, did not survive), Victor Pironne, JBT & Associates, Martin, Murray & Thompson, LLC, Martin Ballingsford, Larry Hudson and Hal Putnam to see how each one was connected to another. He had interviewed Phyllis Strigow at Cleveland Clinic because she had been auditing this JBT's books and there was suspicion that Dan Pironne had a connection to a company called Balpar Industries. JBT was the company holding this account. The board started to look like "finding Elmo". Was Melinda's accident connected to the recent crime that Detective Hudson witnessed? Was the woman who was lying in the morgue Mrs Jacob? He listed each of the detectives and under each name put the names of the others who were in some way being investigated or involved in a case. Daniel Pironne appeared under each of the investigations. Brad knew that the Pironne's were being investigated for crimes perpetrated by the mafia. Victor Pironne had died in a boating accident several years ago and was the Godfather back in his time. They were having a difficult time pinning any actual crimes on Daniel. It would be important to confirm the identity of the dead woman and to talk with Jeff Collins when the doctors allowed him to be questioned.

Chapter XVII
Brighter Days

Hank (Jack Turner) requested a three-week vacation. He spoke with Phyllis several times after she received his letter. She agreed that Millie should not go back to her apartment in Moline. Phyllis had planned for Millie's clothes and other personal items to be shipped to Phyllis's Condo in Indiana. Millie's apartment rent was settled, and the furniture placed in storage. Hank was going to rent an apartment nearby. He hoped to make up for some of his mistakes from the past. Phyllis felt it would be ridiculous to carry resentments. They all needed to move forward and make the best of the years ahead. Jeff was very helpful in arranging for the move. He was worried that someone was out there still hell bent on hurting or killing Millie. Hank was sure it had something to do with the Pironne's, especially when Phyllis shared her suspicions that Balpar Industries was managed by Dan Pironne even though the owner was listed as Arthur Mason. Hank told Phyllis that when he had originally gone in with Victor and Dan, he did not realise they had connections with the mob. After a year, he suspected the investments were illegal and he left the company. After staying clean from gambling for two years, he fell back into his addiction and the saga leading to his disappearance began. He thought for sure Balpar was long gone. He was very surprised that it continued to be managed by highly respected financial consultants at JBT.

Detective Keller was given permission to speak with Jeff for a short time after his meeting with Martin, Larry and Hal.

"Mr Collins, can I call you Jeff? I don't want to cause you any discomfort or overtire you. I am Detective Brad Keller from the Chicago Police Department. Can you tell me why you were in that building when the shooting occurred?"

Jeff had regained more strength to his voice. "Mr Keller, I am in love with Melinda Strigow, I mean Sherman. She was run down by a car in November and almost lost her life. She is getting a divorce from a horrible man that mistreated her. The police questioned him, and he had this lame alibi that he was passed out in some bar. I don't believe him. I followed Ron Sherman for the past two weeks." Jeff coughed and his voice had gradually become weaker and hoarse.

Brad stood and pressed the nurse call button. "Jeff don't try to talk. Let the nurse give you something for your sore throat and allow you to rest. "

"No…" Jeff attempted to clear his throat, but he began coughing and spitting up frothy material. He grabbed for Brad's arm. The look in his eyes was like a deer's in the headlights.

Jeff's nurse, Rebecca, came into the room just as the monitor alarms signaled a drop in Jeff's oxygen level. Another nurse came into the cubicle and asked Brad to step outside. Rebecca grasped a tube and began suctioning the secretions from Jeff's mouth. The other nurse administered medication into the IV tubing and Jeff began to relax and close his eyes. His color had become ashen when he began to cough. It was returning to a more normal color. A Respiratory Therapist came into the room, changed the oxygen cannula to a face mask and worked with the dials on the oxygen equipment. "I'll give him a treatment as soon as he had rested." The nurse told Brad that she would call him in the waiting room or the small office they had given him when Jeff had rested and felt able to resume their conversation. Brad returned to the small office. He looked at the board on which he had listed all the persons somehow entangled in a crazy melee circumstances, scratched his head and added the name of Ron Sherman.

"May I please speak to Ms Phyllis Strigow? This is Harold Putnam of the Davenport Police." Hal spoke to Phyllis's secretary at MM&T.

"Mr Putnam, I am so glad you called. Ms Strigow is out of town. She went to Cleveland Clinic to pick up her sister. Is something wrong?"

"No, I just needed to ask her some questions. If she calls, could you have her contact me at 612-449-7078? It is important I get hold of her." Hal thanked the secretary.

Millie was sitting on her bed, then in a chair, then scanned her room for the third time. Phyllis was late. She couldn't remember if Phyllis was ever late. Somewhere in the memory portion of her brain it gave her the feeling that this was unusual. *Maybe the traffic was bad. I haven't heard from Jeff for a few days either.* She tried to push the anxious feelings away. *It's probably the jitters. I don't know how to feel about going to stay with her. Everything is so crazy. Jack or Hank is my real father. Sally was my mother. Someone tried to kill me. I can barely recall my life before the accident. Who wouldn't be antsy!* She opened the small suitcase and refolded the few outfits Phyllis and Jeff had brought her. She looked at herself in the mirror and wondered who she would be if her memory fully returned. Jeff had begged Francesca to hold the position Millie was supposed to have filled the day she was run down. Francesca seemed more distracted than usual. She was always quite cold and distant to those she supervised. Jeff missed the casual, sly humor of Martin Balingsford who had been his supervisor before Mrs Jacob had become a partner and oversaw the technical accounting department. Jeff thanked her profusely when she begrudgingly agreed to keep the position open for another six months. Millie checked the clock again. Phyllis was over an hour late. Millie's nurse came in to see if she was okay.

"Did my sister or Jeff call lately?" Millie asked.

"No, Millie, I hadn't heard that anyone called. I'll check with the unit clerk. I'm sure you are anxious to get back home. Traffic is crazy all the time in this city, but more so during workdays. I'll be right back. Are you finished with your lunch tray? Dear, you hardly ate anything. Need to put some fat on those skinny bones."

Millie thanked the nurse. She picked up the phone and dialed the extension to Hank's physical therapy department. She knew he was loaded with clients, trying to make up for the time he would be in Indiana. He had given the extension numbers to his department and his office to Millie and told her to call him anytime. "Hello, this is Melinda Sherman Strigow in room 1204 Rehab Unit. Is Mr B…Turner available?" Mille smiled as she almost asked for Hank Baldoni.

The tech that had answered the phone had been told, as had the other employees in Hank's department, to let him know if Melinda called, no matter what he was doing. "Ms Sherman. I hear you are being discharged today. I wish the very best for you. Jack is with a patient. I will tell him you need to speak with him." The tech looked around the large workout area and spied Jack standing near a patient working on the overhead bars. "Jack, Melinda Sherman is on the phone for you. I told her you were with a patient." The tech was nearly knocked over as Hank excused himself, told the tech to take over, and rushed to the phone.

"Millie, are you all right? I though Phyllis would have you on your way to the apartment by now."

"Dad," Millie checked to make sure her door was shut. "Phyllis isn't here yet and Jeff hasn't called in a few days. It's not like either of them. I'm getting worried. The nurse said neither of them have called. Oh, God, I hope nothing had happened to them! I… do you think the people who hit me might do something to them?"

"Millie, honey. Let me take this in my office. Hang on. I'll be in there in a flash." Hank put the phone on hold and began to sort through all the possibilities, even the bad ones. He had warned Jeff and Phyllis to keep their distance from the Pironne family and Ron Sherman. They both had suspicions that there was a connection from them to Millie's accident. "Millie, I can talk a little easier here. I hope it is just the traffic or them readying things at the apartment for your arrival home. I'll try to contact Mr Putnam in Davenport. He can do some checking. He knows Jeff. *I hope he didn't get the crazy idea to follow that Ex of hers,* He said to himself. "Don't worry, Millie, we will get you home and keep everyone safe until they lock up these characters." Hank was worried. Phyllis never would have abandoned Millie. They were doing well repairing their relationship. Jeff called Millie every day she was in the hospital. No matter how busy he was, he either came to visit or called. He was so excited the last time they had all been in Millie's room when the doctor told her she could be discharged that next Tuesday. Jeff had been included in the saga of Hank Baldoni. He was determined to protect Millie even more now that the truth had come out about her real mother and Hank.

Hal went back into the room where Brad was staring at the maze of names and connections on the board. "Brad, I'm afraid you need to add Phyllis Strigow to your artwork. She is Melinda Sherman Strigow's sister, uh… stepsister, whatever, and she has been performing audits for JBT for years. She recently questioned some things surrounding Balpar Industries. She also knew that Hank Baldoni was really Melinda's father. She told Melinda. Hank Baldoni is alias Jack Turner. Jack Turner is Melinda's physical therapist in Cleveland Clinic and … (buzz, buzz). Excuse me, I need to get this." Hal looked at his pager and saw a message to call a number from Cleveland Clinic. He grabbed the phone while Brad looked at Hal's distressed face. "Hello, this is Officer Harold Putnam. Who is calling?"

"Mr Putnam, this is Jack Turner, from the Rehabilitation Center at Cleveland Clinic. I have been caring for Melinda Sherman, you may also know her as Melinda Strigow. She is to be discharged today to stay with her sister, Phyllis, in Indiana. We are concerned because it had been almost two hours past the time Phyllis was to pick up Ms Sherman. There have been no calls from her and from Millie's, Melinda's friend, Jeff Collins." Hank's voice grew louder as he was updating Hal.

"Mr Turner, are you also known as Hank Baldoni?"

Hank felt like his insides were rolling into his chest. How did this guy know about his alias? Did Jeff tell him? "Yes, I was…am Hank Baldoni. Please, whatever you know about me is not important. I'm really getting worried. I understand you guys haven't found the creeps that ran over Millie. They might have done something to Jeff and Phyllis. Can you help me?" He didn't care anymore about himself. What mattered was his daughter and those she had come to trust.

"Hank, or Jack, believe me I am now even more concerned. Jeff Collins was shot in an altercation outside of Gary. He is doing okay, but there was another person, a woman, who was shot and killed in the same event." Hal heard Hank's grown. "I am working with the Chicago Police Department on this case. It seems that you may be one of the key factors in a very convoluted series of events going back to your participation in Balpar Industries many years ago." Brad looked at Hal and then back at his board. He circled Hank Baldoni, Phyllis Strigow, Melinda Sherman and Jeff Collins names. Hal squinted at the board and his face paled as he could see that every one of them could be traced to Balpar and Dan Pironne.

Chapter XVIII
Paranoia

Paranoia is an unrealistic distrust of others or a feeling of being persecuted. Extreme degrees may be a sign of mental illness. Symptoms are doubting the loyalty of others, being quick to become angry or hostile. Some drugs or alcohol can trigger episodes of this psychosis. Francesca was extremely angry and paranoid when she went to confront Dan Pironne in his office. Douglas had questioned her about Balpar Industries after Samantha's presentation of her project during the board meeting. *That bitch will pay! They all will pay! That mole, Martin, hasn't the balls of a mouse. He thought he was such a catch I would have sex with the schmuck. He had better get his ass in here and back me up. I'm glad I showed those pictures to Dougie Pooh.* Her paranoia was mounting. The results of crossing the line burned a trail of lies and deceit. Dan Pironne trusted no one, not even the three-hundred-pound brute who had been his bodyguard for the past ten years. That Francesca babe was peeing all over herself about some chick that brought up questions about Balpar. Dan didn't care what happened to that company. He just needed to distance himself from that albatross. The best way he knew how to deal with a roadblock in his selfish, narcissistic way of living was to destroy it. His whore of a wife, Alyssa, had been taught a lesson when she got entangled with a student in her computer class. He taught that slob a lesson. She had been kept anchored to their mansion ever since. Rarely allowed to go anywhere without one of his henchmen accompanying her, she had shrunk into herself, barely talking to anyone. Dan would rape her whenever he needed to release himself. He would beat her if she refused. He had a plan that would eliminate these problems. He told Francesca she needed to trust him to take care of Balpar. Trust a narcissistic killer, rapist and gangster! He had Rolfe, his bodyguard, take Francesca to the mansion. He told her that he had one of his men plant a bomb in the basement of the building where JBT was located. She could watch the news when the creep that had dared to have an affair with his wife, Francesca's husband and the other partners and employees were blown to bits. He had his bodyguard undress Francesca, rape her and put her clothes on the practically catatonic Alyssa. Francesca screamed and fought the massive hulk that laid on her, slobbered all over her body and hit her when she fought him. He threw Alyssa's torn dress over her, tied her hands and feet, and shoved her bruised body into a dark closet. Dazed and terrified, a small part of her tried to reach back over that line. Memories of the gentle love-making and good life Doug had offered her; the hurt in his eyes when he questioned her earlier that day about Balpar; the tears he shed when she blamed Martin for the improprieties. She showed him pictures of the supposed sexual encounter with Martin saying she had them taken because she thought she could bribe him to let her out of "the deal". Tears burned her eyes and ran down her cheeks as she shook with a terror she had never known. She had to find a way to warn Doug. She had to!

Detective Brad Keller, Chief of Homicide, and Hal Putnam called their precincts and ordered SWAT teams to meet them outside the Pironne mansion. Larry Hudson and Martin were asked to call Douglas Jacob and Henri Treacher to see if they had heard anything from Francesca. Douglas was worried. He didn't believe that crazy story about Martin raping her though he was upset that Martin had even gone up to their apartment with her. He needed an explanation. Martin had tried to calm him down. He told him he was drugged, and those pictures were set up. Francesca had gotten herself involved with Dan Pironne's dealings and was covering illegal business practices for Balpar Industries. Dan Pironne had an evil reputation. The police were closing in on his involvement with the mob.

Samantha Reynolds was sitting in Doug's office waiting to meet with him. She had a feeling that something bad was happening. No one had seen or heard from Francesca or Martin for several days. Douglas and Henri appeared harried. The door opened. Henri and Douglas walked in looking somber. Henri touched Sam's shoulder as he passed her chair, sat in the chair beside her and waited for Doug to speak.

"Miss Reynolds, we have reviewed the details of your project and want to compliment you on the thoroughness of the report. It has come to our attention since the board meeting that Balpar Industries has been used as a front for indiscriminate businesses abroad. Our auditing service has discovered some irregularities over a significant amount of time. There will be investigations by the Federal Government Securities Division, the Chicago Police Department and perhaps other investigators. Since you were key in the discovery of some irregularities, you will be asked to work with all these entities." Samantha squirmed in her seat and looked over at Henri. He reached for her hand and nodded to her. "I'm sure this will be a monumental task and may involve legal action against JBT. We wanted to make sure you realise the seriousness of this nightmare. You may be subpoenaed to testify in court."

"Samantha, we have been blindsided by this debacle. We are sorry that you have become entrenched in this Balpar craziness. It is on us that we trusted the veracity of this account to someone who became entangled in unethical practices. We will support and defend you during this investigation. We may have to close down JBT while this is being reviewed." Henri watched Samantha as she fidgeted in her chair and wrung her delicate hands around the cloth of her shirt. Her exquisite face had turned pale and anxious.

Samantha had approached the line with thoughts of overperforming Francesca and obtaining a higher position in the company. Her initial plan to entrap Henri and Martin with her feminine whiles had been expunged because she had fallen in love with the austere, nonengaging Henri. Under that icy exterior she had discovered a passionate, loving man.

"Miss Reynolds, we will compensate well for your cooperation and assistance. If JBT can come out of this disaster and regain its enviable position in the market, we will offer you a partnership. Henri has assured me that he has undeniable trust in your ethics and abilities. We wouldn't be at all surprised if you wish to leave our firm after the investigation no longer requires your input. Henri and Douglas waited for Samantha to speak. They had just hit her with a huge brick. Several minutes passed while she watched the hands of celebratory clock on the wall tick its minutes quietly. The rim of the clock was gold and the words *Jacob, Balingsford, Treacher & Associates, Fifteen Years of Integrity, Astute Practice, Ethical Principals.*

"Mr Jacob, Mr Treacher, I am so sorry that this has happened to this stellar company and to all of us who work for JBT. I am honored that you think highly of me. I will cooperate with any part of the investigation into Balpar. I also will express my belief that this company has always conducted itself according to legal and ethical business practices. Should I retain legal counsel during this process?"

"That would be wise, Ms Reynolds. We will reimburse you for any financial burdens you incur related to the investigation." Douglas cleared his throat. His voice cracked when he asked Samantha if she had heard from Francesca. Samantha was touched by the pain in Douglas's eyes. She felt ashamed that she had originally walked close to demonising Francesca in order to gain wealth and position.

"No, sir. The last time I spoke with Mrs Jacob was prior to giving my presentation. She seemed distressed so I made an appointment to meet with her to see how we could work together on Balpar Industries account.

Hank tried to call Phyllis. He needed to think of some excuse for Jeff not calling. He didn't want Millie to know that Jeff had been shot. What a mess! Now he was frightened that something might have happened to Phyllis. He cancelled the rest of the day's appointments, made a quick call to his supervisor. He explained that there was a family emergency and he would have to leave a couple of days early for his vacation. He grabbed his street clothes, keeping his scrubs and lab coat on and rushed to the elevators. On his way to Millie's room, he put together a story he hoped she would believe.

"Millie, I wasn't supposed to tell you, but Phyllis and Jeff are planning a surprise welcome home party for you and lost track of time. Between moving your things from the apartment and work, they feel awful about worrying you." *Suppose the woman they found at the scene where Jeff was shot was Phyllis! That would be so devastating for Millie. I can't think that way.* They called me and asked me to take you to Phyllis's. They are so sorry." Hank hoped he looked convincing. Millie stared at him and started to laugh.

"You look like the cat that swallowed the canary! Why didn't you tell me when I called you? I just want to get home. We'll talk on the way. No more lies! I can't take any more lies. No matter what, I need to hear the truth. I can deal with it, Dad…Hank…Jack." Millie handed him her suitcase, buzzed the nurse to let her know she was ready to leave. Hank hung his head and waited until the nurse arrived with the wheelchair.

File # 614378 (Summary)

Caucasian female, 5' 6" in height, age 39

Succumbed to gunshot wound to left side of face and left shoulder. Additional gunshot wounds to abdomen and chest.

Estimated Time of Death: January 8, 1978; 11:45 pm

Identification—fingerprints of one Alyssa Marie Gregory (Pironne)

The preliminary report was faxed to the Homicide Division, Chicago Police Department at 6 pm. It was placed on Chief Keller's desk.

The wind was rattling the wrought iron gates leading to the Pironne mansion. It was 7:30 pm and the darkness mixed with the chilly December air lent an eerie atmosphere to the approach of SWAT vans and police vehicles. There headlights had been turned off several yards from the gated entrance. In the distance lights from several of the windows in the mansion cast a cadaverous face to the main structure. From a tactical van containing surveillance equipment that was able to tap into the security system of the estate, three experts gradually froze the system's ability to alarm. No change would appear on the observation display housed and monitored in the mansion. The entrance gate locks clicked open. Ten men and women dressed in SWAT bullet-proof vests, gas masks, weapons, teargas cannisters and walkie-talkies silently ran through the gates, through the bushes about thirty feet from the driveway leading to the mansion. They had fifteen minutes before the security system would resume and alarm a breach. There were spotlights with motion detectors along the driveway with a range of twenty feet on either side.

His acrid breath spat obscenities. Ron Sherman paced back and forth in front of the drowsy woman bound to the chair. Her head bobbed up and down and side to side trying desperately to orient herself.

"Tell me where that bastard sister of yours is!" He slapped her again across her swollen and bruised face.

"I…I don't know…I haven't talked …" Phyllis began to drift back into the oblivion she had experienced when this horrible man broke into her condo. He had knocked her down, stuffed a pungent rag over her nose and mouth, dragged her down a flight of stairs and put her in the trunk of a blue sedan.

Ron Sherman was losing it. He hadn't slept since the shooting at the abandoned building where he was hiding. That was three days ago. He needed the rest of the money Dan Pironne's bodyguard had promised him months ago. He was supposed to take a black car parked under the overpass near his Ex-wife's apartment, wait until she was waiting for the bus and run her over. He had no problems with paying the bitch back for leaving him. The payoff would get him out of the God forsaken quad cities. He had bought a one-way bus ticket to Mexico with the first payment. The rest was promised after the deed was done. When one of Pironne's henchmen met him in Marti's bar and told him he wouldn't get the rest of the money until Millie was found and brought to the Pironne mansion, he was livid. He was so paranoid when he left the bar, he zig—zagged through side streets in his beat-up red truck and took the back roads to his abandoned hide out near the highway outside of Gary. He had a couple of guns hidden in a drawer of the desk that he needed to protect himself. He hid the truck in the woods behind the building. He could only think of two people who would know where Millie was. That Jeff who he was sure talked Millie into divorcing him and that uppity sister of hers, Phyllis Strigow. He knew where Phyllis's condominium was in Indiana. He had no idea where Jeff lived. Just as he was patting himself on the back for devising a plan the door to the building was kicked open. Ron grabbed both guns as bullets sprayed around the room. He shot repeatedly at the opening where he thought the door was. The desk lamp had dropped over the side of the desk and was dangling by its cord. Silence. He listened, breathing heavily, then inched his way around the desk. He stepped over the two bodies on the floor and haltingly slid against the wall towards where he could feel the edge of the splintered doorway. His heart pounded as he peered outside. The moonlight sent shadows moving about the ground in the wind. The cold air blew against the sweat dripping from his brow as he blinked his eyes to try to see if the coast was clear. Ron ran as fast as he could towards the highway. Suddenly, hands almost the size of Ron's face clamped over his mouth and jaw. He was slammed against the cold turf in a ditch with so much force he could barely breathe. The sting of an icy metal rested against the side of his head.

"Asshole, what were you thinking, huh? Were you running like the skinny hyena you are, huh? The boss told you to finish the job. You have one more thing to do before I shoot your pea-sized brains out. You are going to lead me to that Melinda person, and I'll make sure the job and you are finished, Kapeesh?" Ron lost his bladder contents. He shook his head yes as well as his whole body. Rolfe dragged him across a ditch near where the blue sedan was hidden along the roadside. Ron Sherman knew that this might be his last chance to survive. With all the strength he could muster, he kicked Rolfe in the balls, grabbed the gun and shot him in the head twice. The big man lunged at Ron just before he collapsed near a ditch. Ron kicked at the body to make sure he was dead, rolled him over and rummage through his pockets. He took a wallet filled with credit cards and cash, another gun, grabbed the keys to the car and headed towards Indiana. He still thought he could get the rest of the payment for killing Millie.

Hank and Millie arrived at Phyllis's condo at 11:30 pm. What they found when they approached sent shivers down their spines. The door to her condo had been broken open. A table near the entrance was lying on the floor and there was a blood stain on the carpet not far from the door. Millie gasped and ran into the other rooms calling for Phyllis. Hank grabbed the phone and called the local police. He then called the number for Hal Putnam he had been given. Hal was waiting in the communication van outside Dan Pironne's estate.

"Hal, God am I glad to get you. Phyllis Strigow's condo has been broken into. There is blood on the floor. Looks like there was a struggle. Phyllis in not here!" Millie came running into the room, crying hysterically. "I just brought Millie home from the hospital because Phyllis never showed."

"Hank, Millie is not safe there. They found Ron Sherman's red truck behind the building where Jeff and that woman were shot. They also found the body of a big guy in a ditch not far from the building. I'm thinking it might have been Ron looking for a way to finish the job on Millie. He probably thinks Phyllis knows where she is. Did you call the police there?"

"Yes, man. In fact, I hear a squad car now."

"Tell them I said to take both of you to the station and keep you there until I contact them. They know me there. Don't worry, we will get him." Hal told the officers in the van that he needed to track down an accomplice in this crazy scenario. He ran to his squad car and took off towards

Davenport. If he knew anything about a low life like Ron Sherman it would be that those types of pigeons always flew home at some point.

The SWAT team stealthily approached the mansion. They could see that lights in the house were only visible on the far side of the building. They had six minutes left before the alarm system revealed their positions. Brad Keller knew that there would be gunfire as soon as they blew the lock on the door. The first wave of officers would have metal shields while the second team fired repeated rounds into the onslaught he predicted. As always, he said a quick prayer that no officer would be injured or killed. That was the risk these seasoned police took with every altercation. One of the team attached an explosive to the massive oak door. Five seconds later the door blew apart and a spray of machine gun bullets echoed throughout the entrance. There was an eerie few moment of silence only broken by a groan and gravely cough, then silence again. Two figures jumped from behind a doorway past the entrance and fired multiple shots. The two were quickly eliminated by the advancing SWAT officers. Brad scanned the bodies on the floor and saw none were any of his crew.

Dan Pironne heard the explosion and the gunfire that followed. He ran to his desk and pulled out his howitzer. He ran to the closet where Francesca was cowering, grabbed her off the floor and held her in front of him. He called for Rolfe. Then he suddenly remembered he had sent him with Alyssa, dressed as Francesca, to find Ron Sherman. He had noticed a man wearing a custodian uniform outside his office when Francesca had come there to beg him to release her from her connection to Balpar. His paranoia made him suspicious of everyone. Thinking the custodian spent more time than necessary emptying wastebaskets, he had Rolfe accompany Francesca to her car. The custodian went down the stairway exit just after Rolfe and Francesca entered the elevator. Assuming this guy might be a detective for JBT he contacted Rolfe at the mansion and told him to exchange Francesca's clothes for Alyssa's, dress Alyssa in Francesca's clothes and drive her to Sherman's hideout. He knew about his dingy hideout near Gary. He wanted Ron to bring Millie to the mansion so he could lure Hank Baldoni into rescuing her. His twisted mind focused on fulfilling the vendetta his father had against Hank. With all of them gone, JBT destroyed he would be heralded as the Godfather over all the mobs in the area.

The door to Dan's study burst open. Guns were aimed at the two standing near a door not far from the huge desk Dan's father had occupied. Francesca's eyes were bloodshot and filled with terror. Dan held the gun to her temple.

"I'll kill her. This is Douglas Jacob's wife. Aren't you, Frannie, dear?" Dan could have easily portrayed the devil. His face was dark with anger and the look in his eyes was that of a madman. He moved towards the door that led to a secret passageway to one of the many garages on the estate. Victor had amassed a large collection of sportscars over his tenure. They were stored in several buildings connected by a series of tunnels.

"Mr Pironne. Put down the gun. You cannot escape this. Let Mrs Jacobs go. If you kill her, we will have to kill you. I have officers all over this estate. Be reasonable. We just need to talk with you," Brad said in a firm, calm tone.

"You cops have always been out to get my family. If you try to shoot me, it will be this bitch you kill." If he could make it through the steel reinforced door behind him and slam it shut before a shot got to him, they would not be able to follow him. Francesca summoned all the strength she had left in her beaten body. *This is for you, Doug, she thought as she bit into Dan's arm. He loosened his grip for a second and she fell away from him as the bullets hit his gyrating body.*

Francesca screamed "There is a bomb! Please get to the Prudential building! He called his goon to set the timer for 9 am. He wants to kill my husband and everyone in JBT! Please! Please get someone there!" Brad and a couple of the other officers helped Francesca to a chair and took down the information. Brad immediately notified the bomb squad at his Chicago precinct. The squad was dispensed at 8:10 am. Francesca only knew the bomb was somewhere in the basement. Four squad cars were dispensed to the Prudential building to facilitate an evacuation.

The bomb squad searched the basement of the building. One of the officers noticed a red light blinking from a pipe in the ceiling. He approached it tenuously. He signaled his men. Gingerly following the trail of wires attached to an explosive device, he cut one of the wires. At 8:48 am the bomb was defused. The building remained evacuated until the squad had searched every floor, every office and closet to be assured there were no other devices. Doug, Samantha and Henri were stunned. A police car drove up behind the many squad cars at the scene. Martin ran from the car to embrace the three who just melted into his strong arms.

Hal radioed the precinct closest to Ron Sherman's house. He had been sure that Ron's flimsy alibi was untrue. Now that it seemed he was a small part of a much bigger scenario; he was sure the supporter of his alibi was probably encouraged to lie about his being at Marti's when Millie was run down. If Sherman had abducted Phyllis and probably killed the woman and man found at his hideout, he was extremely dangerous. He told the police to park their cars some distance from Sherman's house. He told them to cautiously, surround the house and wait for further orders.

It was 9 am on a brisk, cloudy day by the time he arrived near the other squad cars. He signaled the police to remain where they were while he sneaked up to the house to see if he could see anything in the dingy windows. There was a figure in a chair slumped over. He or she seemed to be tied to the chair. No one else could be seen from Hal's line of vision. Then he heard muffled shouting. Ron Sherman held a gun to the person's head and was yelling at him or her. Hal was sure the person was Phyllis. He motioned to the other officers to approach the front of the house and on his signal, establish entry with guns ready. This had to be timed perfectly.

Hal jumped through the window, rolling over the shattered glass. Ron pointed the gun at the figure lying on the floor just as the rest of Hal's team burst through the front door and shot Ron in the arm holding the gun. Ron howled and tried to run but was stopped by two of the cops. Hal had some nasty cuts but ignored them to run over to Phyllis. She was unconscious and had been beaten but was still alive. The ambulance arrived and she was taken to the same hospital where Jeff was recovering from his ordeal.

Millie and Hank were taken by Hal's policemen to Chicago Memorial Hospital to meet with Phyllis and Jeff. There were tears and hugs and tales to tell that had to be interrupted by the doctors wanting the two patients to get some much-needed rest. Francesca was hospitalised under police guard. She begged Doug to forgive her. She was convicted of fraud and conspiracy. Douglas Jacob stood by her during her eight—year prison sentence. He, Martin and Henri spent many years reimbursing clients for their losses due to the illegal practices of Balpar Industries.

During the next three years, JBT was rebuilt into the original, ethical business the partners had envisioned. When Francesca was paroled for good behavior in six years, she was content to stay out of JBT's business. She taught seminars to university students on how to recognise fraud and graft in the financial world. Samantha Reynolds became a partner in the newly named JBTR Financial Consultants, Inc. She married good old Henri. She stood by him when he became depressed over Alyssa's violent death, thinking it was his fault.

Millie took a position in JBTR as a technical computer analyst in her husband Jeff's Department. Hal Putnam was Chief of Police in Davenport until he retired in 1984. Brad Keller became Mayor of Gary Indiana after receiving accolades as Chief of the Homicide Division of the Chicago Police Department and street cop for sixteen years.

Brad also had the courage to ask Phyllis out on several dates. She never got used to his fetish of putting hot sauce on ice cream. Hank Baldoni assisted with the plans for the house Millie and Jeff were having built in Davenport. He insisted on designing the extra bedroom so it could accommodate the grandkid he kept bugged them to have. He retired from Cleveland Clinic and worked part-time as a physical therapist in Moline Hospital. Ron Sherman spent the rest of his life in prison.

Millie and Phyllis were having lunch one day in December at a small coffee house near Millie's and Jeff's home, one year after their crazy nightmare. They looked out the window decorated with tiny colored lights for the coming holidays. Tiny sparkling snowflakes kissed the sunshine. A rainbow appeared just above the clouds before they moved in to dump more snow. Millie patted her ever growing belly. She smiled as she felt a little flutter.

"Look, Philli! There are rainbows in December!"